ARTIFICIAL THINGS

Karen Joy Fowler

SPECTRA™

BANTAM BOOKS

NEW YORK • TORONTO • LONDON • SYDNEY • AUCKLAND

For Joy

ARTIFICIAL THINGS
A Bantam Spectra Book

PUBLISHING HISTORY
Bantam edition published December 1986
Bantam reissue / December 1992

SPECTRA and the portrayal of a boxed "s" are trademarks of Bantam Books,
a division of Bantam Doubleday Dell Publishing Group, Inc.

*The stories listed below originally appeared in the following publications. All others are
published for the first time in this volume.*

From Isaac Asimov's Science Fiction Magazine:

"Praxis," copyright © 1985 by Davis Publications, Inc. Appeared in March 1985 issue.
"The Lake Was Full of Artificial Things," copyright © 1985 by Davis Publications, Inc.
Appeared in October 1985 issue.
"The War of the Roses," copyright © 1985 by Davis Publications, Inc. Appeared in
December 1985 issue.
"The Dragon's Head," copyright © 1986 by Davis Publications, Inc. Appeared in August
1986 issue.

From The Magazine of Fantasy and Science Fiction:

"The Poplar Street Study," copyright © 1985 by The Magazine of Fantasy and Science
Fiction.
"Wild Boys," copyright © 1986 by The Magazine of Fantasy and Science Fiction.
"Face Value" copyright © 1986 by The Magazine of Fantasy and Science Fiction.

From L. Ron Hubbard Presents Writers of the Future, Volume I:

"Recalling Cinderella," copyright © 1985 by Karen Joy Fowler. Published by Bridge
Publications.
*The short story title "The Lake Was Full of Artificial Things" is a line from the poem
"Notes Toward a Supreme Fiction" by Wallace Stevens from The Collected Poems of
Wallace Stevens copyright 1954 by Wallace Stevens. Copyright renewed. Reprinted by
permission of Alfred A. Knopf, Inc.*

All rights reserved.
Copyright © 1986 by Karen Joy Fowler.
Cover art copyright © 1992 Jim Burns.
*No part of this book may be reproduced or transmitted in any form or by any means,
electronic or mechanical, including photocopying, recording, or by any information
storage and retrieval system, without permission in writing from the publisher.*

ISBN 0-553-26219-X

Published simultaneously in the United States and Canada

*Bantam Books are published by Bantam Books, a division of Bantam Doubleday Dell
Publishing Group, Inc. Its trademark, consisting of the words "Bantam Books" and the
portrayal of a rooster, is Registered in U.S. Patent and Trademark Office and in other
countries. Marca Registrada. Bantam Books, 666 Fifth Avenue, New York, New York
10103.*

PRINTED IN THE UNITED STATES OF AMERICA

OPM   0 9 8 7 6 5 4 3

FOREWORD

After I had published a few stories, Shawna McCarthy, the editor of *Isaac Asimov's Science Fiction Magazine*, but recently moved to Bantam Books, called and asked if I would write a novel for Bantam. I was surprised, flattered, and not at all tempted. I had only begun to sell. I still hadn't mastered the short form. (Still haven't; no longer expect to.) I had a television-age attention span and no ideas that couldn't be thoroughly explored in fourteen pages. I thanked her and turned her down.

Several weeks later, I attended a convention in Sacramento. Since I had, at this time, published only three stories, I was surprised at the number of people who knew of me. But I quickly came to understand that most of these people had not actually seen my work. "Karen Joy Fowler!" they'd say, glancing at my name tag. "I know who you are. You're the person who won't write a novel for Bantam."

I see now that I developed a bit of an attitude. I love short fiction. I read the short fiction of famous novelists and I generally prefer it to the novels. So I continued to write short stories and if people asked me, as astounding numbers of them did, when was I going to write that novel, I responded with a snarl.

McCarthy must share some of the blame. She did, after all, eventually buy this collection of my short fiction, a development that encouraged me and my attitude enormously. This new printing seems an appro-

priate place in which to remember and to repeat my
thanks to her.

Because these stories represent the time in my life
when I first began to realize some success with my
writing, I will always be fond of them. They are very
personal in a very specific way. I wrote most of them
with no assurance they would sell. I wrote them to
entertain myself and my family or my friends. I wrote
"The Gate of Ghosts" for my daughter, Shannon. "The
Dragon's Head" was for Ryan, my son. In other ways the
stories are quite distant from me now. I can read through
them with an occasional sense of genuine surprise.
Although I remember writing the stories, I don't always
remember writing the sentences; I don't remember
every thought. Did I write that? I'll ask myself. It doesn't
seem likely.

A mere six years later I did manage to produce a
novel. It was more fun than I expected it to be. I have
every hope of writing another. I found that I liked
spending the longer period of time with the characters.
My children developed a code for people who called
while I was working on the novel. "She can't come to
the phone," they'd say. "She's playing with her imaginary friends."

But I still love the flash of short fiction. And I do
understand that no novel or short story I have yet to
write could ever bring me the unalloyed fame I once
enjoyed at the convention in Sacramento for that novel I
didn't write.

KAREN JOY FOWLER

CONTENTS

THE LAKE WAS FULL OF ARTIFICIAL THINGS

—Wallace Stevens

Daniel was older than Miranda had expected. In 1970, when they had said good-bye, he had been twenty-two. Two years later he was dead, but now, approaching her with the bouncing walk which had always suited his personality so well, he appeared as a middle-aged man and quite gray, though solid and muscular.

Miranda noted with relief that he was smiling. "Randy!" he said. He laughed delightedly. "You look wonderful."

Miranda glanced down at herself, wondering what, in fact, she did look like or if she had any form at all. She saw the flesh of her arms firm again and the skin smooth and tight. So *she* was the twenty-year-old. Isn't that odd, she thought, turning her hands palms up to examine them. Then Daniel reached her. The sun was bright in the sky behind him, obscuring his face, giving him a halo. He put his arms around her. I feel him, she thought in astonishment. I smell him. She breathed in slowly. "Hello, Daniel," she said.

He squeezed her slightly, then dropped his arms and looked around. Miranda looked outward, too. They were on the college campus. Surely this was not the setting she would have chosen. It unsettled her, as if she had been sent backward in time and gifted with pre-science, but remained powerless to make any changes,

1

was doomed to see it all again, moving to its inevitable conclusion. Daniel, however, seemed pleased.

He pointed off to the right. "There's the creek," he said, and suddenly she could hear it. "Memories there, right?" and she remembered lying beneath him on the grass by the water. She put her hands on his shoulders now; his clothes were rough against her palms and military—like his hair.

He gestured to the round brick building behind her. "Tollman Hall," he said. "Am I right? God, this is great, Randy. I remember *everything*. Total recall. I had Physics 10 there with Dr. Fielding. Physics for non-majors. I couldn't manage my vectors and I got a B." He laughed again, throwing an arm around Miranda. "It's great to be back."

They began to walk together toward the center of campus, slow walking with no destination, designed for conversation. They were all alone, Miranda noticed. The campus was deserted, then suddenly it wasn't. Students appeared on the pathways. Long-hairs with headbands and straights with slide rules. Just what she remembered. "Tell me what everyone's been doing," Daniel said. "It's been what? Thirty years? Don't leave out a thing."

Miranda stooped and picked a small daisy out of the grass. She twirled it absentmindedly in her fingers. It left a green stain on her thumb. Daniel stopped walking and waited beside her. "Well," Miranda said. "I've lost touch with most of them. Gail got a job on *Le Monde*. She went to Germany for the reunification. I heard she was living there. The antinuclear movement was her permanent beat. She could still be there, I suppose."

"So she's still a radical," said Daniel. "What stamina."

"Margaret bought a bakery in San Francisco. Sixties cuisine. Whole grains. Tofu brownies. Heaviest cookies west of the Rockies. We're in the same cable chapter so I keep up with her better. I saw her last marriage on TV. She's been married three times now, every one a loser."

"What about Allen?" Daniel asked.

"Allen," repeated Miranda. "Well, Allen had a promising career in jogging shoes. He was making great strides." She glanced at Daniel's face. "Sorry," she said. "Allen always brought out the worst in me. He lost his father in an air collision over Kennedy. Sued the airline and discovered he never had to work again. In short, Allen is rich. Last I heard, and this was maybe twenty years ago, he was headed to the Philippines to buy himself a submissive bride." She saw Daniel smile, the lines in his face deepening with his expression. "Oh, you'd like to blame me for Allen, wouldn't you?" she said. "But it wouldn't be fair. I dated him maybe three times, tops." Miranda shook her head. "Such an enthusiastic participant in the sexual revolution. And then it all turned to women's liberation on him. Poor Allen. We can only hope his tiny wife divorced him and won a large settlement when you could still get alimony."

Daniel moved closer to her and they began to walk again, passing under the shade of a redwood grove. The grass changed to needles under their feet. "You needn't be so hard on Allen," he said. "I never minded about him. I always knew you loved me."

"Did you?" asked Miranda anxiously. She looked at her feet, afraid to examine Daniel's face. My god, she was wearing moccasins. Had she ever worn moccasins? "I did get married, Daniel," she said. "I married a mathematician. His name was Michael." Miranda dropped her daisy, petals intact.

Daniel continued to walk, swinging his arms easily. "Well, you were always hot for mathematics. I didn't expect you to mourn me forever."

"So it's all right?"

Daniel stopped, turning to face her. He was still smiling, though it was not quite the smile she expected, not quite the easy, happy smile she remembered. "It's all right that you got married, Randy," he said softly. Something passed over his face and left it. "Hey!" he laughed again. "I remember something else from Physics 10. Zeno's paradox. You know what that is?"

"No," said Miranda.

"It's an argument. Zeno argued that motion was impossible because it required an object to pass through an infinite number of points in a finite amount of time." Daniel swung his arms energetically. "Think about it for minute, Randy. Can you fault it? Then think about how far I came to be here with you."

"Miranda. Miranda." It was her mother's voice, rousing her for school. Only then it wasn't. It was Dr. Matsui who merely sounded maternal, despite the fact that she had no children of her own and was not yet thirty. Miranda felt her chair returning slowly to its upright position. "Are you back?" Dr. Matsui asked. "How did it go?"

"It was short," Miranda told her. She pulled the taped wires gently from her lids and opened her eyes. Dr. Matsui was seated beside her, reaching into Miranda's hair to detach the clips which touched her scalp.

"Perhaps we recalled you too early," she conceded. "Matthew spotted an apex so we pulled the plug. We just wanted a happy ending. It was happy, wasn't it?"

"Yes." Dr. Matsui's hair, parted on one side and curving smoothly under her chin, bobbed before Miranda's face. Miranda touched it briefly, then her own hair, her cheeks, and her nose. They felt solid under her hand, real, but no more so than Daniel had been. "Yes, it was," she repeated. "He was so happy to see me. So glad to be back. But, Anna, he was so real. I thought you said it would be like a dream."

"No," Dr. Matsui told her. "I said it *wouldn't* be. I said it was a memory of something that never happened and in that respect was like a dream. I wasn't speaking of the quality of the experience." She rolled her chair to the monitor and stripped the long feed-out sheet from it, tracing the curves quickly with one finger. Matthew, her technician, came to stand behind her. He leaned over her left shoulder, pointing. "There," he said. "That's Daniel. That's what I put in."

Dr. Matsui returned her chair to Miranda's side. "Here's the map," she said. "Maybe I can explain better."

Miranda tried to sit forward. One remaining clip pulled her hair and made her inhale sharply. She reached up to detach herself. "Sorry," said Dr. Matsui sheepishly. She held out the paper for Miranda to see. "The dark wave is the Daniel we recorded off your memories earlier. Happy memories, right? You can see the fainter echo here as you responded to it with the original memories. Think of it as memory squared. Naturally, it's going to be intense. Then, everything else here is the record of the additional activity you brought to this particular session. Look at these sharp peaks at the beginning. They indicate stress. You'll see that nowhere else do they recur. On paper it looks to have been an entirely successful session. Of course, only you know the content of the experience." Her dark eyes were searching and sympathetic. "Well," she said. "Do you feel better about him?"

"Yes," said Miranda. "I feel better."

"Wonderful." Dr. Matsui handed the feedback to Matthew. "Store it," she told him.

Miranda spoke hesitatingly. "I had other things I wanted to say to him," she said. "It doesn't feel resolved."

"I don't think the sessions ever resolve things," Dr. Matsui said. "The best they can do is open the mind to resolution. The resolution still has to be found in the real world."

"Can I see him again?" Miranda asked.

Dr. Matsui interlaced her fingers and pressed them to her chest. "A repeat would be less expensive, of course," she said. "Since we've already got Daniel. We could just run him through again. Still, I'm reluctant to advise it. I wonder what else we could possibly gain."

"Please, Anna," said Miranda. She was looking down at her arms, remembering how firmly fleshed they had seemed.

"Let's wait and see how you're feeling after our next couple of regular visits. If the old regrets persist and, more importantly, if they're still interfering with your ability to get on with things, then ask me again."

She was standing. Miranda swung her legs over the side of the chair and stood, too. Matthew walked with her to the door of the office. "We've got a goalie coming in next," he confided. "She stepped into the goal while holding the ball; she wants to remember it the way it didn't happen. Self-indulgent if you ask me. But then, athletes make the money, right?" He held the door open, his arm stretched in front of Miranda. "You feel better, don't you?" he asked.

"Yes," she reassured him.

She met Daniel for lunch at Frank Fats Café. They ordered fried clams and scallops, but the food never came. Daniel was twenty again and luminescent with youth. His hair was blond and his face was smooth. Had he really been so beautiful? Miranda wondered.

"I'd love a coke," he said. "I haven't had one in thirty years."

"You're kidding," said Miranda. "They don't have the real thing in heaven?"

Daniel looked puzzled.

"Skip it," she told him. "I was just wondering what it was like being dead. You could tell me."

"It's classified," said Daniel. "On a need-to-know basis."

Miranda picked up her fork, which was heavy and cold. "This time it's you who looks wonderful. Positively beatific. Last time you looked so—" she started to say *old*, but amended it. After all, he had looked no older than she did these days. Such things were relative. "Tired," she finished.

"No, I wasn't tired," Daniel told her. "It was the war."

"The war's over now," Miranda said and this time his smile was decidedly unpleasant.

"Is it?" he asked. "Just because you don't read about it in the paper now? Just because you watch the evening news and there's no body count in the corner of the screen?"

"Television's not like that now," Miranda began, but Daniel hadn't stopped talking.

"What's really going on in Southeast Asia? Do you even know?" Daniel shook his head. "Wars never end," he said. He leaned threateningly over the table. "Do you imagine for one minute that it's over for me?"

Miranda slammed her fork down. "Don't do that," she said. "Don't try to make me guilty of that, too. You didn't have to go. I begged you not to. Jesus, you knew what the war was. If you'd gone off to save the world from communist agression, I would have disagreed, but I could have understood. But you knew better than that. I never forgave you for going."

"It was so easy for you to see what was right," Daniel responded angrily. "You were completely safe. You women could graduate without losing your deferment. Your goddamn birthday wasn't drawn twelfth in the draft lottery and if it had been you wouldn't have cared. When was your birthday drawn? You don't even know." Daniel leaned back and looked out the window. People appeared on the street. A woman in a red miniskirt got into a blue car. Then Daniel faced her again, large before Miranda. She couldn't shut him out. "'Go to Canada,' you said. 'That's what I'd do.' I wonder. Could you have married your mathematician in Canada? I can just picture you saying good-bye to your mother forever."

"My mother's dead now," said Miranda. A knot of tears tightened about her throat.

"And so the hell am I." Daniel reached for her wrists, holding them too hard, hurting her deliberately. "But you're not, are you? You're just fine."

There was a voice behind Daniel. "Miranda. Miranda," it called.

"Mother," cried Miranda. But, of course, it wasn't, it was Anna Matsui, gripping her wrists, bringing her back. Miranda gasped for breath and Dr. Matsui let go of her. "It was awful," said Miranda. She began to cry. "He accused me . . ." She pulled the wires from her eyes recklessly. Tears spilled out of them. Miranda ached all over.

"He accused you of nothing." Dr. Matsui's voice was sharp and disappointed. "You accused yourself. The same old accusations. We made Daniel out of you, remember?" She rolled her chair backward, moved to the monitor for the feedback. Matthew handed it to her and she read it, shaking her head. Her short black hair flew against her cheeks. "It shouldn't have happened," she said. "We used only the memories that made you happy. And with your gift for lucid dreaming—well, I didn't think there was a risk." Her face was apologetic as she handed Miranda a tissue and waited for the crying to stop. "Matthew wanted to recall you earlier," she confessed, "but I didn't want it to end this way."

"No!" said Miranda. "We can't stop now. I never answered him."

"You only need to answer yourself. It's your memory and imagination confronting you. He speaks only with your voice, he behaves only as you expect him to." Dr. Matsui examined the feedback map again. "I should never have agreed to a repeat. I certainly won't send you back." She looked at Miranda and softened her voice. "Lie still. Lie still until you feel better."

"Like in another thirty years?" asked Miranda. She closed her eyes; her head hurt from the crying and the wires. She reached up to detach one close to her ear. "Everything he said to me was true," she added tonelessly.

"Many things he didn't say are bound to be true as well," Dr. Matsui pointed out. "Therapy is not really concerned with truth, which is almost always merely a matter of perspective. Therapy is concerned with adjustment—adjustment to an unchangeable situation or to a changing truth." She lifted a pen from her collar, clicking the point in and out absentmindedly. "In any given case," she continued, "we face a number of elements within our control and a far greater number beyond it. In a case such as yours, where the patient has felt profoundly and morbidly guilty over an extended period of time, it is because she is focusing almost exclusively on her own behavior. 'If only I hadn't done x,' she thinks, 'then y would never have happened.' Do you understand what I'm saying, Miranda?"

"No."

"In these sessions we try to show you what might have happened if the elements you couldn't control were changed. In your case we let you experience a continued relationship with Daniel. You see that you bore him no malice. You wished him nothing ill. If he had come back from the war, the bitterness of your last meeting would have been unimportant."

"He asked me to marry him," said Miranda. "He asked me to wait for him. I told you that. And I said that I was already seeing Allen. Allen! I said as far as I was concerned he was already gone."

"You wish you could change that, of course. But what you really want to change is his death and that was beyond your control." Dr. Matsui's face was sweet and intense.

Miranda shook her head. "You're not listening to me, Anna. I told you what happened, but I lied about why it happened. I pretended we had political differences. I thought my behavior would be palatable if it looked like a matter of conscience. But really I dated Allen for the first time before Daniel had even been drafted. Because I knew what was coming. I saw that his life was about to get complicated and messy. And I saw a way out of it. For me, of course. Not for him." Miranda began to pick unhappily at the loose skin around her nails. "What do you think of that?" she asked. "What do you think of me now?"

"What do *you* think?" Dr. Matsui said and Miranda responded in disgust.

"I know what *I* think. I think I'm sick of talking to myself. Is that the best you therapists can manage? I think I'll stay home and talk to the mirrors." She pulled the remaining connections to her scalp and sat up. "Matthew," she said. "Matthew!"

Matthew came to the side of her chair. He looked thin, concerned, and awkward. What a baby he was, really, she thought. He couldn't be more than twenty-five. "How old are you, Matthew?" she asked.

"Twenty-seven."

"Be a hell of a time to die, wouldn't it?" She watched Matthew put a nervous hand on his short brown hair and run it backward. "I want your opinion about something, Matthew. A hypothetical case. I'm trusting you to answer honestly."

Matthew glanced at Dr. Matsui, who gestured with her pen for him to go ahead. He turned back to Miranda. "What would you think of a woman who deserted her lover, a man she really claimed to love, because he got sick and she didn't want to face the unpleasantness of it?"

Matthew spoke carefully. "I would imagine that it was motivated by cowardice rather than cruelty," he said. "I think we should always forgive sins of cowardice. Even our own." He stood looking at Miranda with his earnest, innocent face.

"All right, Matthew," she said. "Thank you." She lay back down in the chair and listened to the hum of the idle machines. "Anna," she said. "He didn't behave as I expected. I mean, sometimes he did and sometimes he didn't. Even the first time."

"Tell me about it," said Dr. Matsui.

"The first session he was older than I expected. Like he hadn't died, but had continued to age along with me."

"Wish fulfillment."

"Yes, but I was *surprised* by it. And I was surprised by the setting. And he said something very odd right at the end. He quoted me Zeno's paradox and it really exists, but I never heard it before. It didn't sound like something Daniel would say, either. It sounded more like my husband, Michael. Where did it come from?"

"Probably from just where you said," Dr. Matsui told her. "Michael. You don't think you remember it, but obviously you did. And husbands and lovers are bound to resemble each other, don't you think? We often get bits of overlap. Our parents show up one way or another in almost all our memories." Dr. Matsui stood. "Come in Tuesday," she said. "We'll talk some more."

"I'd like to see him one more time," said Miranda.

"Absolutely not," Dr. Matsui answered, returning Miranda's chair to its upright position.

* * *

"Where are we, Daniel?" Miranda asked. She couldn't see anything.

"Camp Pendleton," he answered. "On the beach. I used to run here mornings. Guys would bring their girlfriends. Not me, of course."

Miranda watched the landscape fill in as he spoke. Fog remained. It was early and overcast. She heard the ocean and felt the wet, heavy air begin to curl her hair. She was barefoot on the sand and a little cold. "I'm so sorry, Daniel," she said. "That's all I ever really wanted to tell you. I loved you."

"I know you did." He put his arm around her. She leaned against him. I must look like his mother, she thought; in fact, her own son was older than Daniel now. She looked up at him carefully. He must have just arrived at camp. The hair had been all but shaved from his head.

"Maybe you were right, anyway," Daniel told her. "Maybe I just shouldn't have gone. I was so angry at you by then I didn't care anymore. I even thought about dying with some sense of anticipation. Petulant, you know, like a little kid. I'll go and get killed and *then* she'll be sorry."

"And she was," said Miranda. "God, was she." She turned to face him, pressed her lined cheek against his chest, smelled his clothes. He must have started smoking again. Daniel put both arms around her. She heard a gull cry out ecstatically.

"But when the time came I really didn't want to die." Daniel's voice took on an unfamiliar edge, frightened, slightly hoarse. "When the time came I was willing to do *anything* rather than die." He hid his face in her neck. "Do you have kids?" he asked. "Did you and Michael ever?"

"A son," she said.

"How old? About six?"

Miranda wasn't sure how old Jeremy was now. It changed every year. But she told him, wonderingly, "Of course not, Daniel. He's all grown up. He owns a pizza franchise, can you believe it? He thinks I'm a bore."

"Because I killed a kid during the war. A kid about six years old. I figured it was him or me. I shot him." Miranda pushed back from Daniel trying to get a good look at his face. "They used kids, you know," he said. "They counted on us not being able to kill them. I saw this little boy coming for me with his hands behind his back. I told him to stop. I shouted at him to stop. I pointed my rifle and said I was going to kill him. But he kept on coming."

"Oh, Daniel," said Miranda. "Maybe he didn't speak English."

"A pointed rifle is universal. He walked into the bullet."

"What was he carrying?"

"Nothing," said Daniel. "How could I know?"

"Daniel," Miranda said. "I don't believe you. You wouldn't do that." Her words unsettled her even more. "Not the way I remember you," she said. "This is not the way I remember you."

"It's so easy for you to see what's right," said Daniel.

I'm going back, thought Miranda. Where am I really? I must be with Anna, but then she remembered that she was not. She was in her own study. She worked to feel the study chair beneath her, the ache in her back as she curved over her desk. Her feet dangled by the wheels; she concentrated until she could feel them. She saw her own hand, still holding the pencil, and she put it down. Things seemed very clear to her. She walked to the bedroom and summoned Dr. Matsui over the console. The doctor was with a patient. She waited perhaps fifteen minutes before Anna appeared.

"Daniel's the one with the problem," Miranda said. "It's not me, after all."

"There is no Daniel." Dr. Matsui's voice betrayed a startled concern. "Except in your mind and on my tapes. Apart from you, no Daniel."

"No. He came for me again. Just like in our sessions. Just as intense. Do you understand? Not a dream." She cut off Dr. Matsui's protest. "It was not a dream, because I wasn't asleep. I was working and then I was with him. I could feel him. I could smell him. He told me an absolutely horrible story about killing a child during the war. Where would I have gotten that? Not the sort of thing they send home in their letters' to the bereaved."

"There were a thousand ugly stories out of Vietnam," said Dr. Matsui. "I know some and I wasn't even born yet. Or just barely born. Remember My Lai?" Miranda watched her image clasp its hands. "You heard this story somewhere. It became part of your concept of the war. So you put it together now with Daniel." Dr. Matsui's voice took on its professional patina. "I'd like you to come in, Miranda. Immediately. I'd like to take a complete read-out and keep you monitored awhile. Maybe overnight. I don't like the turn this is taking."

"All right," said Miranda. "I don't want to be alone anyway. Because he's going to come again."

"No," said Dr. Matsui firmly. "He's not."

Miranda took the elevator to the garage and unlocked her bicycle. She was not frightened and wondered why not. She felt unhappy and uncertain, but in complete control of herself. She pushed out into the bike lane.

When the helicopter appeared overhead, Miranda knew immediately where she was. A banana tree sketched itself in on her right. There was a smell in the air which was strange to her. Old diesel engines, which she recognized, but also something organic. A lushness almost turned to rot. In the distance the breathtaking green of rice growing. But the dirt at her feet was bare.

Miranda had never imagined a war could be so quiet. Then she heard the chopper. And she heard Daniel. He was screaming. He stood right next to her, beside a pile of sandbags, his rifle stretched out before him. A small, delicately featured child was just walking into Miranda's view, his arms held behind him. All Miranda had to do was lift her hand.

"No, Daniel," she said. "His hands are empty."

Daniel didn't move. The war stopped. "I killed him, Randy," said Daniel. "You can't change that."

Miranda looked at the boy. His eyes were dark, a streak of dust ran all the way up one shoulder and onto his face. He was barefoot. "I know," she said. "I can't help him." The child faded and disappeared. "I'm trying to help you."

The boy reappeared again, back farther, at the very edge of her vision. He was beautiful, unbearably young. He began to walk to them once more.

"*Can* you help me?" Daniel asked.

Miranda pressed her palm into his back. He wore no shirt and was slick and sweaty. "I don't know," she said. "Was it a crime of cowardice or of cruelty? I'm told you can be forgiven the one, but not the other."

Daniel dropped his rifle into the dirt. The landscape turned slowly about them, became mountainous. The air smelled cleaner and was cold.

A bird flew over them in a beautiful arc, and then it became a baseball and began to fall in slow motion, and then it became death and she could plot its trajectory. It was aimed at Daniel, whose rifle had reappeared in his hands.

Now, Miranda thought. She could stay and die with Daniel the way she'd always believed she should. Death moved so slowly in the sky. She could see its progress moment to moment. It descended like a series of scarcely differentiated still frames. "Look, Daniel," she said, but he refused to look up. "It's Zeno's paradox in reverse. Finite points. Infinite time." How long did she have to make this decision? A lifetime. Her lifetime.

Daniel reached out his hand to touch her hair. Gray, she knew. Her gray hair under his young hand. He was twenty-four. "Don't stay," he said. "Do you think I would have wanted you to? I would never have wanted that."

So Miranda moved from his hand and found she was glad to do so. She began to think her way out, tried to feel the bicycle between her legs, the pedaling movement of her feet, her hands gripping too hard. "I always loved you," she said as if it mattered to Daniel, who dimmed before her eyes. He looked through her as though she were already gone. She just glimpsed the soldiers who materialized beside him and death which grew to accommodate them. But they wouldn't all die. Some of them would survive in pieces. She remembered this. And some would survive whole. Wouldn't they?

THE POPLAR STREET STUDY

The 600 block of Poplar Street was known for its nice lawns. The Desmonds, who lived on the corner, had the very nicest—a tasteful display of seasonal flowers under the arch of an oriental bridge. The Narrs next door worked endlessly to keep the Desmonds' grass out of their ornamental strawberries, but this irritation had never blossomed into gunfire the way the Simpson/Martin dogfight had.

Two years ago the Martins had acquired a dog—a nervous terrier who never stopped barking. People farther down the street were able to ignore the noise. It was so steady it became no more troublesome than the occasional jet overhead, or the comforting sound of power mowers on a Sunday morning. But the Simpsons, who shared a fence with the Martins, compared it to Chinese water torture. One night Mr. Simpson hysterically demanded a solution. Mr. Martin, who really had tried to train the dog, responded nastily that the only thing he could do was to shoot it. "The blood will be on your hands," he said coldly, closing the door on Mr. Simpson's hysteria. He walked calmly into the backyard and discharged a pistol into the air. He enjoyed it, picturing the guilt Mr. Simpson must be suffering, but the terrier, who had stopped barking in surprise at the sound of the gunshot, resumed its noise almost im-

mediately, so the tableau was not really a convincing
one.

Two months later the Simpsons moved out and the
Andersons moved in. The Anderson were both black and
Jewish, a nice family with two boys and a dog of their
own. The barking seemed to trouble them less, although
they did tell the Aldritches that the Simpsons had not
mentioned the dog to them during the sale of the house
and had described the neighborhood as "quiet." Mrs.
Aldritch imagined this was a complaint, although nothing in Mrs. Anderson's tone suggested it.

At this point the trouble center of the block shifted
to the Kramer house. Everyone knew that the Kramers'
marriage, which had survived for twenty miserable
years, was gasping its last few breaths. Mr. Kramer had
told them so. "A man has certain needs," he hinted. Mr.
Kramer had a drinking problem, which he displayed at
every opportunity. He was overweight, balding, and
flirtatious. Mrs. Kramer was a saint. Everyone said so.

The people of the 600 block knew each other
without actually being friends. They were, for the most
part, professionals, gone all day and tired at night. They
took pride in their homes and protected their privacy.

There were only a few children: the Anderson boys,
David and Joey, who were ten and eight years old,
Sunny Aldritch, age eight, Tommy and Maureen Martin,
eight and two, and the Evert baby, who was too little to
count.

Once a year on the fourth of July they closed both
ends of the street and had a block party with volleyball.
The Kramers and the Andersons sometimes played
bridge together and groups sometimes watched the
world series or the superbowl at the Narrs', where
reception was inexplicably better. When the Simpsons
had gone for four weeks without cutting their grass, Mrs.
Desmond had organized a neighborhood improvement
committee to deal with them. But for the most part, the
600 block was not a social unit. Only the children were
really friends, and spent the weekends riding their
bicycles together, up and down the street.

* * *

The first indication of crisis that Poplar Street had was the six o'clock news, which wasn't on. Mr. Anderson turned on his television to see how the Padres were doing and got "Father Knows Best" reruns instead. On every channel. He went next door to check the Martins' TV, but the Martins were eating and Mr. Martin said, rather shortly, that they never watched television during the dinner hour. Later Tommy Martin came to see if David and Joey could play, and interrupted the Andersons' dinner. Mr. Anderson thought it was deliberate and told his wife that Mr. Martin was a bigot with a lot of repressed hostility. He tried to call and tell him so, but the phone was dead.

Mrs. Narr discovered that her phone was out of order at about the same time. She went to the Desmonds next door, planning to call the phone company and report it, but their phone didn't work either. It was cocktail hour at the Desmonds and they persuaded her to stay and join them. Mrs. Desmond and Mrs. Narr got along well, in spite of their warring gardens. They were both attractive, well-groomed, ambitious women in their thirties. They were both married to older, admiring men. Mrs. Desmond worked in city government and Mrs. Narr sold real estate. Confident that someone else would eventually report the phones, they sipped martinis and complained about the Aldritches, who lived on the other side of the Narrs, but had so many cars they continually parked the oldest one in front of the Narrs' house. "There's a grease spot there nothing will ever remove," Mrs. Narr said.

The Aldritches were a young couple with strange friends. Mrs. Aldritch must have been a child bride and she was totally ineffectual in controlling her daughter, Sunny, whose real name was Sunshine and who knew an astounding number of vulgar expressions. The Desmonds were sympathetic to Mrs. Narr's complaints and sent her home with the comfortable feeling that she had been heard. Mrs. Desmond had even spoken of rejuvenating the Neighborhood Improvement Society, "if push came to shove," she said. Mrs. Narr went to bed happy, one of the last on Poplar Street to turn out her light.

Only Mr. Kramer remained awake, having a solitary scotch and thinking that something was different. He thought of his wife, already asleep, and had another drink, still puzzling over the change until, at last, it came to him. It was amazingly quiet out. No planes. No trains. Even the Martins' dog seemed muted. He sat out on the back patio for a long time, listening to the whisper of the natural world.

Friday morning came early to the 600 block, with so many people trying to get to so many offices, schools, and childcare centers on time. Mrs. Aldritch discovered she had no banana for Sunny's cereal. She had raisins, but Sunny didn't really like raisins, and Mrs. Aldritch thought she had time to get to the store if she took the car and made only the one purchase. She drove to the end of the block, then, suddenly, the car went dead. "Damn," she thought. It had started up smoothly enough, although she had noticed it dripping oil. Mrs. Aldritch got out with the intention of looking under the hood, but was immediately distracted by an enormous presence on the Desmonds' lawn. "My god, look at that!" she said to herself. At one end of the oriental bridge sat what appeared to be a piece of modern sculpture, huge, iridescent, with an obsidian slickness that made it appear permanently wet "The Desmonds were the ones," she thought, "who made that huge fuss when the Kramers wanted to put those little gnomes in their yard and now they go and put up something like this." The sculpture resembled an eight-foot mood ring. She could hardly wait to go home and tell her husband about it.

She turned, but peripherally she saw a slight tremor and looked back. Now there were two sculptured pieces and they began to grow horizontally in a movement which became the lifting of many arms. Suddenly the bulges at the top were clearly clusters of eyes, and she could make out, she thought, lips, too, rolled back to display drooping incisors. Each creature held an object in front of it in a single hand. The objects were identical, small, metallic boxes, perfectly square and they extended them toward Mrs. Aldritch, making her scream and then freeze as still as her car.

The sound of her scream brought the Desmonds to their front door and Mr. Anderson to her side. Mr. Anderson's morning paper had not been delivered and the early news had been replaced by a Dean Martin/Jerry Lewis movie. Mr. Anderson had come outside with the intention of finding out what in hell was going on when he heard Mrs. Aldritch. He stood beside her now, his hand floating just above her shoulder, his mouth still open for the question he'd never asked. The creatures responded to his presence by waving their arms wildly and rubbing them together. The friction of their arms created a high, hollow sound, like a flute far off in the distance. Then a mechanical voice, lisping slightly and off-pitch like a record played a bit too fast, came from within the boxes. "Retain your composure if possible," it said. "No one is going to be hurt."

Down the street a door slammed and Sunny's plaintive voice was heard. "Mommy! I thought you were making my breakfast! I'm starving to death. . . ." She appeared in front of the Aldritch house, caught sight of her mother, and began to run toward her. Mrs. Aldritch whirled, calling to Sunny to get back in the house *instantly* and to stay there. Sunny did not even pause and her mother caught her as she came, wrapping her arms about the child protectively. From inside her mother's clutch, Sunny located the creatures. "Gross out," she said. "Really."

They heard Mr. Kramer's car pull out and head in the opposite direction. At the end of the block it went dead, and moments later, Mr. Kramer ran toward them, white-faced and panting. Mr. Anderson caught his arm as he went past, slowing Mr. Kramer sufficiently to notice the creatures in his way. "My god," sobbed Mr. Kramer. "My god. We're surrounded."

The 600 block of Poplar Street lived inside for two whole days. Mr. Martin and Mr. Aldritch, independently, tried to climb their back fences. They found that they froze upon reaching the top, and then some irresistible force gently pushed them back. Mr. Aldritch kept trying until he sprained his wrist. He had an over-the-fence acquaintance with his rear neighbors and tried to call to them. Mr. Anderson stood in *his* backyard and signaled repeated SOSes with bathtowels and flashlights. Neither received any response. As nearly as they could tell, the blocks on every side of them were deserted.

The Narrs began to run out of food. Saturday had always been their big shopping day. Sunny, David, Joey, and Tommy began to find it tiresome indoors. They were active children, used to running and bicycling, and being children, they found it impossible to sustain an atmosphere of alarm. The creatures had remained on the corners and made no attempt to enter the block itself. "The Best of Johnny Carson" was the only show on television.

Sunny was the first child to defy her parents and venture outdoors. She rode her bicycle enticingly back and forth in front of the Andersons' until David and Joey joined her and soon the Martin children were out, too, pedaling around as though it were a normal weekend. They discovered a wonderful new game. If they rode as hard as they could into the Poplar/Maxwell intersection, the bicycle would freeze up suddenly, then be spit back into Poplar Street. The Anderson boys rigged a jump so that they could be aloft at the moment of freezing.

The creatures arm-wrestled at the corners and ignored them. Mrs. Desmond watched from her window. At last she made herself open the door. She walked by the creatures, catching a quick whiff of an odor rather like tuna fish, forcing herself not to move too fast. The Narrs' door opened just enough to let her in.

Mrs. Narr wanted to talk about food. The Desmonds had purchased catastrophe supplies of dried foods when Reagan became president. Mrs. Desmond chose not to mention these now, but listened to Mrs. Narr's concerns as though she shared them. "Why are they here?" said Mrs. Narr at last, and her voice went hoarse as she said it. "What do they want with us?"

Mrs. Desmond, with her greater political aware-
ness, suggested that the Andersons might be the key.
She tried to explain the quota system to Mrs. Narr, who
didn't listen. The conversation about familiar issues and
complaints began to soothe Mrs. Desmond. She was a
professional; she was used to being in charge. Her self-
confidence began to return to her. "Well, why don't we
just ask them?" she said in a voice almost girlish.

But Mrs. Narr refused to join her. Not that she
didn't think it was a good idea. But it struck her as rash.
Mrs. Narr never behaved rashly, she reminded Mrs.
Desmond. Unless she was certain the occasion called for
it.

This was irritating and shook Mrs. Desmond's
resolve slightly. But only slightly. She pointed out to
herself that she had to pass right by the creatures to get
home anyway. She smiled politely and told herself Mrs.
Narr was a wimp. She took a deep breath, holding
herself very straight, and opened the door. It was her
lawn they were camped out on, after all. She was
entitled to an explanation. She attempted a confident,
purposeful stride and wished she had dressed with more
care. What were her clothes saying about her?

The creatures watched her approach, beginning to
wave their arms. She heard a faint sound like wind
chimes. The tuna odor intensified. That and their sleek
skins reminded her of the seal pool at Marine World.

"I believe I speak for the entire neighborhood," she
said formally, "when I say I think we have a right to know
what's going on."

There was a pause, then the boxes answered. The
synthetic voices reminded her of Alvin, the singing
chipmunk. "Information will be provided as it is purposeful," they answered.

What did that mean? Mrs. Desmond wondered.
She grew more specific; her tone was aggressive. "How
long are we to be kept here?" she asked. "I have a job to
go to. We're in the middle of budgeting and I really
cannot be spared. The children have school."

She waited for the response. "These things are no
longer necessary," she was told.

It chilled Mrs. Desmond. She was suddenly aware of her husband, watching her through the window. His silent support brought an unprofessional quaver to her voice. She lost her courage all at once. "We cannot stay here indefinitely," she forced herself to say. "We are running out of food."

"We are prepared to assume responsibility for your nutritional needs."

The teeth which loomed above her were so clearly carnivorous. The wet skin suggested a fatty diet. Mrs. Desmond felt faint. She began to cry. "You've no right to keep us here," she said. "What are you going to do to us?"

"No one will be hurt," the boxes answered. "Information will be provided as needed." The two creatures sank back into the lawn, lowered the metallic boxes. Their arms intertwined.

Mrs. Desmond went into her house and let her husband put his arms around her. "I've made you a cup of coffee," he said. "I'll go and get it."

He looked so concerned Mrs. Desmond forced herself to smile. "Put some powdered milk in it," she told him. "We might as well get used to dried foods."

She took a long time over her coffee. If she had been at work she would have been drinking coffee just like this. She would have been making decisions, redpenciling the glut out of proposed expenditures, drafting memos. She sipped her drink. "Honey," she said. "We all need to talk. Don't you think? I mean the whole neighborhood. We need to have a meeting."

"Will they let us?"

"Let's see. Are you with me? We'll go knock on doors."

"I'm with you," her husband told her. "Whatever you say."

"Or—" Mrs. Desmond's voice was thoughtful. "If we all put on our swimsuits we could say we were going to the Kramer's for a swim. That would be even better. We could say we do it every Sunday."

Mr. Desmond thought she was clever and said so. He went to slip into his suit and flipflops. But at the last moment Mrs. Desmond chose a sundress for herself. It had occurred to her that she could easily dominate a group of people in swimsuits if she dressed appropriately. And leadership was going to be critical now. A unified response. One leader.

The creatures seemed to pay no attention to them as they stepped outside, but had a disconcerting ability to look in many directions at once, each eye independent of the others. Mr. Desmond waved his towel in their direction. "Pool party," he called and proceeded hastily to the Narrs' front door.

Sunny Aldritch came skidding up on her bicycle. "Did they invite us to go swimming?" she asked excitedly. "Really? I'll get my suit. Far out! I'll go tell my Mom. She didn't think they were *ever* going to ask us."

The Everts wouldn't answer their door, but the rest of the neighborhood assembled quickly at the Kramers'. A quantity of beer was produced—to help with the cover—and they began to drink it. Mrs. Desmond opened a can and looked for a place to throw the fliptop. "We must be thinking about escape," she said. "After all, there are only four of them."

Sunny Aldritch took a sip of her mother's beer. "Oh, there are lots more than that," she said.

"What do you mean, sweetheart?" said Mrs. Desmond icily. "Two in front of my house, two down by the Everts'."

"But not always the same two," said Sunny. "The two at your house now are different than the first two we saw."

Mrs. Desmond felt something bitter rise in her throat. "Are you sure? How can you be sure? They all look alike."

"Not to me," said Sunny saucily.

"Even if there were only four," said Mr. Anderson. "What good would it do us? We're webbed in here. We're no match for them."

"It's a force field," said Mr. Aldritch knowledgeably. "I've seen them on 'Star Trek.' What we have to do is find out how they generate it. A picked team of us will have to turn it off at the source while the rest of us create a diversion."

"What if the source is outside the field?" asked Mr. Anderson.

"The key is those little boxes," said Mr. Kramer. "One of them pointed that at me and I went weak all over. We have to get those little boxes."

The children began a game of Marco Polo in the pool. Mrs. Desmond felt the meeting was slipping away from her. "What kind of weapons do we have?" she asked.

There was a pause. "Mr. Martin has a gun," said Mr. Desmond. "We all know that. And Mr. Narr has a hunting rifle."

"Three rifles," Mr. Narr told them.

Mr. Aldritch nodded. "Keep those ready. They might be just the diversion we need." He sipped his beer. "Aliens invade suburban neighborhood," he said. "I saw it on 'Twilight Zone.' The important thing now is that we don't begin to turn on each other."

"Why?" said Mrs. Narr.

"Why what?"

"Why did aliens invade a suburban neighborhood?"

Mr. Aldritch shrugged. "For entertainment? For research?" He lowered his voice so the children wouldn't hear. "For food."

Mrs. Narr sniffled slightly. "Suppose we could get off the block," she said. "have you looked at the houses behind us? The grass is growing, but no one mows it. No one lives in those houses anymore."

"We haven't been mowing our lawns, but we're still here," Mr. Martin objected.

Mr. Anderson finished his beer. "But Mrs. Narr is right. Those houses are deserted. No noise, no lights. Our radios don't work. They may be holding the whole city."

"So what can we do?" asked Mrs. Desmond. "That's what we have to decide."

"Mommy!" Sunny's voice was loud and indignant. "Tommy keeps opening his eyes underwater."

"Am not," said Tommy.

"Are, too."

"You're just a baby. Can't stand to get caught."

"Can, too!"

"Can not."

"I wish we could signal," said Mrs. Aldritch quietly.

There was a pause while the neighbors thought nostalgically about the Simpsons' CB radio, which had so infuriated everyone by interfering with prime time television reception. "We have flares in the car trunk," Mrs. Desmond said at last.

"Oh, so do we," said Mrs. Aldritch. "In all the car trunks."

"We can set some out tonight," Mr. Anderson agreed.

Mr. Kramer reached for the last Coors. They were down to the light beer now. "I wonder how the Padres are doing," he said.

"Do you think they're playing?" said Mr. Anderson. "They were scheduled against the Braves today. And what are we getting? Did you look this morning? 'Gilligan's Island.'" His wife moved in closer to him. She thought he was beginning to get drunk. "You know Garry Templeton, the shortstop?" Mr. Anderson continued. "Did I tell you he went to the same high school I did?" There was a long silence. "Damn it! It irks me to just sit here." Mr. Anderson stood up. "I'm going to go find out what's what."

Mrs. Desmond rose, too, one hand on her husband's arm, pulling him to his feet at the same time. "We'll come," she said.

"And us," said Mr. Aldritch, "except for Sunny." Sunny climbed out of the pool instantly and came to drip on his shoes.

"Except for Sunny what?" she asked.

The other neighbors looked uncomfortably away. It was a small and silent delegation. Mr. Anderson's anger propelled them down the street. "I want some questions answered," he told the two sentries in the Desmonds' yard. They had draped themselves over the oriental bridge which, as a result, was creaking in the center. The creatures straightened and began to rub their arms together. Mr. Anderson paid no attention to the faint music. "And I want them answered now," he said.

"Information will be provided as it is purposeful," the boxes answered. The creatures were not even holding them today, but had them slung about their bodies like tourist cameras.

"We want to contact our friends and family outside."

"Regretfully, we cannot permit it."

"I—" Mr. Anderson's voice was dangerously quiet and distinct. Beer and baseball, thought Mrs. Desmond irritatedly, that's what it takes to get a man to act like a man. "*I*," repeated Mr. Anderson, "refuse to be kept here."

The boxes made their customary pause. The sound of the creatures' arms rose in pitch. "We have no interest in interfering in your lives," they said. "Please continue to function normally."

"Normally! Normally!" Mr. Anderson's voice rose to match the boxes. "Do you imagine any part of the last few days has been normal for us? You imprison us in our homes. Cut us off from our friends. Deprive us of our sources of food and information. Even the television is nothing but reruns."

There was a longer pause. Then the boxes responded like a choir of dwarves. "We have continued the television," they said, "because we believe it to be an integral part of your routine. We welcome programming suggestions."

Mr. Anderson sneered. "*Invasion of the Body Snatchers*," he said.

"*The Invaders*," said Mrs. Aldritch.

"*War of the Worlds*," said Mr. Aldritch.

"'Joanie Loves Chachi,'" said Sunny.

The next day the aliens delivered the first shipment of food. Four additional aliens appeared to distribute it. They greeted each other with a weaving of arms which was almost sexual, Mrs. Desmond thought, and somewhat disgusting. When the boxes were opened they contained small, hard pellets like dog food.

"Do you believe this?" Mrs. Desmond asked. She

was anxious to reestablish her authority. She felt Mr. Anderson's actions after the pool party had threatened it slightly. "Are we supposed to eat this?" she asked the alien next to her. It focused three of its jellied eyes on her, but did not respond.

Mr. Aldritch picked up a pellet and tasted it. "It tastes just like it looks," he told them.

"It looks like the food you buy in the zoo for animals," said Mrs. Desmond.

"It looks like shit," said Sunny. "Rat shit. I'm not eating it."

The voice boxes spoke. "The foodstuffs are of a high quality. They are noncarcinogenic and contain slight doses of fluoride in addition to vitamins. . . ."

"We need a variety of foods," said Mrs. Narr despairingly.

"No, these will meet your nutritional needs."

"We like a variety of foods."

Mr. Evert had joined them today. He looked wan and unsteady. "The baby can't chew these," he pointed out.

"The food has been sorted according to residence. In the box labeled with the number of your residence you will find a powdered variant which may be mixed with water." Mrs. Desmond began to pass out the packages. The aliens retreated back down the street to their usual corners. "Starting tomorrow," the voice boxes chorused, "we will expect you to take weekly physicals."

Mr. Kramer's mouth went dry. "Physicals?" he said.

"We are taking care of you. We have assumed responsibility for you." The voices grew faster. "Check your televisions. There is a film festival on."

Mr. Anderson picked up a handful of food and let it slip through his fingers. "Rat *food,*" he said. "Lab rats. That's it. It's a study."

Eight additional aliens appeared in the morning for the physicals. Each could wield several instruments at once so things went very fast. Despite Mr. Kramer's premonitions, the physicals were just physicals. Tissue samples, blood, urine, mucus, and stool samples were collected from each neighbor. Each neighbor was weighed and measured, their voice pitches were recorded, their posture was analyzed. There were balance tests, reflex tests and questionnaires. "'I have the feeling people are out to get me,'" Mr. Anderson read aloud off his personality profile. "'Usually true, sometimes true, rarely true.' Jesus Christ!"

At the end of the week the aliens made another announcement. The rubbing of their arms was particularly harmonious. They had brought five boxes of Whitman's candies as a special treat.

"Great," said Mr. Narr. "When do we get them?"

The synthetic voices were annoyingly even. "They've been hidden. You must hunt for them."

There was a long dumbfounded silence. "You must be kidding," said Mr. Anderson. He felt a clutch inside him, a furious contraction. "We've cooperated with your physicals; we've answered your questionnaires. But we're not going to hunt for chocolates."

"I will," said Sunny. "And I bet I find them."

The children fanned out, leaving behind an angry and bewildered group of adults. "This is to humiliate us," said Mrs. Desmond. "This is a psychological ploy to break us completely. Mr. Martin, get your gun. Enough is enough."

Mr. Martin reached slowly into his shirt. "It won't work," he said. "I've already tried it."

He handed the pistol to Mrs. Desmond, who aimed in the direction of her front yard. The creatures gave no sign of noticing. "Not like this," said Mr. Anderson. "We need a plan, we need the boxes. . . ." His voice faded as Mrs. Desmond pulled the trigger and heard dead air.

"Are you sure . . . ?" she began.

"Oh, it's loaded," said Mr. Martin.

"Let me try." Mr. Kramer reached for the gun. His hand shook violently and left a sweaty film on Mrs. Desmond's own dry skin. Mr. Kramer had been looking quite ill recently. His flirtatious, easy manner had vanished with the last of the alcohol. Now, in one sharp movement, he pointed the gun to his forehead and pulled the trigger. The silence continued. "Damn," said Mr. Kramer, beginning to cry. "Damn."

Sunny came racing back down the street. "I found one box in the Anderson's ivy," she called. "And another under our car. I get all the chocolate creams."

David Anderson appeared with a Whitman sampler. "Here, Mom," he said.

Mrs. Anderson opened the box. "There's a rum chocolate," she said. "You take it, Mr. Kramer." She passed the rest around.

Mrs. Narr took a caramel. "David is a good boy," she said quietly to Mrs. Aldritch, who nodded, chewing thoughtfully.

"A nice kid," Mrs. Aldritch said. "But just a little repressed. You'll never see Sunny stifled like that."

"No," Mrs. Narr agreed. "I know I won't."

After that the creatures began to hide the daily food supplies and to time the hunts. One day the neighbors couldn't find the food at all. They appealed to the creatures for help, but were told to look harder. A week later they came across the missing boxes in the Aldritches' garage.

"I'm surprised we *ever* found them," said Mr. Martin nastily. "It's lucky you've got the whole street to park along. It's lucky you don't have to try and fit a car in here."

Mrs. Desmond took charge of the extra food—their insurance against another failed search. She felt she was the most trustworthy since she and her husband still had their dried foods, but she did not explain this to the neighbors. The fact that the Desmonds were still drinking coffee was something they kept just between the two of them.

In the third week Mr. Anderson was asked to remain at the physicals for additional testing. A single alien did the extra work-up; it was the first time Mr. Anderson had seen one alone. He had begun to notice differences in the individual creatures—enough to know that Sunny was right. There were a great many of them. They even smelled different at times. The one drawing blood samples for him now had the customary tuna odor with a sort of garlic overlay. Mr. Anderson supposed that

their diets varied. He tried to count up exactly how
many there were, but couldn't. He thought of the
hopeless flares they had lit, night after night, when there
were no humans in the air to see them. He felt
completely dispirited.

The voice box spoke in its high-pitched, expressionless way. "You seem to have an abnormality in your
ability to use sugar."

"You're talking about diabetes," said Mr. Anderson.
"No, I'm not diabetic."

"Our tests confirm that you are."

"I would have thought we were on a pretty low-
sugar diet. But, if you're right, I'll need insulin."

"There are a number of possible treatments. Each
one necessitates greater contact between you and us
than we can allow. Such intercourse may contaminate
the control group. It will be necessary to remove you."

Mr. Anderson felt cold. "The control group?" he
asked, his own voice high and false somehow. "We're the
control group?" There was no answer. "Don't take me,"
he said. "Please."

"It is regrettable. You were one of the brighter
subjects. We have always enjoyed your questionnaires.
And you have assumed some leadership. Someone else
must replace you. That, in itself, will be interesting to
see. Mrs. Aldritch, perhaps? Or Mr. Kramer?"

This was more than any of the creatures had ever
said to Mr. Anderson. In the sheer volume of information he was receiving, Mr. Anderson saw the hopeless-
ness of his position. He was not going back. Not even to
say good-bye. There was no reason not to be frank with
him. "My family is there," he pleaded. "My children."

"The children are proving adaptable to anything.
The important element is the integrity of the control.
None of our other experiments can be evaluated without
it."

Mr. Anderson maneuvered himself closer to the
alien. Its arms were nearly around him, the smell was
very intense. Almost, he was out of the creature's line of
vision, almost too close to be seen. The eyes loomed
above him like clusters of fish eggs. He grabbed for the

voice box, held on to it though it burned his hand. It became shapeless, melted into his palm, and his last hopes melted with it. The creature ignored this action, merely grasped him gently by the shoulders and lower down the arms, thrusting him out farther away. The mountain of eyes focused on him.

"You're all wrong," said Mr. Anderson. "If you imagine that you've created a control situation in there. It's laughable, really." He felt his cheeks go wet, his nose fill. He wiped it. "I mean if you think for a moment what's going on out there is normal." The creature created a gentle friction with its arms, like wind in the trees. What it meant, Mr. Anderson didn't know, but he thought, he imagined, that the fishy eyes were looking at him intently, and that the movement of the arms was thoughtful.

Five years passed before they saw him on Poplar Street again. The creatures had been mistaken in their predictions. Neither Mrs. Aldritch, nor Mr. Kramer, nor Mrs. Desmond despite her hopes and plans had emerged as the natural block leader. It was Sunny who mediated between the neighbors and the creatures, organized the foodhunts, and planned holidays for their entertainment. She discovered quite quickly that there were patterns to the ways in which the food was hidden, and although the patterns changed, twenty minutes was the longest she ever had to hunt. She used this expertise to bully the reluctant grown-ups into doing what she wished. Gradually the resentment disappeared and it began to seem natural to listen to Sunny and agree with Sunny and do what Sunny said. When the Martins' dog died in a hysterical fit and Sunny wanted the entire neighborhood to attend a burial in the Martins' backyard, everyone did so.

Mrs. Narr let her garden go to weed and learned to make dandelion salads, which were enjoyed with the same ardor as the occasional Whitman's candies. Mr. Kramer began an evening tradition of story-telling, in which his stories were acknowledeged the best. They were, Mrs. Aldritch told him wistfully, as good as the soaps.

He was continuing an old favorite, a tale about warriors as slender as reeds who lived in glass houses on green hills at the end of the world, on the evening when Mr. Anderson reappeared. When they first saw him, in the last light of the day, he was magnificent. His skin gleamed moistly, he waved his arms when he talked and his words were a kind of singing. He had been living with aliens, he told them. But now he was back. They thought he was some sort of Messiah come to lead them to their freedom. He even thought so, himself. Unless it was another experiment. There was really no way to be sure.

FACE VALUE

It was almost like being alone. Taki, who had been alone one way or another most of his life, recognized this and thought he could deal with it. What choice did he have? It was only that he had allowed himself to hope for something different. A second star, small and dim, joined the sun in the sky, making its appearance over the rope bridge which spanned the empty river. Taki crossed the bridge in a hurry to get inside before the hottest part of the day began.

Something flashed briefly in the dust at his feet and he stooped to pick it up. It was one of Hesper's poems, half finished, left out all night. Taki had stopped reading Hesper's poetry. It reflected nothing, not a whisper of her life here with him, but was filled with longing for things and people behind her. Taki pocketed the poem on his way to the house, stood outside the door, and removed what dust he could with the stiff brush which hung at the entrance. He keyed his admittance; the door made a slight sucking sound as it resealed behind him.

Hesper had set out an iced glass of ade for him. Taki drank it at a gulp, superimposing his own dusty fingerprints over hers sketched lightly in the condensation on the glass. The drink was heavily sugared and only made him thirstier.

A cloth curtain separated one room from another, a blue sheet, Hesper's innovation since the dwelling was designed as a single, multifunctional space. Through the curtain Taki heard a voice and knew Hesper was listening again to her mother's letter—earth weather, the romances of her younger cousins. The letter had arrived weeks ago, but Taki was careful not to remind Hesper how old its news really was. If she chose to imagine the lives of her family moving along the same timeline as her own, then this must be a fantasy she needed. She knew the truth. In the time it had taken her to travel here with Taki, her mother had grown old and died. Her cousins had settled into marriages happy or unhappy or had faced life alone. The letters which continued to arrive with some regularity were an illusion. A lifetime later Hesper would answer them.

Taki ducked through the curtain to join her. "Hot," he told her as if this were news. She lay on their mat stomach down, legs bent at the knees, feet crossed in the air. Her hair, the color of dried grasses, hung over her face. Taki stared for a moment at the back of her head. "Here," he said. He pulled her poem from his pocket and laid it by her hand. "I found this out front."

Hesper switched off the letter and rolled onto her back away from the poem. She was careful not to look at Taki. Her cheeks were stained with irregular red patches so that Taki knew she had been crying again. The observation caused him a familiar mixture of sympathy and impatience. His feelings for Hesper always came in these uncomfortable combinations; it tired him.

"'Out front,'" Hesper repeated, and her voice held a practiced tone of uninterested nastiness. "And how did you determine that one part of this featureless landscape was the 'front'?"

"Because of the door. We have only the one door so it's the front door."

"No," said Hesper. "If we had two doors then one might arguably be the front door and the other the back door, but with only one it's just the door." Her gaze went straight upward. "You use words so carelessly. Words from another world. They mean nothing here." Her eyelids fluttered briefly, the lashes darkened with tears. "It's not just an annoyance to me, you know," she said. "It can't help but damage your work."

"My work is the study of the mene," Taki answered.

"Not the creation of a new language," and Hesper's eyes closed.

"I really don't see the difference," she told him. She lay a moment longer without moving, then opened her eyes and looked at Taki directly. "I don't want to have this conversation. I don't know why I started it. Let's rewind, run it again. I'll be the wife this time. You come in and say, 'Honey, I'm home!' and I'll ask you how your morning was."

Taki began to suggest that this was a scene from another world and would mean nothing here. He had not yet framed the sentence when he heard the door seal release and saw Hesper's face go hard and white. She reached for her poem and slid it under the scarf at her waist. Before she could get to her feet the first of the mene had joined them in the bedroom. Taki ducked through the curtain to fasten the door before the temperature inside the house rose. The outer room was filled with dust and the hands which reached out to him as he went past left dusty streaks on his clothes and his skin. He counted eight of the mene, fluttering about him like large moths, moths the size of human children, but with furry vestigial wings, hourglass abdomens, stick-like limbs. They danced about him in the open spaces, looked through the cupboards, pulled the tapes from his desk. When they had their backs to him he could see the symmetrical arrangement of dark spots which marked their wings in a pattern resembling a human face. A very sad face, very distinct. Masculine, Taki had always thought, but Hesper disagreed.

The party which had made initial contact under the leadership of Hans Mene so many years ago had wisely found the faces too whimsical for mention in their report. Instead they had included pictures and allowed them to speak for themselves. Perhaps the original explorers had been asking the same question Hesper posed the first time Taki showed her the pictures. Was the face really there? Or was this only evidence of the ability of humans to see their own faces in everything? Hesper had a poem entitled "The Kitchen God," which recounted the true story of a woman about a century ago who had found the image of Christ in the burn-marks on a tortilla. "Do *they* see it, too?" she had asked Taki, but there was as yet no way to ask this of the mene, no way to know if they had reacted with shock and recognition to the faces of the first humans they had seen, though studies of the mene eye suggested a finer depth perception which might significantly distort the flat image.

Taki thought that Hesper's own face had changed since the day, only six months ago calculated as Travel-time, when she had said she would come here with him and he thought it was because she loved him. They had sorted through all the information which had been collected to date on the mene and her face had been all sympathy then. "What would it be like," she asked him, "to be able to fly and then to lose this ability? To outgrow it? What would a loss like that do to the racial consciousness of a species?"

"It happened so long ago, I doubt it's even noticed as a loss," Taki had answered. "Legends, myths not really believed perhaps. Probably not even that. In the racial memory not even a whisper."

Hesper had ignored him. "What a shame they don't write poetry," she had said. She was finding them less romantic now as she joined Taki in the outer room, her face stoic. The mene surrounded her, ran their string-fingered hands all over her body, inside her clothing. One mene attempted to insert a finger into her mouth, but Hesper tightened her lips together resolutely, dust on her chin. Her eyes were fastened on Taki. Accusingly? Beseechingly? Taki was no good at reading people's eyes. He looked away.

Eventually the mene grew bored. They left in groups, a few lingering behind to poke among the boxes in the bedroom, then following the others until Hesper and Taki were left alone. Hesper went to wash herself as thoroughly as their limited water supply allowed; Taki swept up the loose dust. Before he finished, Hesper returned, showing him her empty jewelry box without a word. The jewelry had all belonged to her mother.

"I'll get them when it cools," Taki told her.

"Thank you."

It was always Hesper's things that the mene took. The more they disgusted her, pawing over her, rummaging through her things, no way to key the door against clever mene fingers even if Taki had agreed to lock them out, which he had not, the more fascinating they seemed to find her. They touched her twice as often as they touched Taki and much more insistently. They took her jewelry, her poems, her letters, all the things she treasured most, and Taki believed, although it was far too early in his studies really to speculate with any assurance, that the mene read something off the objects. The initial explorers had concluded that mene communication was entirely telepathic, and if this was accurate, then Taki's speculation was not such a leap. Certainly the mene didn't value the objects for themselves. Taki always found them discarded in the dust on this side of the rope bridge.

The fact that everything would be easily recovered did nothing to soften Hesper's sense of invasion. She mixed herself a drink, stirring it with the metal straw which poked through the dust-proof lid. "You shouldn't allow it," she said at last, and Taki knew from the time that had elapsed that she had tried not to begin this familiar conversation. He appreciated her effort as much as he was annoyed by her failure.

"It's part of my job," he reminded her. "We have to be accessible to them. I study them. They study us. There's no way to differentiate the two activities and certainly no way to establish communication except simultaneously."

"You're letting them study us, but you're giving them a false picture. You're allowing them to believe that humans intrude on each other in this way. Does it occur to you that they may be involved in similar charades? If so, what can either of us learn?"

Taki took a deep breath. "The need for privacy may not be as intrinsically human as you imagine. I could point to many societies which afforded very little of this. As for any deliberate misrepresentations on their part—well, isn't that the whole rationale for not sending a study team? Wouldn't I be farther along if I were working with environmentalists, physiologists, linguists? But the risk of contamination increases exponentially with each additional human. We would be too much of a presence. Of course, I will be very careful. I am far from the stage in my study where I can begin to draw conclusions. When I visit them . . ."

"Reinforcing the notion that such visits are ordinary human behavior . . ." Hesper was looking at Taki with great coolness.

"When I visit them I am much more circumspect," Taki finished. "I conduct my study as unobtrusively as possible."

"And what do you imagine you are studying?" Hesper asked. She closed her lips tightly over the straw and drank. Taki regarded her steadily and with exasperation.

"Is this a trick question?" he asked. "I imagine I am studying the mene. What do you imagine I am studying?"

"What humans always study," said Hesper. "Humans."

You never saw one of the mene alone. Not ever. One never wandered off to watch the sun set or took its food to a solitary hole to eat without sharing. They did everything in groups and although Taki had been observing them for weeks now and was able to identify individuals and had compiled charts of the groupings he had seen, trying to isolate families or friendships or work-castes, still the results were inconclusive.

His attempts at communication were similarly discouraging. He had tried verbalizations, but had not expected a response to them; he had no idea how they processed audio information although they could hear. He had tried clapping and gestures, simple hand signals for the names of common objects. He had no sense that these efforts were noticed. They were so unfocused when he dealt with them, fluttering here, fluttering there. Taki's ESP quotient had never been measurable, yet he tried that route, too. He tried to send a simple command. He would trap a mene hand and hold it against his own cheek, trying to form in his mind the picture which corresponded to the action. When he released the hand, sticky mene fingers might linger for a moment or they might slip away immediately, tangle in his hair instead, or tap his teeth. Mene teeth were tiny and pointed like wires. Taki saw them only when the mene ate. At other times they were hidden inside the folds of skin which almost hid their eyes as well. Taki speculated that the skin flaps protected their mouths and eyes from the dust. Taki found mene faces less expressive than their backs. Head-on they appeared petaled and blind as flowers. When he wanted to differentiate one mene from another, Taki looked at their wings.

Hesper had warned him there would be no art and he had asked her how she could be so sure. "Because their communication system is perfect," she said. "Out of one brain and into the next with no loss of meaning, no need for abstraction. Art arises from the inability to communicate. Art is the imperfect symbol. Isn't it?" But Taki, watching the mene carry water up from their underground deposits, asked himself where the line between tools and art objects should be drawn. For no functional reason that he could see, the water containers curved in the centers like the shapes of the mene's own abdomens.

Taki followed the mene below ground, down some shallow, rough-cut stairs into the darkness. The mene themselves were slightly luminescent when there was no other light; at times and seasons some were spectacularly so and Taki's best guess was that this was sexual. Even with the dimmer members, Taki could see well enough. He moved through a long tunnel with a low ceiling which made him stoop. He could hear water at the other end of it, not the water itself, but a special quality to the silence which told him water was near. The lake was clearly artificial, collected during the rainy season which no human had seen yet. The tunnel narrowed sharply. Taki could have gone forward, but felt suddenly claustrophobic and backed out instead. What did the mene think, he wondered, of the fact that he came here without Hesper. Did they notice this at all? Did it teach them anything about humans that they were capable of understanding?

"Their lives together are perfect," Hesper said. "Except for those useless wings. If they are ever able to talk with us at all it will be because of those wings."

Of course Hesper was a poet. The world was all language as far as she was concerned.

When Taki first met Hesper, at a party given by a colleague of his, he had asked her what she did. "I name things," she had said. "I try to find the right names for things." In retrospect Taki thought it was bullshit. He couldn't remember why he had been so impressed with it at the time, a deliberate miscommunication, when a simple answer, "I write poetry," would have been so clear and easy to understand. He felt the same way about her poetry itself, needlessly obscure, slightly evocative, but it left the reader feeling that he had fallen short somehow, that it had been a test and he had flunked it. It was unkind poetry and Taki had worked so hard to read it then.

"Am I right?" he would ask her anxiously when he finished. "Is that what you're saying?" but she would answer that the poem spoke for itself.

"Once it's on the page, I've lost control over it. Then the reader determines what it says or how it works." Hesper's eyes were gray, the irises so large and intense within their dark rings, that they made Taki dizzy. "So you're always right. By definition. Even if it's not remotely close to what I intended."

What Taki really wanted was to find himself in Hesper's poems. He would read them anxiously for some symbol which could be construed as him, some clue as to his impact on her life. But he was never there.

It was against policy to send anyone into the field alone. There were pros and cons, of course, but ultimately the isolation of a single professional was seen as too cruel. For shorter projects there were advantages in sending a threesome, but during a longer study the group dynamics in a trio often became difficult. Two were considered ideal and Taki knew that Rawji and

Heyen had applied for this post, a husband and wife team in which both members were trained for this type of study. He had never stopped being surprised that the post had been offered to him instead. He could not have even been considered if Hesper had not convinced the members of the committee of her willingness to accompany him, but she must have done much more. She must have impressed someone very much for them to decide that one trained xenologist and one poet might be more valuable than two trained xenologists. The committee had made some noises about "contamination" occurring between the two trained professionals, but Taki found this argument specious. "What did you say to them?" he asked her after her interview and she shrugged.

"You know," she said. "Words."

Taki had hidden things from the committee during his own interview. Things about Hesper. Her moods, her deep attachment to her mother, her unreliable attachment to him. He must have known it would never work out, but he walked about in those days with the stunned expression of a man who has been given everything. Could he be blamed for accepting it? Could he be blamed for believing in Hesper's unexpected willingness to accompany him? It made a sort of equation for Taki. *If* Hesper was willing to give up everything and come with Taki, *then* Hesper loved Taki. An ordinary marriage commitment was reviewable every five years; this was something much greater. No other explanation made any sense.

The equation still held a sort of inevitability for Taki. *Then* Hesper loved Taki, *if* Hesper were willing to come with him. So somehow, sometime, Taki had done something which lost him Hesper's love. If he could figure out what, perhaps he could make her love him again. "Do you love me?" he had asked Hesper, only once; he had too much pride for these thinly disguised pleadings. "Love is such a difficult word," she had answered, but her voice had been filled with a rare softness and had not hurt Taki as much as it might.

The daystar was appearing again when Taki returned home. Hesper had made a meal which suggested she was coping well today. It included a sort of pudding made of a local fruit they found themselves able to tolerate. Hesper called the pudding "boxty." It was apparently a private joke. Taki was grateful for the food and the joke, even if he didn't understand it. He tried to keep the conversation lighthearted, talking to Hesper about the mene water jars. Taki's position was that when the form of a practical object was less utilitarian than it might be, then it was art. Hesper laughed. She ran through a list of human artifacts and made him classify them.

"A paper clip," she said.

"The shape hasn't changed in centuries," he told her. "Not art."

"A safety pin."

Taki hesitated. How essential was the coil at the bottom of the pin? Very. "Not art," he decided.

"A hair brush."

"Boar bristle?"

"Wood handle."

"Art. Definitely."

She smiled at him. "You're confusing ornamentation with art. But why not? It's as good a definition as any," she told him. "Eat your boxty."

They spend the whole afternoon alone, uninterrupted. Taki transcribed the morning's notes into his files, reviewed his tapes. Hesper recorded a letter whose recipient would never hear it and sang softly to herself.

That night he reached for her, his hand along the curve at her waist. She stiffened slightly, but responded by putting her hand on his face. He kissed her and her mouth did not move. His movements became less gentle. It might have been passion; it might have been anger. She told him to stop, but he didn't. Couldn't. Wouldn't. "Stop," she said again and he heard she was crying. "They're here. Please stop. They're watching us."

"Studying us," Taki said. "Let them," but he rolled

away and released her. They were alone in the room. He would have seen the mene easily in the dark. "Hesper," he said. "There's no one here."

She lay rigid on her side of their bed. He saw the stitching of her backbone disappearing into her neck and had a sudden feeling that he could see everything about her, how she was made, how she was held together. It made him no less angry.

"I'm sorry," Hesper told him, but he didn't believe her. Even so, he was asleep before she was. He made his own breakfast the next morning without leaving anything out for her. He was gone before she had gotten out of bed.

The mene were gathering food, dried husks thick enough to protect the liquid fruit during the two-star dry season. They punctured the husks with their needle-thin teeth. Several crowded about him, greeting him with their fingers, checking his pockets, removing his recorder and passing it about until one of them dropped it in the dust. When they returned to work, Taki retrieved it, wiped it as clean as he could. He sat down to watch them, logged everything he observed. He noted in particular how often they touched each other and wondered what each touch meant. Affection? Communication? Some sort of chain of command?

Later he went underground again, choosing another tunnel, looking for one which wouldn't narrow so as to exclude him, but finding himself beside the same lake with the same narrow access ahead. He went deeper this time until it gradually became too close for his shoulders. Before him he could see a luminescence; he smelled the dusty odor of the mene and could just make out a sound, too, a sort of movement, a grass-rubbing-together sound. He stooped and strained his eyes to see something in the faint light. It was like looking into the wrong end of a pair of binoculars. The tunnel narrowed and narrowed. Beyond it must be the mene homes and he could never get into them. He contrasted this with the easy access they had to his home. At the end of his vision he thought he could just see something move, but he wasn't sure. A light touch on the back of his neck and another behind his knee startled him. He twisted around to see a group of the mene crowded into the tunnel behind him. It gave him a feeling of being trapped and he had to force himself to be very gentle as he pushed his way back and let the mene go through. The dark pattern of their wings stood in high relief against the luminescent bodies. The human faces grew smaller and smaller until they disappeared.

"Leave me alone," Hesper told him. It took Taki completely by surprise. He had done nothing but enter the bedroom; he had not even spoken yet. "Just leave me alone."

Taki saw no signs that Hesper had ever gotten up. She lay against the pillow and her cheek was still creased from the wrinkles in the sheets. She had not been crying. There was something worse in her face, something which alarmed Taki.

"Hesper?" he asked. "Hesper? Did you eat anything? Let me get you something to eat."

It took Hesper a moment to answer. When she did, she looked ordinary again. "Thank you," she said. "I am hungry." She joined him in the outer room, wrapped in their blanket, her hair tangled around her face. She got a drink for herself, dropping the empty glass once, stooping to retrieve it. Taki had the strange impression that the glass fell slowly. When they had first arrived, the gravitational pull had been light, just perceptibly lighter than Earth's. Without quite noticing, this had registered on him in a sort of lightheartedness. But Hesper had complained of feelings of dislocation, disconnection. Taki put together a cold breakfast, which Hesper ate slowly, watching her own hands as if they fascinated her. Taki looked away. "Fork," she said. He looked back. She was smiling at him.

"What?"

"Fork."

He understood. "Not art."

"Four tines?"

He didn't answer.

"Roses carved on the handle."

"Well then, art. Because of the handle. Not because of the tines." He was greatly reassured.

The mene came while he was telling her about the tunnel. They put their dusty fingers in her food, pulled it apart. Hesper set her fork down and pushed the plate away. When they reached for her she pushed them away, too. They came back. Hesper shoved harder.

"Hesper," said Taki.

"I just want to be left alone. They never leave me alone." Hesper stood up, towering above the mene. The blanket fell to the floor. "We flew here," Hesper said to the mene. "Did you see the ship? Didn't you see the pod? Doesn't that interest you? Flying?" She laughed and flapped her arms until they froze, horizontal at her sides. The mene reached for her again and she brought her arms in to protect her breasts, pushing the mene away repeatedly, harder and harder, until they tired of approaching her and went into the bedroom, reappearing with her poems in their hands. The door sealed behind them.

"I'll get them back for you," Taki promised, but Hesper told him not to bother.

"I haven't written in weeks," she said. "In case you hadn't noticed. I haven't finished a poem since I came here. I've lost that. Along with everything else." She brushed at her hair rather frantically with one hand. "It doesn't matter," she added. "My poems? Not art."

"Are you the best person to judge that?" Taki asked.

"Don't patronize me." Hesper returned to the table, looked again at the plate which held her unfinished breakfast, dusty from handling. "My critical faculties are still intact. It's just the poetry that's gone." She took the dish to clean it, scraped the food away. "I was never any good," she said. "Why do you think I came here? I had no poetry of my own so I thought I'd write the mene's. I came to a world without words. I hoped it would be clarifying. I knew there was a risk." Her hands moved very fast. "I want you to know I don't blame you."

"Come and sit down a moment, Hesper," Taki said, but she shook her head. She looked down at her body and moved her hands over it.

"They feel sorry for us. Did you know that? They feel sorry about our bodies."

"How do *you* know that?" Taki asked.

"Logic. We have these completely functional bodies. No useless wings. Not art." Hesper picked up the blanket and headed for the bedroom. At the cloth curtain she paused a moment. "They love our loneliness, though. They've taken all mine. They never leave me alone now." She thrust her right arm suddenly out into the air. It made the curtain ripple. "Go away," she said, ducking behind the sheet.

Taki followed her. He was very frightened. "No one is here but us, Hesper," he told her. He tried to put his arms around her but she pushed him back and began to dress.

"Don't touch me all the time," she said. He sank onto the bed and watched her. She sat on the floor to fasten her boots.

"Are you going out, Hesper?" he asked and she laughed.

"Hesper is out," she said. "Hesper is out of place, out of time, out of luck, and out of her mind. Hesper has vanished completely. Hesper was broken into and taken."

Taki fastened his hands tightly together. "Please don't do this to me, Hesper," he pleaded. "It's really so unfair. When did I ask so much of you? I took what you offered me; I never took anything else. Please don't do this."

Hesper had found the brush and was pulling it roughly through her hair. He rose and went to her, grabbing her by the arms, trying to turn her to face him. "Please, Hesper!"

She shook loose from him without really appearing to notice his hands, continued to work through the worst of her tangles. When she did turn around, her face was familiar, but somehow not Hesper's face. It was a face which startled him.

"Hesper is gone," it said. "We have her. You've lost her. We are ready to talk to you. Even though you will never, never, never understand." She reached out to touch him, laying her open palm against his cheek and leaving it there.

THE DRAGON'S HEAD

HALLOWEEN 1955

Mrs. McLaughlin was terribly old. Penny's father said that she was living in that same house, already an old woman, when he was a boy. No wonder she was eccentric, he implied, as if she were the kind of harmless old woman who knits.

Clifton Bell, a classmate of Penny's, said Mrs. McLaughlin was a witch. She looked like one, all right, with her bony elbows, that cloud of thin, white hair, and those strange fogged eyes. Mrs. McLaughlin was often out working in her roses during those times of the day when children passed by on their way to or from school. Occasionally she would seize some child in a grip kept strong by gardening or some supernatural force. She would lean her face into the child's face, asking "Who are you? What's your name?" without listening to the answer as her victim twisted to get away. "You wouldn't steal the apples from an old woman's tree, would you?" she might continue, in a voice of dreadful amusement. "Oh, no. Not you. You wouldn't strip a vine of nice, fat tomatoes. Must have been the crows." And truthfully, it must have been. Not a child in the school would have eaten anything from Mrs. McLaughlin's garden, much less gone in to get it. Penny never even walked down her side of the street.

Penny was not a cowardly child. She could hold

worms in her bare palm and thought of snakes merely as
bigger worms. She liked to play in the basement. Its
cobwebs, small, gritty windows, and damp corners made
it a wonderful landscape for all sorts of games. She was
not afraid of the dark. But the thought of witches did
give her an uncomfortable, shivery feeling in her
stomach and a coldness at the base of her neck and this
was really her mother's fault for letting her go to see *The
Wizard of Oz* when she was only five years old. Her
mother's memories of the movie had centered on Judy
Garland—the ruby slippers, the charming voice, the
surprising moment when black and white turned into
Technicolor. She had forgotten how effective the per-
formance of the witch was. Penny had slept between her
parents that night and had suffered from nightmares for
several nights afterward. A tree outside her room cast
moon shadows through the windows; the shapes of the
branches distorted into long, extended hands.

Penny had confided these fears to Clifton Bell while
they were still friends and it was really unfair that he
would taunt her with them now that they were not. "Go
play with Clifton," Penny's mother would suggest when
she grew tired of having Penny underfoot. Penny had
not played with Clifton in more than a year, but Penny's
mother never seemed to notice. Clifton only played with
boys now and Penny was practically a boy herself, but
Clifton didn't care. Couldn't she hit a baseball out of her
own yard and into Mr. Sillman's? How many boys could
do that? Mr. Sillman was their neighbor and their
postman. He would deliver the ball back to them with
their mail. "Hell of a swing she's got," he would say to
Penny's mother and then apologize quickly for his
language. "I'm going to tell the Yankees." And wasn't her
mother always complaining about the state of her clothes
or her knees or her hair? "I might as well have had a
boy," Penny's mother would say, looking her over and
shaking her head.

Penny's personal opinion was that she was a boy
trapped inside the body of a girl. She had heard this
interesting phrase at her mother's bridge party. Maggie
Cantor had been telling the women about her cousin

from Chicago who should have been married this week, but the wedding had to be canceled when her fiancé turned out to be a woman, too. "Angie is just as pretty as a picture," Maggie said, over her coffee. "Just as sweet as they come. And the invitations were already out and they have tickets to New York for their honeymoon and her fiancé says there's something she'd better know before the wedding. Thoughtful, wasn't she? Well, did you ever hear anything like it?"

Penny's mother was celebrated for her levelheadedness. "No, I never did," she said. "Do you really believe it?" and then noticing, suddenly, how quiet the house was, called out "Penny?" Penny had answered reluctantly, aware that she was closer than she should have been during such an adult conversation. "Go and play with Clifton," Penny's mother had told her, and while Penny was standing on the porch, the door just creaking shut behind her, she had heard one more scrap of conversation . . . "a boy trapped inside the body of a girl" . . . and had not known for sure whether the words referred to her or to Angie's fiancé.

Down the street Clifton and Brian Goodman were repairing Clifton's treehouse. Penny ambled through her own yard, stopping to catch and release a ladybug, to chew the sour petals of a buttercup, to look briefly for four-leaf clovers. It was practically by accident that she ended up under Clifton's tree. He looked efficient and capable, hammering a new nail into a cross-piece. "Can I help?" Penny had offered, and he had reminded her that she was a girl.

"So what?" she said angrily. "I'm as good as any boy," and she grew even angrier when she saw Clifton smile at Brian. Clifton's right hand, the one which held the hammer, dropped back against his leg. He leaned onto the narrowing trunk, one foot resting on a branch slightly higher than the other foot. Brian was stretched out on the platform of the treehouse. He inched forward so that Penny could see his face, white among the leafless branches. "I can do anything any boy can do," Penny added.

"Oh, really," said Clifton. "Well, Brian and I were

just remembering what we did last Halloween and you could never do it. Right, Brian?" He glanced up at Brian, who smiled, his eyes narrowing from the movement of his mouth. Perhaps he nodded his head. The head was all Penny could see of him and so she wasn't really sure. But the way he stayed there, looking down at her, was irritating.

"I could, too," she said. "If you did it, I can do it."

Clifton raised his hammer and went back to work. He paused between blows. "Promise?" he asked casually.

Penny had her first moment of doubt. "Promise."

"It was nothing really," said Clifton. "We went trick-or-treating at old lady McLaughlin's." Brian laughed aloud. Clifton looked at Penny. "So, I'll pick you up. Halloween." And Penny had walked away with those cold, fluttery feelings, wincing everytime she heard the hammer hit the nail.

The days before Halloween passed slowly, like a nightmare she woke up to each morning. Everyone at school knew that she was going trick-or-treating at Mrs. McLaughlin's all alone to prove she was as good as any boy. Penny could see no way out unless she got sick and even then it would have to be something like chicken pox that everyone could see. Penny had always thought being a boy would be easy until this week when she faced the prospect of being as brave as one.

"Are you really?" Shelley asked at recess, her own face tight with sympathy. "I wouldn't for *anything*. I'd die of fright."

"Don't," Marybeth told her shortly. "You don't have to, Penny."

"Penny's not afraid," Clifton told them, his smile angelic. "Are you, Penny?"

The cold flutters moved into Penny's throat and solidified there, like a stone she had swallowed until it stuck. Eating was impossible. She moved her food around her place, but her mother was not fooled. "What's wrong?" she asked Penny.

"Nothing."

"I can see there's something. Maybe I could help."

Penny wound spaghetti around her fork until she had a coil too big to fit her mouth. "Are there witches?" she asked finally. "I mean, I know there aren't the kind who fly around on broomsticks, but is there another kind?"

"No." Her mother's voice was assured. "No such thing."

"Remember," said her father, leaning forward and pinching her nose, "this is the same woman who told you there *was* a Santa Claus."

"Ed!" Her mother was irritated. "Can't you see she's serious?" She turned back to Penny. "What's all this about?"

"Mrs. McLaughlin."

"Oh." Penny's mother set her fork down and wiped the corners of her mouth with a napkin. She shook her head at Penny. "I hope you children aren't planning some sort of Halloween prank on that poor old woman."

"Oh, no," Penny assured her. A prank? On Mrs. McLaughlin? What a dream world her mother lived in. "It's just that some of the kids in my class think she's a witch. She *is* creepy."

"She's awfully old," said Penny's father. "I wouldn't be surprised if she was a hundred. She was already old and living in that same house when I—"

"There's no such thing as witches," Penny's mother interrupted.

"There's no such thing as witches," Penny told herself at night. The branches of her tree, once more denuded of their leaves which blurred their forms all summer, reached their shadows to her through the glass. "There's no such thing as witches," she told her concerned classmates at school, who agreed with her hastily. "There's no such thing as witches," she said to Clifton, who did not look convinced.

He shrugged. "I'll pick you up Halloween," he said. "We'll see, right?"

He was the first one to ring their doorbell Halloween night. Penny's mother put a Tootsie Roll in his bag. "Come in, Clifton," she said. "We haven't seen you in so long."

Clifton was annoyed by the ease with which Penny's mother had recognized him, Penny could tell. He was costumed as Dracula and had smeared himself with green makeup as well as inserting a set of false teeth. Penny was a gypsy in a long skirt and gold bracelets. She wore her mother's blouse, and a heavy jacket underneath it, which gave her figure an odd, lumpy look. It was a cold night, with an even colder wind.

A group of children waited for them outside. "We're going straight to the Murphys'," Clifton told her, removing his teeth. "We'll wait on the porch there while you go to old lady McLaughlin's. You sure you want to go through with this?"

The Murphys lived on the other side of the street and two houses down. Too far away if she should need help. "Fine," Penny answered. "*if* you're too afraid to get any closer."

"Hey, I did this last year." Clifton's face was triumphantly green. "She's gonna grab you. Just like the witch in *Hansel and Gretel*. Lucky for you you're so skinny."

Penny went on from the Murphys' alone. Her heartbeat was hard and high; she felt her throat contract and expand around it. It made breathing difficult. Her empty bag slipped from her cold fingers in the middle of the street and she stooped to pick it up. The shapes of the parked cars became mammalian.

Mrs. McLaughlin's house was set far back from the street at the end of a gravel path. Penny counted the steps she took to get to the porch. Forty-two. Her bracelets jangled with each; her shoes scrunched through the gravel. Up three stairs and onto the wooden porch. One of the boards was warped and creaked underfoot. Step. Step. Step. Penny forced herself to raise her empty hand. She made a fist and she knocked.

There were lights inside, but no one came. She knocked again, slightly louder. Still no one. Penny felt relief wash warmly over her. Mrs. McLaughlin had gone out. Mrs. McLaughlin was not coming. She turned to leave, then heard the door handle catch and the door open behind her. Turning back she saw Mrs. McLaughlin standing in the yellow light from inside. Mrs.

McLaughlin had a towel around her shoulders; her hair was wet and dripped onto it. Her face was unfriendly.

"Trick or treat." Penny's voice was hoarse and expressionless.

"Who are you, child?" Mrs. McLaughlin asked sharply. She waved one hand in front of her face as if something was preventing her from seeing.

"Trick or treat," said Penny again, in a whisper.

There was a long silence. "Wait here," said Mrs. McLaughlin at last, closing the door. Penny didn't want to wait. Neither did she want to turn her back to the door and start down the steps. There was something horrifying in the notion that Mrs. McLaughlin might come at her from behind. She took a couple of small steps backward. The door opened again. "I'm supposed to give you something, am I?" Mrs. McLaughlin's question held the hint of an accent, more of a difference in inflection than pronunciation. Mrs. McLaughlin held out her hands. "Put these in your bag." She gave Penny five walnuts and three old copies of *The Reader's Digest*.

"Thank you," said Penny, and then Mrs. McLaughlin's right hand reached out farther and closed over Penny's arm. Penny found herself looking directly into the opaque eyes; a scream began to push its way up into her throat. Before it surfaced, Mrs. McLaughlin released her. She stroked Penny's cheek with her warm, dry hand. The bag rattled in Penny's shaking fingers.

"Come back tomorrow," said Mrs. McLaughlin, "and I'll give you something else. Something very special."

Penny began to edge away from her without turning around. "Will you come? Don't forget." Mrs. McLaughlin shook her head, water flew from it. "I have something for you."

"All right," Penny said and watched the door shut.

She returned quickly to the Murphys' front porch. "What did she say?" Shelley asked. "Weren't you scared?" And "What did she give you?" said Clifton.

"Some nuts and some old magazines. What did you get last year?"

"Same thing." Clifton's tone was casual. "What a weird old lady."

"She told me to come back," Penny said. "She says she'll give me something else tomorrow."

Clifton replaced his teeth and chewed on them thoughtfully. When he spoke again, the words were slightly slurred, but his voice was quiet and friendly. "You don't have to do that," he said.

Her mother said the same thing next morning when, having stuffed herself with Baby Ruths and candy corns, Penny was trying to face a breakfast of scrambled eggs. Holding her fork irresolutely in one hand, Penny told her mother she had been to Mrs. McLaughlin's the night before. "She must be a very interesting lady," her mother answered. "Mr. Sillman says her father was a missionary and she's lived all over the world. She showed him her stamp collection once. I bet she could tell some fascinating stories." She scraped a thin layer of Welch's jelly over her toast and looked at Penny's face. "You don't have to go, darling," she said gently. "Even if you said you would. By today she's probably forgotten she asked you."

"She said she had something to give me."

"She's probably forgotten that, too."

So Penny thought she wouldn't go until she got to school and found that the prestige she had gained the evening before was practically forgotten by the afternoon. "You were okay last night," Clifton told her, and his very capitulation was irritating. He went to play basketball and left her with the other girls.

"I'm visiting her again today," Penny announced loudly, in his presence. "She invited me. She wants to give me something special."

"I still think she's creepy," Marybeth said. "And you were scared last night. I could tell. Even afterward."

"Well, I'm not scared now," Penny told her. "She's going to give me something. She said it was very special." They speculated on the gift, guessing it would be jewelry, an heirloom, perhaps, brought back from the Orient and very valuable. Poor Mrs. McLaughlin had no one else to give her treasures to.

Mrs. McLaughlin was out in the garden when Penny arrived. If she had not been, Penny might have skipped the visit, after all. The last hour of school, during a spelling bee in which Penny had stumbled on the word "vice-president" since she had thought surely it would be capitalized, Penny had suffered a slight return of those symptoms which had plagued her all week. "Something special"—it could mean anything. It could be horrible. But Mrs. McLaughlin was clearly expecting her. She tucked the pruning shears into her garden basket with a shake of her head. "They should have all been cut back weeks ago," she told Penny. "I just can't seem to keep up with things these days." Penny looked at the roses, which, despite Mrs. McLaughlin's continual care, looked as leggy and unkempt as her hair. "Come inside, child," Mrs. McLaughlin said. "I'll make us some tea."

She led Penny over the porch, through the hall, and into a small, musty living room, then excused herself to go and heat the water. The room was crowded with all manner of exotic bric-a-brac and smelled of dust and medicine. There were carved elephants, trunks raised in permanent alarm, smooth wooden Madonnas, and long strips of bright material embroidered with mirrors. There were shelves of blue and white china and, on the wall, two watercolors of pale herons, and a large brass platter with the raised figures of sailors on a boat with a square sail.

When the tea was ready, Mrs. McLaughlin called Penny into the dining room, put two thin cushions on a chair to give her just a little more height, and handed her a small, round cup half filled with cream. Mrs. McLaughlin poured tea over the cream and disappeared again. When she returned she had a sleepy, gray kitten in one hand. "Perhaps you might like a cat to hold," she said, dropping it into Penny's lap, where it curled against her palm and slept as if unaware that it had even been moved.

Penny took a cookie with her other hand and ate it. Mrs. McLaughlin had put on a bright blue oriental

housecoat with embroidery and loose sleeves. She
gestured meaninglessly over her cup. Her excessive
sleeves gave her hands a curiously unsupported look.
They floated free as birds in the steam. The continual
movement made Penny uneasy.

"He's a lovely kitten," she said.

Mrs. McLaughlin did not respond. Penny sipped at
her tea. She had never had tea before and found it
neither pleasant nor unpleasant. She preferred Kool-
Aid, though. "My mother says you've traveled so much
you must have seen many fascinating things," Penny said
at last.

"I've seen a woman burned to death," said Mrs.
McLaughlin, not looking at Penny, but turning her
strange eyes inward. "I saw her thrown into the flames. I
saw her face when she felt the fire." She sat for another
moment, then her eyes cleared suddenly. "That was in
India where I was born. Not really a story for a young
girl, of course. I don't suppose that's what you meant."

Penny looked down at the kitten. When she looked
up again Mrs. McLaughlin's face had taken on a rather
sly look. "I was thinking of the dragon, actually," she
said, her eyes fixed upon Penny, who stared back. "That's
what made me remember it. The dragon who has two
heads and one of them is fog and one of them is fire."

The kitten stretched in Penny's lap, but Mrs.
McLaughlin never shifted her eyes. There was an
uncomfortable silence. "I was thinking about its two
heads," Mrs. McLaughlin repeated, looking pleased.
"Have you ever seen the dragon?"

"No," said Penny.

"Of course you haven't. It's too big to be seen. Just
pieces of it, sometimes. Sometimes." Mrs. McLaughlin
paused to take a sip of her tea. "I've seen the breasts of
birds," she added, "brighter than their backs. When you
see something all lit up from below like that you know it
can't be the sun. It has to be the dragon's breath." She
drained her small cup in a few gulps. "Drink your tea,"
she said. "Drink it all and tell me what you see."

Penny drank and uncovered the form of a dragon,

painted in the bottom of her cup. She laughed in surprise and Mrs. McLaughlin smiled at her. "He's only got one head," Penny pointed out.

Mrs. McLaughlin made a gesture of dismissal with one of her hands. "The man who painted that never saw the dragon. I told you it was too big to be seen. And it does have two heads, I promise you. Like yin and yang." Mrs. McLaughlin's sly look returned. "When does one person have two heads?" she asked. "It's a riddle. It's the dragon's riddle."

"I don't know," said Penny.

"And I won't tell you. It's one of the rules. A person has to solve the dragon's riddle for herself." Mrs. McLaughlin began to rock slightly, back and forth in her chair. Her gaze went inward again. "You don't see the dragon coming. But it gets you. Then you find out, it's had you all along."

Penny set the kitten down on the rug. It yawned prettily, showing its tiny, pointed teeth. "I've had a lovely time," she said carefully. "Thank you for the tea." She stood to show she was going home now. Mrs. McLaughlin continued to rock. "Mrs. McLaughlin?" There was no response. "Mrs. McLaughlin? You said you'd give me something."

Mrs. McLaughlin smiled. "I already have."

"Oh. Of course," said Penny, quickly, trying not to sound disappointed. It was the tea, then, or perhaps the conversation. Grown-ups were always giving you advice, as if anything could be less of a gift. But Mrs. McLaughlin gestured downward.

"It's the kitten, of course," she said. "If you want him. I've never had a sweeter one. And if it's all right with Mum."

"Oh!" Penny retrieved the kitten gently. "Oh, thank you, Mrs. McLaughlin. He's lovely . . . I love him . . . thank you!"

Penny named the kitten Smoke. She stopped by Mrs. McLaughlin's the next day to tell her so, but Mrs. McLaughlin wouldn't answer the door. Penny could see her inside, through the living room window, wrapped in an afghan by the fireplace, staring into the flames. She knocked repeatedly, but Mrs. McLaughlin ignored her.

"Perhaps she didn't hear you," Penny's mother suggested. "She's so awfully old."

"She heard fine on Halloween and she was washing her hair," Penny objected. "She heard fine when we were talking." Smoke attacked Penny's shoelace, his small tail twitching with menace. They watched the struggle. Now Smoke was on top. Now the shoelace had flipped him onto his back and pinned him there.

Penny's father laughed. "How did Mrs. McLaughlin seem," he asked, "when you were talking?"

"She was nice. But real strange." Penny rescued the cat. "She made me tea, you know. And . . . she told me she'd seen a woman burned to death."

"Did she?"

"Really! In India, she said." Penny stroked Smoke's chin to hold him still. "Do you think it could have been a witch? Didn't they use to burn witches?"

"Penny." Her mother sighed. "Listen to me. No witches. Not now. Not ever. Many years ago innocent, ordinary women were accused of witchcraft and burned for it. Or drowned. It was a tragedy caused by ignorance and it happened a very long time ago."

"A hundred years?" asked Penny. "Like when Mrs. McLaughlin was a little girl?"

"More like three hundred. And not in India. At least, I don't think so. Mrs. McLaughlin is old enough to be confused about such things. Don't let it worry you."

"It is always women they're burning, though," said Penny's father. "Did you ever notice that? Witches and female military geniuses and unfaithful queens."

"Who are you thinking of?" Penny's mother asked. "Queens get decapitated."

"What does that mean?" said Penny. Her parents turned to her, both at once. She thought her mother seemed slightly surprised by the question, as though she had forgotten just for the moment, that Penny was there. "What does that mean, 'decapitated'?" Penny repeated.

Her father grinned at her, drawing his index finger

across his throat slowly. "'Off with her head,' the red queen said."

Penny's mother looked at him disapprovingly. It made him laugh. "Hangings," he said heartily. "Now, there's a punishment for a man. Why did the executioner want to examine the corpses?"

"Ed." Penny's mother's tone was a warning. Her father ignored it.

"He wanted to make sure they were well——"

"Ed!" said Penny's mother. But when she left to start dinner she was smiling.

The next day Mrs. McLaughlin was dead. Clifton told her so on the playground before school. He lowered his scarf from his face to talk and his breath ghosted into the air around his mouth.

"Dead for days," he said. "They just found her body."

Penny felt a horrible sensation in her stomach as though she might throw up. "I saw her yesterday," she told him. "Sitting in her chair."

"No. She was dead then."

Penny turned and ran home. She stayed on the Murphys' side of the street and moved as fast as the layers of winter clothing permitted, as fast as she was able with tears fogging her vision and soaking into the knitted muffler at her neck. Her mother caught her as she came through the door and held her, trembling.

"Penny . . . Penny . . . what's wrong? What happened?"

Penny was sobbing so she could hardly answer. "Mrs. McLaughlin," she said.

Her mother petted her hair. "Yes. Mr. Sillman was just telling me. Honey, when someone very old like that dies, there's something right and natural about it."

"You don't understand. I saw her! Yesterday! I saw her ghost!"

"Nonsense. Who's been telling you such rubbish?" Penny's mother held her away to look at her face. "Mr. Sillman says they found her in the backyard just this morning. He thinks she froze out there, but it's possible

her heart just stopped. In any case it must happened
sometime last night." Her mother pulled Penny into her
again and held her tightly. "She'd had a long, long life
and she didn't suffer. You mustn't be upset."

"Clifton said she'd been dead for days."

"Nonsense," her mother repeated. "She died last
night."

"How do you know?"

Her mother's voice was firm. "Mainly because of
you. You saw her yesterday in her living room. How can
you have any doubts about it?" Her words were exas-
perated, but her tone was merely sad. She held on to
Penny until Penny's body began to relax and the sobbing
stopped. Then she gave Penny a kiss on the forehead.
"You know," she said, "ever since I heard, I've been
asking myself why I wasn't a better friend to her. Why
none of us ever visited her the way you did. Why I never
took her my Christmas bread the way I do all the other
neighbors. I simply never thought to. That poor, lonely
old lady."

Penny looked up at her mother's face. It looked
older, sagged at the mouth, and her eyes were red. That
large wet spot near her mother's breast—Penny had
made that with her tears. But her mother was crying,
too. Penny had never seen her mother cry before. Her
mother had hardly known Mrs. McLaughlin; she had
just finished saying so. Why was she crying? Her mother
returned the stare. "Do you want to know something
amazing?" she offered. "Mr. Sillman says she has a
daughter. They found her address in Mrs. McLaughlin's
desk. She lives in England. Mr. Sillman can't understand
how Mrs. McLaughlin even came to have the address.
He's been delivering her mail for twenty years and he
says there's never been a letter from England."

"Who will take care of her cats?" Penny asked.

"I imagine the neighbors will keep them. We didn't
do much else for her; I guess everyone's feeling a bit
guilty. Her daughter will get the house and everything
else, I suppose. Strange to think, she must be quite an
old lady herself." Her mother touched Penny on the

cheek. "I'm going to put you back to bed, darling. Let's skip school this morning, shall we? You can go after lunch if you feel like it."

And Penny found she actually was tired in spite of having just gotten up. She lay in bed with Smoke until his purring became the dragon's hoarse and even breathing in her dreams.

Later, it felt odd to be walking back to school all by herself with the sun high and the streets deserted of children. She heard the sounds of her own steps and walked more and more slowly. When she was opposite Mrs. McLaughlin's house she stopped. Everything looked just the same. You'd think a dead person's house would be different, Penny thought. You'd think there'd be some sign. Penny crossed the street. She stood at the edge of the walk and stared into the living room window. It was too far away to see inside. Penny was frightened, but no more so than she'd been on Halloween and she'd gone to the house then. She started up the walk.

A rose branch caught at her sleeve. Poor Mrs. McLaughlin never had finished her pruning. Penny reached out to detach herself and there, by her hand, was an unseasonal bud. Penny stretched her fingers toward it, but it began to open in front of her eyes. The bud twisted, then shook itself loose. It was red and perfect and then, just a moment later—Penny had hardly had time to admire it—it was past perfection; it was overblown. Instead of dropping, the petals shriveled from their outer edges in as if they had been set on fire. When the flower was black and dead Penny touched it, her hand trembling so she made the petals fall.

It was a message from Mrs. McLaughlin; Mrs. McLaughlin was speaking to Penny in the voice of her garden and if the message was enigmatic and confusing, well, all of Mrs. McLaughlin's words had been riddles to Penny. But one part of it was clear. I am here, Mrs. McLaughlin said. I am still here, and this was not frightening to Penny at all, it was comforting. If I went all the way up to the window and looked in, Penny thought, I could see her sitting in her chair just like yesterday and this was so obviously true Penny never needed to actually do it.

For years afterward, whenever she sat and looked into a fire, she saw the petals of roses bloom and then wither in the flames.

CHRISTMAS 1975

Penny's husband turned off the television and came to lie beside her. He raised her nightgown and ran his hands over the globe her stomach had become. "How are you feeling?" he asked.

Penny stroked his hair. "I was just thinking that this is an awfully old-fashioned way to have a baby. I can't believe that in all this time they haven't found a way to shorten the procedure. Why can't I just send to Detroit for the most recent model? Why can't Disney collapse the whole thing through the miracle of time lapse photography?" She circled his ear with her fingers. "It's a boy," she told him.

"You're very sure of yourself. Women's intuition?"

"It's a boy trapped inside the body of a girl."

Penny's husband shifted his head so that his other ear was above the protrusion of her navel. "You may be right," he said at last. "I'm getting a clear SOS here." The baby stirred suddenly and pushed outward. Her husband raised his head. "Look," he said. "Look at this."

While the child pushed, its form could be seen, just faintly. It was as if a new continent had suddenly arisen. Her husband pointed out one peninsula. "It's a foot." He was excited. "Penny, it's a foot, I swear. There's a real baby in there."

Penny reached down and gave the foot a push. She got a kick in response. She pushed on other, less identifiable parts of the form and found something hard. She felt it carefully. "Did I ever tell you the dragon's riddle?" she asked her husband. "I learned it from a witch when I was just a little girl."

"No," her husband answered. "How did you happen to meet a witch?"

"She was my neighbor." Penny stopped and considered her answer. "She was my friend," she added, a little self-consciously.

Her husband reached for her hand, kissing the palm and laying it over his own eyes. He had turned onto his back. "What a brave little girl you must have been, Penny." His voice was sleepy.

Penny lay and looked out the bedroom window. There was a great movement in the sky; half a moon floated in the upper right corner of the window, clouds covering and uncovering it like smoke. Still the same moon, Penny thought. Always the same moon. But no, now it had footprints on it, large prints like those the Abominable Snowman left in the snow. Right at this second, she wondered, right now were the prints in the dark or in the sunlight? She pulled her hand back and rolled to her side to face her husband. "Yes," she agreed. "Yes, I was." Her husband smiled. "Listen," she continued. "I'm quite serious about this. Are you listening?" She waited until he had opened his eyes and was looking at her. "This witch was born in India where, she told me, she once saw a woman burned to death. I was eleven. This was 1955. Now, I looked it up later and sati was abolished by the British in 1829. Let's say, being generous, that in order to remember it she must have been at least four years old. That means when I knew her this witch was somewhat older than a hundred and thirty."

"No," her husband protested. He sat upright, stuffing his pillow behind his neck. "India is a large country. Parts of it were never controlled by the British and lots of it was only nominally controlled. I'm sure there were countless violations. For decades."

"How would a little English girl get to see an illegal procedure? A murder?"

"How would she see it even when it was legal? What kind of a family takes a four-year-old to a funeral pyre? Not a *British* family." Her husband closed his eyes and tilted his chin upward. "Sorry, Penny. It doesn't make sense. Did she say specifically it was a sati she saw?

Maybe it was an accidental death. Or something she saw as an adult. Now it's brides they're burning, isn't it? Dowry murders."

Penny picked at the white tufted bedspread with her fingers. "You're just like my mother," she complained. "You always have some simple explanation for any astounding occurrence. Thank god I know better."

Her husband crossed his arms behind his head. "I just believe in exhausting the probable before clutching at the impossible. You're pregnant so you get to be irrational. You women have all the fun." Penny reached over and pinched him. "Ouch," he said. He leaned toward her stomach and spoke to the baby. "We could poke back," he told it, "but we're bigger than that. Though if you feel like kicking this might be a good time."

"All right," said Penny. "I have another amazing story for you to explain. An elderly woman lives by herself in a small town. She lives there some fifty years. Neighbors come and go, pretty soon she's been there longer than anybody. She spends a lot of time in her yard. Everyone in town knows her by sight; most of them know her name. But not until she dies does anyone in that town know she was a mother. She has a daughter living in England, and for at least twenty years and probably more, not one word has passed between them."

"How do you know?" her husband asked.

"Letters from overseas are rare and the postman is nosy."

"What about phone calls?"

"No. They'd have to go through the operator."

"Well." Her husband closed his eyes again. "That's a sad story, but I wouldn't call it an amazing one."

"Put your hand on my stomach," Penny suggested, "and say that again." They were both silent a moment. "When does one person have two hearts?" Penny asked. "That's the dragon's riddle, or that's my version of it. It's a very feminine riddle."

"What do I get if I can answer it, too?" her husband

asked. He kissed her on the forehead, just where a witch would kiss her to protect her. He left his hand lying softly on her hair.

"I don't know, Stephen," she said. "It's a wonderful thing, isn't it?" She took his hand and directed it down over her face to the hollow of her throat, between her breasts and then onto her swollen belly. "Wonderful," she repeated. "But I think maybe you get just a little scared."

THE WAR OF THE ROSES

I never thought of my village as a flowering place. It was homes, built closely together, fields and gardens, reserved for practical crops which could be eaten, sold, or woven into cloth. Such crops have their own blossoms, of course. We didn't use them, so I didn't notice them. And there must have been wildflowers. Somewhere in my memory is the bitter taste of buttercups, the sweet suckings of clover. How could I know such things? These are weeds. The enemy. We rid ourselves of these before they ever came to flower.

I am being honest with myself. I have done the best that I could do. I never thought I was chosen to lead the assault on the rose guild through any particular merit. I was a poor shot and an indecisive leader. Two qualities, I believe, recommended me to the committee. The first was my age. I was sixteen, born after the revolution, and therefore sounder politically than my elders, who'd had much to unlearn in their lives. The second was my expendability. Not that the assault was considered hazardous. The rifles were for show only; we knew the rose guild would have no weapons. But the time frame was uncertain. It might take a month. It might take six months. I had not begun specialized training of any kind. I was not ready to bear a child. However long I was gone I would not be missed. Those who accompanied me were also essentially unnecessary.

I thought Silas too old to make the trip, yet he was chosen as our guide. We were ferried over the river, then Silas led us up our side of Sleeping Man Mountain. Years ago, he had walked this route in reverse, being outside the border when the revolution called its children home. He had passed the rose guild, already building—"and the trellises before the roofs," he said—in a valley the mountain hid from us. When he told this to our new leaders, many had wanted to go after the rose guild at once, angered that they would flee the revolution, steal their time and labor from the people. Instead, the committee had voted to close the borders. Forget them, the committee said. We will go for them when we need roses. It became our saying for the time which never comes. "When we need roses . . ."

I spent the first days of the journey watching my feet, trying to put them where Silas had put his. The terrain was rough; the land opposed us. Although we are used to labor, this kind of work was new. On a long journey, from my village, say, to the next, fatigue can be conquered with a kind of mindlessness. You forget yourself, become walking, become one foot in front of the other. Here there was no path. Each footstep required a decision. The straps of my pack rubbed twin lines of red skin on my shoulders and I longed to lighten myself of the ridiculous rifle. Yet none of us complained. Not Ruben, who at thirteen was the youngest. Not Angel, a childless widow of thirty-four. Not Silas, who moved more and more slowly uphill. And not me. I was proud of us. We are the new men and women, the flower of the revolution. We carried our guns and our demands against the rose guild, against people who had chosen before to use their skills to grow roses when children were starving around them. I could not even imagine such wickedness.

Later I was able to look up and about me at the land we crossed. I had never seen a wild country and as Silas's progress became more painfully slow, I could take in the trees, the plants that grew in their endless shadow, the water running white, always finding the easiest way downhill. There was a special silence, beyond our footsteps, below the noise of the water, an homage the forest paid to us, the intruders. And finally, after many days, we stood and looked down at the roofs of the rose guild and even the roofs had gardens on them.

I felt as though we could jump from here to there; instead it took another two days to reach the guild. We spent our last night in a meadow and woke to find a herd of deer cropping the weeds between us. The deer were aware of us, but strangely unafraid. Perhaps the guilders walked in this meadow often, I thought. Perhaps people were not so unusual here. "I wonder if we shall ever have to eat meat," Angel said quietly. It was the only reference I remember to the fear which triggered the assault. Then Ruben rolled to his rifle, sighted down it. The bullet entered the deer's chest which went red. Its thin legs folded beneath it. I saw the eyes, wide and startled, dim before they comprehended. The rest of the herd vanished.

I was angry. "Why did you do that?" I demanded. "Killing with no point to it. And the valley will have heard."

"Let them hear," said Ruben. "Let them know what kind of people are coming to them now. Let them spend the day expecting people with guns."

"I will decide what is shot and when," I told him, and he would not look me in the face, gave me no answer. My eyes went beyond him to Angel and I remembered her words. It was hard to see the corpse, the compact fit of flesh to bone, and think of it as food. It was sickening to try. We moved away from it to eat our usual breakfast of cereal and coffee. No one spoke to Ruben. I had to force myself to chew, force myself to swallow. The killing had awakened me at last to the realities of the assault. Not that I would be shooting anyone. Merely threatening it convincingly. I asked myself for the first time if I could do that.

Late that afternoon we stood outside the gates of the guild, ancient iron gates which I examined with awe. They must have been brought here. Some people had traveled the same route as we, but had carried these enormous grills. I pictured them, bent like a dozen turtles under a single shell, the gate on their backs, picking their way up Sleeping Man Mountain. But I knew the picture was wrong. No one could do that. There must have been another way. Silas reached through the grill to open the gate from the inside. It swung away from us and we entered.

Outside, the walls had been bare. Inside, they appeared to be little more than excuses for the trellises nailed along them. At the base of each trellis was the squat, severely pruned trunk of a rose bush, no flowers, just a knot of old wood and thorn. Ahead of us was the guildhouse. I don't know what I had expected. Perhaps the opulence of corruption. Instead the guildhouse looked much like our own homes, simple, unadorned, though much larger. We learned later that what we had assumed initially to be several small dwellings was, in fact, one large hall. The guildhouse was built in a square around an inner courtyard and the entire guild lived in it.

A man came to the central door and called out to us, ritual words of greeting so ancient their meaning was lost on me. His clothes, which in cut and fit were loose and utilitarian, had been dyed a shade of purple seen only in the sunset. I was conscious of Ruben, shifting his rifle beside me, and I gripped his arm tightly enough to carry a message of discouragement.

"We are representatives of the people's revolution," I said. "We wish to make a proposal to the rose guild."

"Then come inside," the man answered, but Silas, Angel, Ruben, and I were frightened suddenly and uncertain. Or perhaps I should speak only of my own feelings. On the journey, being a leader had seemed to mean only that others would do as I asked. I was sixteen. I had no sense of the leader's responsibility to those who followed, had done nothing to win their loyalty or their respect. I needed neither since the committee had both. Now I saw the decisions which lay ahead of me and how much depended upon making them correctly. It was up to me to bring the rose guild home and I knew they would not come willingly. So I stood just inside the gate and the uncertainty of that first decision almost overwhelmed me. Should we enter the guildhouse? Could it be a trap? Would I look foolish and cowardly if I refused to enter? Could I send Silas before me?"

I raised my eyes to examine the man again. I judged him to be in his middle twenties, old, he seemed to me then. His posture was relaxed; he waited with apparently an endless patience for my answer. "Ruben and I will go," I said to Silas. "You and Angel must wait at the gate." I still held Ruben's arm; now I pulled him forward with me. The man stood to one side, forcing us to precede him through the door. It closed behind us. We were in the center of a long, bare hall. I smelled the clean wood smell of the forest. Facing us was a second door, which the man indicated by extending his hand. "Go into the garden," he said. "I will bring you coffee and also for those who chose to stay outside."

In my dreams there are still times when I am confronted by doors. I open one and there is another behind it, and another behind that, and I must force myself to keep opening them, all the while aware I am coming closer to something I will not want to have found. My uncertainty made me snap at Ruben. "Do exactly as I tell you," I said, "and nothing I have not told you. If they have prepared a trap for us, it will be because they were expecting us, and if they were expecting us, it will be because they heard your stupid shot this morning."

Ruben showed no signs of remorse. "The rose guild prohibits the use of coercion," he said. "Didn't the committee tell you that? For hundreds of years their rules have always been the same.'

"I know," I answered sharply. "Did you think the committee would choose me to lead and then brief you more thoroughly? Don't be so stupid." The exchange left me even more insecure. If I couldn't convince Ruben of my authority, what hope had I in persuading the guild? I opened the door and stepped into the garden. I did it to show Ruben I could.

"Garden" is a word we use also, but never to describe such a place as that courtyard. It was cold, as wintry as anywhere we had passed on the mountain, yet

roses bloomed about us, scented the air, scattered petals
thick as snow upon the ground. Black roses, blood roses,
blue roses. A woman about my age and similar to me in
other ways, dark hair, gray eyes, knelt beside the black
flowers with a pair of shears. She rose to a height slightly
above mine. Her face did not welcome us. "You may sit
over there." She gestured with the scissors to a protected alcove which held a small table and four chairs. To
my surprise, we were warm enough. The sun was bright
and the courtyard admitted little wind. I looked again at
the roses, noting their differences—large, loose buds,
small and perfect flowers, rose trees, rose vines, stalks of
roses. And their similarities—the lushness, the health of
the plants, the courage to bloom through the winter. I
had never doubted the committee, yet for the first time I
began to *believe* that the help we needed was here.

The coffee came, the man who brought it enough
like the woman to be her brother. I thanked him, but he
left without a word. I drank and felt warm and comforted
by the beauty around me. And then I felt angry, because
no one came to speak to us and we were being kept
waiting like petitioners instead of soldiers of the revolution and once again I was convinced I was doing it
wrong.

I called out to the woman, who had continued to
prune, collecting the severed blooms into baskets,
examining each leaf for something she did not find. "I'm
not in a mood to wait any longer," I said and shifted my
rifle conspicuously. She spread the blades of her shears
before a vine of blue roses, set her mouth in a straight
line, the lips pressed together. I could see the effort it
took, but she responded politely.

"There is no one free to speak with you now. The
guild is at work. We have made you as comfortable as we
can—if your friends outside are less comfortable it is not
because we lacked the courtesy to invite them in.
Grandfather is holding class. In an hour, perhaps more if
there are questions, he will come and speak to you." She
turned back to the vine and the blades she had opened
before she spoke, closed now over a budding stem.

I stood, angry at the answer, embarrassed before

Ruben. But I let my rifle dangle slack at my side. If I used it now, just to begin the interview, what would I have to threaten with later? "Go and get your grandfather," I said and tried to suggest with my tone that I anticipated no argument.

She looked at me for one long moment, then dropped the shears onto the basket of clippings. "Very well," she said curtly and disappeared through a door on our left. She returned behind an old man, hairless except for the white beard on his face, older even than Silas. His garment was a pale yellow.

He seated himself at our table and looked into our faces without seeming to notice the guns. "It is nice to see children from home," he said, almost as if he believed it.

"We are not children," I told him, trying not to sound as if we were. Not awkward. Not frightened. Amused, as an adult might be amused by a joke she understood, but did not expect anyone else to. "We are the sons and daughters of the people's revolution. Your home no longer exists, and we are all new men and women there."

Now it was his turn to be amused. "Yes?" he asked and glanced at last at our rifles. "How like the old men and women you look." He motioned to the young woman to continue her work, accepted coffee from the young man who appeared, served it, and disappeared. "A nice day," he said, taking a sip. "Inside the garden, spring. Outside, fall creeping into winter. An unusual time for a trip through the mountains. Why have you come?"

I looked into the black cloud of coffee in my cup. The sunlight gave it a pearled surface; many colors floated on the one. I tried to frame my answer with the right combination of force and of appeal. "The revolution has been endangered by crop failures," I told him. "The wheat has rotted at the roots and produced nothing which could be eaten or planted. The new seeds shrivel before we put them into the ground."

"Are all wheats equally affected?" he asked with interest. "In all soils?"

"There is only one wheat. A high-yielding strain created for the revolution. In the first year it tripled our harvest. This surplus is all that keeps us from starvation now."

The old man rested his elbows on the table, pressed his palms together in a prayer. "All the fields gone to one wheat? It was a great risk. Surely this was understood."

"We needed the big harvests. The revolution is surrounded by enemies. And is still so young. . . ." I bit off the word, instantly regretting having made the revolution sound weak and insecure. At the words "so young" the man's eyes had rested on me.

"Your revolution is doomed," he said mildly. "The rose guild has survived many famines. But governments never do."

His tone was sympathetic; his words were unforgivable. My own voice swelled, grew adolescent and shrill. "The revolution is not a government. The revolution is us. Let us be absolutely honest. When you say that the revolution is doomed, you mean that the people are doomed. In another three seasons the surplus will be gone. If we cannot bring in a harvest we will begin to starve. The children will die first, their bones pushed outward through the surface of their skin. We will eat our dogs and then our cows, but we will die anyway. Unless you help us. The committee believes that you can. They say we can plant immediately, that you can make things bloom in the snow." I looked around at the lush surroundings. "They say you can reach inside the seed itself to change the shape of the stem, the color of the blossom." I leaned across the table to look directly into his red-rimmed eyes. "Is it true?"

He met my gaze. "There is truth to it. It will not help you. Hardiness is increased by hybridization; it takes generations. Those who created your wheat must have known this. You modify a few plants at a time, backcross them, or clone them. After months of work you have a dozen plants. But you are talking of an entire crop. It is impossible."

"No," I told him. "Everyone will help. It cannot be impossible. The revolution is rich in people all of whom will work as though their lives were at stake." He did not respond and I allowed myself to hope I was persuading him. "I am no farmer. Those suited to this work have remained behind, have started without us. They can explain the problem better than I; they can implement the solution. We are asking for your help," I laid the rifle delicately on the table between us, "but I cannot permit your refusal." A mistake. A mistake. He put his hands over his face, the yellow sleeves slipped down to expose the bones of his wrists. He had gardeners' hands, strong, thick at the knuckles, though old and prominently veined.

His voice became sharp. "In the history of the guild," he said, and uncovered his eyes, "you are not the first to make this—request. I will go so far as to say you are not the second. We survive you, although our answer is always the same. We are the rose guild. Our duty is the roses. Your famine is someone else's duty."

"People will die." I had been prepared for this answer, still I couldn't believe I had heard it. "Are roses more important than people?"

"It's not a question I can answer. Important to whom? Important for what? We will regret the deaths very much." His voice was sincere. This sincerity was the wickedest part of all. It strengthened me for what must come next. I saw Ruben's hand moving on the stock of his rifle and I reached out to stop it. Then I stood, raised my own gun, and sighted along the wand at the young woman's blue coat. She stood with her back to me, reaching into the black rose tree. I picked out a square of blue material just under the collar. I could never hit it at this distance. But who was to know that?

"Very regrettable," I agreed, "the deaths of those you do not know and need not see. But the death of someone close to you—that's something more than regrettable." I heard the old man set his cup onto the saucer. The china rattled as it came together. I told myself his hands were shaking. "I will kill her," I said quietly. "Or you will come with me."

He raised his voice to reach the young woman's ears. "Anna? My little flower?"

"Yes, grandfather."

"You must prepare to die." The woman turned. The patch of blue coat swirled out of my sights, replaced by many moving colors. I looked up to her eyes, dark and startled. It would not do to look at them.

"Must I?" she said, and her voice was high and trembled.

"Yes," he answered gently.

"I am not talking now," I said loudly, "to the old man whose life is nearly over. I am talking to the young woman. If you will come with us and help us, you will save many from suffering and death. If you will not, I will kill you. Is this really a hard choice to make?"

She would not look at me. Tears gathered in her eyes and rolled out; she raised her hand, but did not wipe them away. She looked only at the old man's face.

"Must I?" she asked again.

"Yes," he said.

"How will I die, grandfather?" She was so frightened. I couldn't bear to hear her voice. I would shoot her just to silence it, I thought, although I knew I couldn't. But for the revolution? For my friends? For myself?

"Quickly," the old man answered. "Bravely. We shall all follow you soon."

The long minutes passed. Ruben shifted in his seat beside me. "Go to your room, Anna," the old man said. "Leave the basket. You are not dying today, after all." Anna walked slowly to the nearest door, never moving her eyes from his, step after frightened step. The door closed behind her. My rifle had followed her progress, saw the door swing shut. I lowered it.

Now I had failed. I tried to close my mind to the consequences of my failure, searched for a thought which would make it not matter. "The revolution will send someone else. If there is no other way to solve the problem, they will have to. I failed because you didn't believe me."

"And if we had believed you," the old man's voice was cheerful, natural, "our answer would have been the same. You trusted the power of your rifle; that was your mistake. It is just to avoid this fallacy that the guild

prohibits weapons. Coercion is the weakest manifestation of power. Better is persuasion. And most effective of
all is that authority which creates loyalty. Others in the
guild may listen to you. They may even agree with you.
But they will still die if I tell them to. Only I have power
here."

"Then you are the one we should kill," said Ruben.
He began to raise his gun. Perhaps I should let him, I
thought, even as my hand moved to his shoulder, but the
old man forestalled him.

"Anna has already heard my answer. The guild will
die to honor it. I would be even more powerful as a dead
man." He watched with satisfaction as Ruben relaxed.
"You see?" he said to me. "You see the power of
persuasion?"

We heard the central door opening; Angel and Silas
were joining us. "Good," said the old man heartily.
"Come here and be warm."

It was a poorly timed entrance. I was sick with
failure already. As they came sheepishly to our table, I
turned on them. "I told you to stay by the gate. Why
have you disobeyed?"

"The wind was very cold," said Angel. "And Silas
began to cough. It seemed to us a long time had passed
and we wondered if we might be more useful else-
where." Her dark hair was matted about her face. She
pushed it back from her eyes. "Do you wish us to return
to the gate?" she asked.

"I wish you had stayed," I told her angrily. "I wish I
didn't have to repeat my orders." Every exchange
lowered the credibility of my leadership and therefore
that of the mission. I was too young. Why had I been
sent? The sudden sound of a shot made my throat close
over. I looked to where Ruben stood, his rifle still
pointing into the garden. He pulled the trigger again.
Another shot. I saw the petals of a large red rose
explode. Ruben always hits what he wants to hit.

He turned to me, grinning. "It's so simple," he said.
"We'll kill the roses." And I only watched him. I had
ceased to be a participant in the assault at all. I only
watched and wondered that, of all of us, it should be

Ruben who was the killer. You'd think it would be Silas, who'd grown up in oppression and poverty. Or Angel, who'd been young and home when the revolution was bloody. Angel had seen her own husband hacked to pieces in the final rally of reactionary forces. Angel had killed before. But Ruben was like me—accepting the need for violence in a theoretical framework, but completely unfamiliar with it. To us the revolution meant plowing fields, factory shifts, vigilance against the old hierarchies. Where had Ruben learned to kill?

Ruben walked out into the garden. He raised his rifle like a club, its handle in both his hands, and brought it down on a young rose tree. Wood met wood; a branch broke. Then Anna darted from the side door. She seized the shears and held them closely against her. Other doors opened. The guild came, though no one had called them. Apparently they had all been gathered, been watching. They ran into the garden, even the children. When Ruben raised his club against the red roses, they stopped his blows with their arms, held him off with their hands. "Let me go," he told them. His voice was threatening. He shouted it. "You'd better let me go!"

The old man left the table and went to stand in front of Ruben. "Be quiet," he said and when Ruben was, he signaled for the rose guild to release him. "To kill the roses, you will have to kill us. It amounts to the same thing."

Ruben stood, holding his rifle loosely, his face angry and uncertain. He looked at me and looked away. "Kill us," the old man continued, "and the knowledge you came for dies with us. Kill us and your mission fails in the most complete way possible."

"If you will not help us," said Ruben, "we lose nothing by killing you."

"And gain nothing."

"I don't know which to choose." He really didn't. I could hear it in his words, and I think the old man heard it, too, and in spite of his bravado earlier, he was shaken. His next words came slowly.

"We cannot leave the roses," he repeated. "We cannot risk them in any way. But perhaps we can help you and serve the roses at the same time." A slight breeze swept the courtyard. Petals fell and no one moved. "When we fled the revolution," the old man said, "we were forced to abandon a great deal of valuable equipment. Does your revolution have these things?"

"I don't know," I told him. "The revolution thinks that people are valuable. The revolution doesn't value machines."

"The revolution doesn't have machines. This is not doctrine, this is a fact of life your committee must live with," said the old man. "Never mind. We might be willing to trade training for the return of our property."

"I can't promise this."

The old man looked from me to Ruben. "I am willing to gamble on your good faith," he said. "We will make one offer of help. You and he"—he moved his hand, palm up, from me to Ruben—"may stay. We will show you how to change the seeds. It will take time; I cannot say how much. Nor can I promise it will help." He never moved his eyes from Ruben. Ruben was our natural leader. It was Ruben to whom he offered his bargain and he grew more persuasive. "A great gift. Unprecedented in the long history of the guild. But you must understand, the training is knowledge and discipline. While you are here, you submit to the laws of the rose guild. When you leave, you will not be the same person you were." It was the challenge Ruben responded to.

"All right," he said while I spoke quickly, if futilely.

"We accept," I told the old man, pretending it was up to me. And then turned to Silas and Angel. "You must go back. Tell the revolution we will return and we will have the knowledge to help."

The old man held out a gnarled hand. It took me a moment to comprehend its purpose. Then I put my rifle stock into it; it was a relief to be free of that weight. Ruben was more hesitant. "What will you do with it?" he asked.

"I will put it by the main door. The door closest to the gate. No one will touch it. Is that acceptable?"

Ruben swung the rifle upward, aimed it at the trunk

of the largest rose tree, then raised the sight abruptly. His final shot sounded its passage over the roofs of the guildhouse. "Now it's empty," he said, turning the rifle to point at himself, laying the stock in the old man's hand. Although, of course, it wasn't.

I was glad to have salvaged some measure of success to report to the committee, though I knew none of the credit was mine. And so I reject all blame for what came later. Although embarrassed by my public shortcomings, I admired Ruben for his results. And I was frightened of him. I gave no more orders and followed carefully those the rose guild gave to me. I felt an unaccustomed concern for Angel and Silas, taking the trip home, only the two of them.

We stood together in the early morning of the next day, our breath illustrating our words with white clouds. The sun had not yet appeared over the mountains. It always reached the valley late. Silas and Angel shifted on their feet before me, their backs bent under the weight of the food the guild had packed for them. I knew they would have preferred a longer rest before returning.

"They'll be fine," the old man told me as we watched their slow beginnings up the dirt-packed trail. "Mikhal has just come in from the mountain. He says the weather won't break for another two weeks yet, and if Mikhal says this, then it is so."

"Who is Mikhal?" I asked, and he pointed out to me a shadowy figure in black, stooped slightly over the roses on the guildhouse roof.

"Mikhal is our wanderer," he said, then called out "Mikhal!" so that the figure straightened abruptly, waved to us, blew me a sudden kiss. The gesture surprised and embarrassed me. I lowered my eyes at once, turned again to the small backs of Silas and Angel, already almost level with the figure on the roof. I wondered what report of me they would give the committee.

It was the last time I allowed myself such a thought. Then I went inside and became, as I had promised, a guilder. It was not as difficult a transition as I might have expected. The guild proved to be as austere in its material surroundings as the revolution. In both cases this was a matter of doctrine as well as one of necessity. And the camaraderie was much the same. The guilders told stories and sang when they worked together. The more unpleasant the job, the brighter the music. They accepted me the first time I dirtied my hands. Hard, useful work made me happy.

As Ruben was not. No matter how small, no matter how reasonable the rule, Ruben made a point of disobedience. He would not work his shift in the kitchen, though this is a discipline the revolution also demands. He told the guild he had not come to learn to cook, though he ate well enough and often. The guild's fruits and vegetables were undeniably larger and more flavorful than those we grew at home. He refused to tend the roses. Sent out to find and remove suckers, he severed an entire plant.just above the bud union. He said it was an accident, but perhaps he shouldn't be asked to prune again? Every time we saw each other he asked me when I thought we would be taught to open the seeds.

I was enjoying the gardening. I drew a shift with Mikhal who taught me how to shape the growth and tend the grafts. Mikhal was only a few years older than I and certainly no taller. He had a long curved nose and the heavy-lidded eyes of a reptile. Do I make him sound unattractive? I did not find him so. Mikhal had returned to the guild for the winter and the gardening, which is a guild discipline required for all. But his main responsibility was the wild roses. What improvements could nature make? What had nature done that was new? Mikhal went out on long expeditions to find and bring back cuttings and seeds. He held the guild's own roses somewhat in contempt, I think, for the care they required. It was the wild roses that he loved.

For three days we worked together, binding the exposed plants on the guild roofs against the winter. We pruned them back almost to the ground, wrapped the stumps in undyed cloth. Mikhal sang or told me stories of his travels. Last year he had failed to come home before the first snowfall, had been forced to share a cave with a hibernating bear. "Really," he said, against my smiling mistrust. "I crept as close to it as I dared and woke up all night long every time it *stopped* snoring." His most recent trip had been to Snake's Tongue River and along its banks he had found something extraordinary. The blossoms of the wild roses were simple, utilitarian, just as much fuss as a bee required. But these had been a deep pink in color and more strongly scented than any he had ever found before. The samples he brought back would enable the guild to transfer the new perfume to one of their own creations. We stopped work each morning to watch the sun rise. I saw Mikhal's face and hands with the clarity of morning mountain light.

Mikhal's samples would also allow the guild to preserve the wild strain without modification. The old man told me this was the chief difference between the guild and the revolution. "The revolution," he said, "would like to sweep the past away."

"The past is a prison," I answered. "We must leave it to be free," but he shook his head.

"There are many designs in the world, many plans. When you choose one, then you are imprisoned. Then you have doomed yourself never to rise above its weakest aspect. No, freedom involves the preservation of old choices and work is the creation of new ones." He took me to the library to show me the history of the guild, or what they had been able to save of it; plated pictures of noisette roses, the pedigree of a damascus climber, an ancient account of a rose festival in which rose petals were spread so deep a few of the celebrants suffocated in them. The pedigree went back a thousand years.

I found it all rather distasteful. "Your roses are aristocrats," I said, choosing a word I knew well, but had never used before.

"The guild has survived the rise and fall of dynasties as the pedigrees show," the old man agreed proudly. "A thousand years of uninterrupted work. Until your revolution. When we fled we had to leave centuries behind us."

"So you admit that the revolution is different?"

"Oh, yes." The old man had found a watercolor of a golden rose. The palest inner petals just matched the material of his sleeves. "Tell me," he asked. "What did your revolution name its wheat?"

"The People's Wheat," I answered and was forced to smile myself at his laughter. "All right," I told him. "And what is the name of this golden wonder?" I indicated the flower in the painting.

"This is one of my own," he said. "An early work. I named it Firebird, because I had heard that the feathers of the new phoenix take on the golden color of the flame. A prophetic name, as it turned out. But all the yellow roses come originally from a single stock and its name was Peace."

My hostility toward the old man had worn away. I called him "grandfather" as everyone else did. And I refused to think of his calloused politics. I found them impossible to forgive, so I tried to forget them. I was helped in this by his genuine interest in the People's Wheat.

He believed the root rot was parasitical. He lectured me and Ruben on the subject, excusing the rest of the guild since the subject matter was already familiar to them. "Susceptibility," he said, "is a product of the host plant—and it's good you brought samples—the pathogen, and the soil's microbial population, which is always in flux. You might be able to control the disease through soil preparation. This would certainly be simplest. If not, we have to resort to cytogenetic techniques. Before the revolution, I remember great successes with these, particularly in wheats where whole chromosomes can be transferred from one variety to another. Much depends on the characteristics of the old strains, those which have survived, and I think you'll find that many have. The past is not so easy to obliterate." He consulted a list of tables, located the genes which controlled the relevant expression of resistance. "I see two possibilities," he continued. "We can inject cloned genes into the early embryo. Or we can use a viral vector to transfer the genes." He closed his eyes, the lids were paper thin, the lashes almost invisible. We sat for a long and silent moment. Then he looked at Ruben with a smile, turned to include me. "Wheats are not my specialty," he reminded us apologetically. "I suppose I had better instruct you in both techniques."

Ruben had a flair for the work, the same sense of physical competence which made him such an excellent shot, and a deeper understanding than I was able to achieve. I ground the plant cells, used the solvents I was instructed to use, operated the centrifuge, separated fragments of rose DNA by electrophoresis. But I was never able to assemble the pieces of the process into one purposeful image. I told myself it didn't matter. I didn't need to understand the work. I was just a technician. All I needed was to be able to reproduce the procedures. Perhaps I was too awed by the unexpected world of machines, their dull exteriors, their amazing abilities. Like the work, I could learn to use them. But I could never see into them, never penetrate their secrets.

Ruben was less impressed. "You have a great gift," said the old man. "And a greater arrogance. You must work in the garden. Learn the patience of the seasons. Compare your own small powers to the wisdom of nature."

"Yes, grandfather." Ruben did not pretend to hide the sarcasm.

"You are an instrument. Merely an instrument." The old man raised his voice until it cracked, tangled his fingers helplessly in his beard. "*You do not grow the roses*. You tend them. Do you see the difference?"

"I do neither," Ruben reminded him. "I will do neither. Until we need roses." He met the old man's eyes squarely, and finally it was the old man who looked away. Ruben was completely isolated within the guild. He refused to dress in the loose, brightly colored clothing of the guild. This was of no consequence. But there were also rumors that Ruben had made demands of Anna, and the reluctance of everyone to discuss it further told me what the nature of those demands had been.

By contrast, and perhaps for Ruben's benefit, the guild was open and friendly toward me. When the old man told me I had been selected to arrange cut flowers inside the guildhouse, I understood the honor that was done me. Though the guilders themselves usually used the cut flowers with restraint and seldom mixed colors, I was unable to resist, abandoned taste for gaiety, and spread large multicolored bouquets throughout the rooms.

"Very beautiful," Mikhal told me, and his voice turned my breath hot within my throat.

The next night the first snow fell and I awoke to a muffled world. Outside I worked to raise the temperatures in the gardens, the snow melted and watered the plants. Inside, I lowered the temperatures on the viruses in the lab. Ruben and the old man were arguing again, the wheat seed samples I had brought sprinkled before them on the black tabletop. I picked one up, rolling it between my fingertips. How withered and dry it was. No new life resided here. Whatever codes were locked inside this wrinkled shell were codes for death. I thought of my friends. I thought of the revolution. I thought with a sudden, searing certainty that what the old man was teaching us would not be enough to save them.

Ruben was agreeing. "You must teach us to open the seeds," he said. "We don't have time for back-crossing. We can't wait for generations."

"I'm sorry," said the old man. "I have shown you what we do. I warned you it might not help."

Ruben's voice was beginning to change. He had developed a habit, owing to its unreliability, of speaking quite softly when he was angry. He split through a seed hull with his fingernails. "You must teach us how to reach into the seeds."

"I cannot," said the old man. "We use those words only figuratively. Such work would involve surgery on the molecular leval. This is impossible."

Ruben's voice sank again. "You're lying!" He swept a furious arm over the tabletop, many of the scattered seeds hit the old man's face like a small storm. He did not put up his hands. Ruben turned to me. "Didn't he promise us?" he said. "In the very beginning? Didn't he say he would teach us to open the seeds?"

I shook my head at Ruben. I sorted through my memories and could find no such promise. And yet, I felt from inside a growing sense of futility and betrayal, that we had certainly been allowed to believe this. Ruben had voiced this expectation often enough. No one had bothered to tell him before now that this was merely a figure of speech.

Ruben saw none of my thoughts, only my head moving from side to side. "You are such a fool," he said. He spit the words at me, then left the lab with an unsuccessful attempt to slam the door. We felt the wind of this attempt; it moved the seeds on the table, on the floor, caught in the old man's sleeves. But the door stopped itself abruptly. Swung shut with a quiet click. The old man sank into a silence.

"Can you open the seeds?" I asked him.

He did not answer.

"Have you truly taught us all you can do?"

He raised his face to mine. "You have been here a few weeks. I have worked in the lab all my life. Of course I have not taught you all I can do. But I have taught you all I can teach you."

"It's not enough."

"I told you it would not be." He began to brush at his beard with his gnarled fingers, scattering wheat seeds onto the floor. He shook out his clothing, looked again at my face and softened. "Patience," he said. "In good faith I have taught you what I believed would be most useful. There may still be a famine. There may be starvation. But in time your work will bring relief. Whether the revolution survives to this point or not depends on the revolution."

"I should go home at once," I said.

"In the snow?"

"Yes."

"Come here," said the old man. "Sit down." I sat in the chair vacated by Ruben. I could still feel the heat of his body inside the cushions. The old man drummed his fingers along the tabletop. They met their own images in the shiny surface, fused at the ends, then separated. "The lab is for the young," the old man said quietly. "The older I get, the more comfortable I find the library. What has been is just as incredible as what will be." His hands slackened, the yellow sleeves fell over them, obliterated them. We were silent.

I was not angry. I have no gift for anger. A brief flare, but I cannot sustain it. "I will leave tomorrow," I said.

"Yes. Mikhal is ready to go out again. He will take you over Sleeping Man Mountain. You must arrange a meeting in the spring. Then you can tell us if the revolution will return our equipment to us or not."

"And Ruben?" I asked.

"Ruben must stay with us. We have contributed to his training: now he becomes our responsibility. Ruben is why we have never trained outsiders before—we cannot trust him to use his knowledge judiciously. He has refused the disciplines. But perhaps if we keep him longer . . ."

"Will Ruben be told he is a prisoner of the rose guild?"

The old man reached across to my hands, wove my fingers into his own. "Do not tell him you are leaving. It is the last restriction the rose guild will place upon you. I will tell him you are returning in the spring. I do not think he will attempt to leave. Not alone and over the snow."

Did I make a mistake? I was sixteen and offered the prospect of a mountain journey alone with Mikhal. I agreed to secrecy. But I was truly convinced of its necessity. I was frightened of Ruben, frightened of what he could do to the revolution. Ruben, I thought, was a child completely out of control. If the rose guild was willing to keep him, wouldn't he be relatively harmless there?

"Ruben is the seed," the old man said, "of your revolution. Think what those seeds will bring in another generation."

But I told him he was wrong. Ruben was an aberration, a sport. I knew no one else at home like Ruben. So I left Ruben behind for further modification and walked the silent, wintry trails and thought only of

Mikhal. Mikhal showed me how to find the faint paths of deer, how to walk the pebbled sides of rock without sliding, how to pick the surface of the snow most likely to hold your weight. Mikhal plucked a digitated leaf for me, held it in the icy stream until it turned to silver. Mikhal had names and stories for the stars. Mikhal said he loved me.

We lay together in the sleeping bag. "Over that mountain," said Mikhal, pointing out a blue curved horizon in the distance, "are fields I have never walked to the end of. And horses. Herds of wild horses. The dust from their hooves is as thick as fog." He kissed me. "You cannot imagine how beautiful they are." He kissed me again, more slowly.

"Come home with me," I offered. "You are too young to be blamed for the guild's decision to flee. You would be welcomed."

Mikhal rested his ear on his palm, his elbow bent beneath it. "Are there roses there?" he asked. "Are there wild roses? And what has happened to the roses around the old guild?"

"The guild is a hospital now." I tried to picture the grounds, but could remember no roses. In fact, when I thought of home I could remember no flowers at all. Mikhal refused to come to such a place. We said goodbye at the river, kissing and crying in the cold air, promising to meet in the spring. Mikhal's refusal to join me made him an enemy of the revolution, yet I could understand it. We all have our homes; it is not easy to trade one for another.

My return to *my* home was not what I had expected. The crisis was over; the assault on the rose guild was of no interest to anyone. I was grateful to be spared the necessity of detailing my many failures, but disappointed to find my efforts trivialized. The old strains of wheat had been recovered after all. Harvests would be minimal, but the people were used to making sacrifices. We would survive. We had not needed roses.

No one missed Ruben. Not until I told the committee I thought I could perfect the People's Wheat by substituting a chromosome line from something more vigorous did they show their first interest. They provided a lab. My assistants were all old men; before the revolution they had been agriculturalists and phytochemists. Like the old strains of wheat, these things had never really been lost, after all. So I asked about the equipment. "What happened," I said, "to the laboratory implements in the old rose guild? I could use them now." And they were provided, too, many familiar to me and a few like nothing I had seen. So I knew these strange machines were the ones the old man wanted.

By our second day of work my assistants knew more of what I taught them than I did. I was merely an excuse to bring them together, a political leader, but hardly a scientific one. I asked one of them if he thought it would ever be possible to perform surgery inside the seeds themselves. He responded with surprise. "I'm sure the guild already does this. Did they deny it?"

"They did."

He isolated an unfamiliar utensil for me. "A mass spectroscope," he said. "It provides information about the molecular structure. The rose guild was using these decades before the revolution. Who knows what they're capable of now."

A growing season later we had five plants, vigorous, hardy, abundant. I named the new strain the Old Man's Wheat and no one who saw my assistants or the plants themselves, bearding in the sun, questioned its appropriateness. "A great success," the committee congratulated me, but I had learned to be more cautious.

Shortly before I was due to meet Mikhal I dreamt I was back in the guild library. The old man stood over me, draped all in black, holding out a rose. "Look," he said. "My newest creation."

It was like the rose in the painting, but larger, brighter. Then as I watched, the colors began to move in the petals, flickered and glowed like candles. The light from the flower shone over the old man's face, which was smooth and yellow like the moon. "What is its name?" I asked.

"Death," he said. He held it out to me. "Take it," he

told me. "And don't be sad. All the yellow roses come from one strain and its name is Peace."

The flower was so beautiful it frightened me. I opened my hand to accept it, but woke myself instead, sweating, relieved to return to the unbroken blackness of the night.

The next day I asked the committee for permission to give the smaller pieces of equipment, just those I could carry, back to the guild. "The Old Man's Wheat is their success as well as ours," I argued. "A gift they have given us."

The committee responded that the guild had been reluctant and niggardly with their training. They had given away none of their secrets. What they had shared only slightly exceeded what we already knew.

And I told the committee a lie. I said that these were the techniques of the rose guild. I said that the old man had claimed no secrets and that I had believed him.

Still the committee refused. I went to meet Mikhal as we had arranged, and I was empty-handed. The dirt along the roads was dark, soft, and ready; the river had lost its icy edges and ran full. Mikhal waited for me on the other side. He had grown a beard and his eyes were sunken into round shadows. Before I had time to be alarmed at his appearance, he had fallen into my arms.

"I wintered down-river," he told me. "And when I returned home the rose guild was dead."

I pushed him back to look at his face. I did not understand.

His hair fell forward in unclean locks. "Some of the roses. All of the people."

"How?" I asked him, wonderingly, and then a horror rose into my throat. I could hardly speak past it. "Ruben?"

Mikhal's voice grew harsh. "They had been dead for some time. Some were hard to identify." He looked away from me, reddened eyes fastened on the horizon farthest from his home. "I don't think Ruben was with them," he said. Mikhal pulled me close again, held on to me during the long moments it took me to realize what he was telling me. Perhaps I never did truly realize it. My eyes followed his gaze to the blue mountain. I had climbed a mountain once. I knew about edges and rock. Yet, at this distance, how soft it looked. My own voice spoke to me. "Regrettable," it said. "The deaths of those you need not see," and in that moment I despised myself for the way I always seemed to be protected. As a penance, I tried to imagine their deaths, tried to share in them, but all I could create was a soft picture of bodies smothered in petals, like the victims of an ancient festival, something too distant to be real.

Then Mikhal needed me and I kept him in my arms while he cried for his family, watched him sleep at last after many haunted nights. And while he slept dreamless, I walked awake through my nightmare of doors behind doors. I tried to shut them, but they opened instead on horrible suspicions. Why would the committee send an untried girl to lead a mission on which the survival of the revolution depended? How often had I asked myself that question and neglected the only conceivable answer? They would not. An untested leader would be sent on a mission of no importance at all.

It seemed to me that two paradoxical aspects of the guild had once protected them from the dynasties, the revolution, the disruptions of history. The first was the unimportance of their knowledge. They were ignored because they dealt in trivialities. Time enough to deal with them when we needed roses.

But, as unimportant as their knowledge was, still they had a monopoly on it. What if we did need roses someday? There was only one place to get them. This monopoly was the second aspect which protected the guild. And I had broken it. I had taken the training and spread it among many people. Superficial training, of course. Restricted training, even. But had the committee believed this? I could hear myself assuring them, just yesterday, that the guild had no important secrets. "The gate is open," the committee had said when my lab work began. The committee has great faith in the ability of those motivated by a genuine desire to help the people to walk through an open gate.

What if my mission to the guild was never the real mission? What if I had been only Ruben's escort? I saw the deer falling into itself again. Had the committee known Ruben was a killer? Had they wished to be rid of him? Or had they created him?

I will never answer these questions, so I have stopped asking them. And I have forgiven myself. Always, I did the best that I could do. But in the morning, I stole myself from the revolution. I went home with Mikhal and we have tried to save the guild. No one could be less suited to this work. Mikhal knows more than I and he says of all the guilders he knew the least.

Last spring we lost the last of the black vine roses. Mikhal took it very hard, but of course it is nothing, nothing compared to the human loss. The old man was wrong, after all. It is easy to obliterate the past; a bullet in the right place and the work of centuries is gone. But he was right about the power of loyalty, for it is only loyalty which holds me here. I tell Mikhal I am still a child of the revolution, and he says no, I am a hybrid now. But if anyone ever asks me to choose between a strain of roses reaching back into history and a child's food, I will not hesitate. We are all the product of the centuries. I struggle to regain the guild and the old man's work without ever believing in its importance the way he believed. And I hope the revolution prospers. With all my heart, I believe in the creation of new men and new women.

The seasons pass. I share them with Mikhal and our children and the revolution does not need me. I see Mikhal look often at the distant mountains. He is thinking of his wild roses. They are his loss and his comfort. With or without us, somewhere the roses grow. Some of them must even be yellow.

CONTENTION

Some of us are dreamers.
—Kermit

At dinner Claire's son asks her if she knows the name of the man who is on record as having grown the world's largest vegetable, not counting the watermelon, which may be a fruit, Claire's son is not sure. Claire says that she doesn't. Her son is eight years old. It is an annoying age. He wants her to guess.

"I really don't know, honey," Claire says.

So he gives her a hint. "It was a turnip."

Claire eliminates the entire population of Lapland. "Elliot," she guesses.

"Nope." His voice holds an edge of triumph, but no more than is polite. "Wrong. Guess again."

"Just tell me," Claire suggests.

"Guess first."

"Edmund," Claire says, and her son regards her with narrowing eyes.

"Guess the last name."

Claire remembers that there are more Chinese in the world than anything else. "Edmund Li," she guesses, but the correct answer is Edmund Firthgrove and the world's most common surname is Chang. So she is not even close.

"Guess who has the world's longest fingernails," her son suggests. "It's a man."

Well, Claire is quite certain it's not going to be

97

Edmund Firthgrove. Life is a bifurcated highway. She points this out to her son, turns to make sure her daughter is listening as well. "We live in an age of specialization," she tells them. "You can make gardening history or you can make fingernail history, but there's no way in hell you can make both. Remember this. This is your mother speaking. If you want to be great, you've got to make choices." And then immediately Claire wonders if what she has just said is true.

"We're having hamburgers again." Claire's husband makes this observation in a slow, dispassionate voice. Just the facts, ma'am. "We had hamburgers on Sunday and then again on Thursday. This makes three times this week."

Claire tells him she is going for a personal record. In fact it is a headline she read while waiting with the ground meat for the supermarket checker that is making her rethink the issue of choices now. "Meet the laziest man in the world," it said. "In bed since 1969 . . . his wife even shaves and bathes him."

Claire imagines that a case like this one begins when a man loses his job. He may spend weeks seeking employment and never even make it to the interview. He's just not a self-starter. Thoroughly demoralized, on a Monday in 1969, at the height of the Vietnam War, he refuses to get out of bed. "What's the point?" he asks his wife. She is tolerant at first. He needs a rest. Fine. She leaves him alone for a couple of days, even brings in trays of food, changes the channel on the TV for him.

This is no bid for greatness; this is a modified suicide. "Man collapses watching game show." But staying in bed turns out to have pleasant associations for him. He begins to remember a bout of chicken pox he had as a child—how his mother would bring him glasses of orange juice. He feels warm and cared for; his despair begins to dissipate. "I've got such a craving for orange juice," he tells his wife.

Months pass, he has been in bed an entire year before he realizes what he has become. He's not just some schlub who can't find work. Suddenly he's a *contender*. With stamina, perseverance, and support he can turn tragedy into triumph. He tells his wife that the only thing they have to fear now is a failure of nerve.

How does she feel about this? In the picture which accompanied the story she was shown plumping up his pillow and smiling, a beefy sort of woman, a type which is never going to be fashionable. She may feel, like him, that this is her only shot. His greatness is her greatness, his glory is her glory.

Or her motives may be less pure. Out in the world more, she is bound to be more worldly than he is. He has a vision. He is extending the boundaries of human achievement. She is speculating on the possibility of a movie made for TV. She may suggest that, as long as he is just lying there, he could be growing his fingernails, too.

She is an ignorant woman. You don't just grow your fingernails because you happen to have time on your hands. It requires commitment, a special, gelatinous diet, internal and external fortification. A person's nails, in fact, are at most risk during those precise hours a person spends in bed. She has her own motives, of course. She is tired of clipping his nails. "Why don't you grow your beard out?" she suggests, rouging her cheeks and donning a feathery hat before slipping out to a three-martini lunch with the network executives. She will order lobster, then sell the exclusive rights to the tabloids instead. "Why don't you make a ball out of twine?" The largest recorded string ball is more than twelve feet in diameter. *That* will keep him in bed for a while.

At the restaurant she meets Solero don Guillermo, the world's fastest flamenco dancer. She forgets to come home. Her husband grows hungrier and hungrier. He makes his way to the kitchen five days later, a smashed man. He contemplates slitting his wrists. Instead, while preparing his own breakfast, he manages, in twelve seconds, to chop a cucumber into 250 slices, besting Hugh Andrews of Blackpool by four cuts. The rounds of cucumber are so fine you could watch TV through them.

Forty-two years later—a good twenty-four years off the record—he gets his wife's note, placed in a bottle and tossed off the *Queen Mary.* "Kiss my ass," it says.

"You *know*," Claire's son's voice is accusing, "how much I hate raw hamburgers. This is all pink in the middle. It's gross. I can't eat this."

"I'm tired of hamburgers," Claire's daughter says.

"Is there anything else to eat?" Claire's husband asks.

Claire smiles at them all. She sends them a message, tapping it out with her fork on the side of her plate. It may take years, but she imagines it will get there eventually.

RECALLING CINDERELLA

Raina . . . Raina . . . Raina. . . . The name is like a heartbeat, the sound you hear inside your ear when everything is quiet, a whisper in the dark. "Who named me?" I once asked Elaine.

"It was part of the package," she answered. "It was the first word you spoke. Don't you remember?"

I don't. And since I have no reason to believe that my memory is defective and much evidence of the unreliability of hers, I doubt it happened that way. But if she is right, if I awoke saying "Raina," isn't it much more likely that I was calling to someone else? How often does a person say her own name?

This is what I remember—the sound of soft footsteps, three people walking on rubber-soled shoes. A rustling, from clothing, I suppose, and a loud inhalation of air. And then, a voice—Laura's voice, although of course I didn't know that then. "She gives me the creeps," Laura said.

"Nonsense." That was Dr. Margaret, Laura's mother. She picked up my hand and pulled the fingers back until the palm flattened. "She's just what we ordered. I'm very pleased." Her voice came closer to my face. "Raina . . . Raina . . . Raina . . . open your eyes."

I was in a white bed in a white room and a large woman was removing a tube from a vein in my wrist.

101

Her eyes were gray, her skin slick and oily-looking. Quite unattractive, although of course I didn't notice at the time, having nothing to compare it to. Her jaw was so square it looked out of proportion to the rest of her face. It moved. "How do you feel?" she asked.

How did I feel? I didn't know. I began to explore, to search for feelings inside, but it was all emptiness and the one question. How did I feel?

Dr. Margaret had given me the question like a gift. Now she gave me the answer. She read a series of numbers from a screen beside the bed. Then she smiled at me. "Perfect," she said. "You'll be trained to help us here at the hospital. We have instructional tapes; Laura can show you how to use them." She gestured toward the door, where two other women stood. One of them, the one with reddish hair and a jaw identical to Dr. Margaret's, grimaced slightly. That was Laura. The other was Elaine. No one introduced her. Dr. Margaret was still talking. "All we expect of you is the more routine work," she continued. "I think you can be trained in, say—two weeks?"

As she spoke, Dr. Margaret examined my body. She felt for muscles along my arms, pressed her fingers into my skin, shone a small pinpoint of light into first one eye and then the other. "We catch breakfast and lunch as we can," she continued. "Laura will show you how to use the kitchen. But we make it a point to eat dinner together. It gives us a chance to go over the day's work and exchange ideas. Dinner is at the start of the third period. You won't be hungry today, but come anyway. Laura will show you where." She finished with a slight slap on the bottom of my left foot. "We'll leave you now to dress, Raina. Can you do that?"

And *these* were my first words. "Yes," I said. "I can." The three women left then, first Elaine, then Laura, then Dr. Margaret. I saw the connection between them; I saw it most clearly then, when I had no memories to obscure my vision, but it was a thing I didn't understand. I concentrated on the physical features they shared—the jawline, certain facial expressions, the curve of their backs. A tenuous connection, but I was certain of it. Dr. Margaret and Laura were identically dressed in dark coveralls with scarves over their hair. Elaine was wearing coveralls, too, but hers were blue with a thin green stripe. They had left a pair of coveralls for me on a chair beside the bed.

The chair was a hard orange plastic with a curved seat, and the coveralls were bright green. I got up and put them on and socks and rubber-soled shoes. I was filling myself inside with new colors, new textures, new thoughts, moving farther and farther away from the emptiness of my past. There was nothing to regret or miss in that whiteness, but there *was* something. Something irretrievable, something which had no shape and certainly no name, but which, over time, I began to think of as my family. My past.

I mentioned it once, and only once to Elaine. We were having breakfast. Elaine had cut herself a large slice of spongy yellow bread, and told me it was impossible. "You don't have a family," she said. "You were grown on one of the farms. But you couldn't remember that—you wouldn't have any more memory of that than a baby has of the womb. Top of the line, though. State of the art. Nothing but the best for Mother. I don't imagine there was even a pattern for you; little bit of genetic engineering, I suppose. Language skills, manual skills. The basics. But no personality. You're really only capable of following simple instructions."

Laura joined us at the table, yawning and reaching for the bread. She watched Elaine spread her piece with purple jelly. "Haven't you had enough, Elaine?" she asked.

Elaine is very fat, so Laura continually nags her to restrict her diet. Yet, during our dinnertimes, Dr. Margaret frequently urges her to eat more. Dr. Margaret says that beauty is fleeting and ultimately trivial. She didn't select their fathers with beautiful daughters in mind. She gave them intelligence and money. What more do you need? Why shouldn't Elaine eat as she chooses?

Perhaps this is what Elaine believes. In any case, she looked defiantly at Laura and spooned more jelly onto her bread. "I may not get lunch," she said. "I've got a whole new group on their way to Athens. It'll take me all day to screen them. Mother says I caused the last flu there through carelessness."

"Who named me then?" I asked, and Elaine and Laura turned to me.

"It was part of the package," Elaine answered. "It was the first word you spoke. Don't you remember?"

"Kind of a stupid name," said Laura.

It didn't take two weeks to train me. This prediction of Dr. Margaret's was merely the first instance of her tendency to underestimate me. I helped her in the lab, but my main duties concerned record-keeping and retrieval. It was not demanding work, but it was certainly important. In a hospital, access to information can be the difference between life and death. I worked hard, had little free time, and it occurred to me to wonder how they had gotten along without me.

The hospital is small, but it serves an entire sector, five inhabitable planets with a total population of less than five thousand. "The Outback," Elaine calls it. "The outcasts," is what she calls us. Someday she plans to live in an older, more populous sector. Someday she plans to lose her excess weight.

If I understand the word "outcast" correctly, and it's one which I find difficult in any but the most literal sense, then I think it's a poor choice. Dr. Margaret is known and respected far beyond the sector. It was her work in immunology which opened the outer sectors to settlement in the first place. Every year she receives another humanitarian award from some group or other, a tribute to her willingness to live and work out here with the miners. Dr. Margaret inherited money and all her grants, awards, and patents have added to it considerably. She is rich enough to live wherever she wants. It follows that she wants to live here. Every year she gets requests from students and researchers anxious to come just for the privilege of working with her. But she chose me instead.

The truth is, Dr. Margaret doesn't care for people much. What Dr. Margaret likes is control. Elaine, Laura, me—everything in the hospital—we all do exactly what she tells us.

But once someone didn't. Elaine told me about it. It was the day I first entered her room. I had been at the hospital for two months then, two months and four days. Dr. Margaret had sent me to find Elaine, who had neglected to record her lab results from the previous day.

I looked for her first in the kitchen, then on the ward using the monitor. I knew the location of her room from the tapes and it seemed logical to look there next.

I walked into the empty room, and I remember being struck by the frivolity of the furniture. I imagined her mother fixing her room for her, though it did not seem the sort of furniture Dr. Margaret would choose. Certainly it was not like my room. Many of the larger pieces were actually wooden; I knew from the rings and whorls of the grain. There were pink curtains and a pink and white spread on the bed. A half-eaten box of wafers sat on the bureau and gave the room a pleasant, sweet smell.

I was curious about the curtains. We live several layers inside the hospital, where Dr. Margaret can control temperatures and humidities precisely. I expected the curtains to hide a monitor, perhaps a communication into Laura's or her mother's room. Instead, when I pulled it aside, I found a mirror—three mirrors, really, hinged together so they could be opened and shut.

Inside the mirror was my face, clear skin, even features, and suddenly one side of the mirror swung in so there were several faces, all mine. At the sight of my faces, the thing buried inside me, past emptiness, gave a sudden cry. It stirred and struggled while I stared at the faces and tried to remember . . . tried to remember. . . .

"Raina!" Suddenly there were several Elaines behind me in the mirror, all looking annoyed. Her voice was shrill and aggressive. "Do you think you're pretty, Raina?" she asked.

I turned to her and I imagined what I could not see—that my mirror selves had all turned their backs on me. "Your mother sent me to find you. She wants to know what your lab results were yesterday?"

"Nothing," said Elaine. "What does she expect?"

"She wants you to record them."

Elaine waved a hand in annoyance. "Do you know," she said, "that on the other planets, the time period for one day is set at twenty-four hours? Not long enough for Mother, of course. She has to live here so she can add an extra work-hour." She looked at me closely. "Come here." Her expression was unreadable. "I'll show you a pretty face." She took a picture off her desk, an oval of a young woman from the waist up. She was dressed in the usual coveralls, but her hair was loose, black, and very shiny. Her facial features were larger and less symmetrical than my own, but the effect of the whole was an appealing one. I looked at her closely to learn what a pretty face was.

"Mother could have made any of us this pretty," Elaine said. "If she'd wanted to. This is my oldest sister, Gwen. She left before you came. It destroyed Mother. Gwen went to live with a vehicle technician on Athens 4—not a real mechanic, you know. Strictly assembly-line. Mother hated him. He checked in here with one of those port diseases, if you know what I mean. But Laura would have gone with him if Gwen hadn't. You can't mention her to either of them, you understand? They don't want to hear about her."

Elaine took the frame back, careful not to touch me. "I don't want you in my room unless I've asked you," she said, every word unnecessarily distinct. But then she changed abruptly. She put one strand of her brown hair behind her ear—it was an artful gesture, done for timing—and she forced herself to smile at me.

"We couldn't manage the work without her," she told me. "On top of everything else. That's why we got you." She reached to me, moving a section of my hair in the identical way she had just touched her own. "I miss Gwen dreadfully," she said. "But don't tell anybody."

Gwen was my first secret, if you don't count the one I kept inside, the secret I kept even from myself. The hospital is full of secrets and most I don't share. If anyone had asked me then what a family was, I would have answered that it was an elaborate arrangement of secrets. I don't see why it should be that way.

Laura enjoys her secrets. They make her absent-minded, they give her an adolescent dreaminess she is far too old for. Laura's secrets fill Dr. Margaret with disquiet. I remember one evening when we were washing for dinner. Dr. Margaret was scolding Laura for imprecise measurements in her lab work. "Now it will all have to be done again," she said.

Laura removed her coveralls for sterilization. Her hair rested softly on her green shirt collar, curling under just slightly, softening her jawline. "Sorry," she said unapologetically. "I'm not feeling well. I'm about to start my monthlies." She looked at me, anticipating the question I would not have asked. "You don't need to know," she said, a curious lilt in her voice. "Lucky you."

"That's a ridiculous excuse," said Dr. Margaret, pouring a disinfectant into her palm. "I won't even respond to that."

"Why keep running the same tests, anyway? Look what can be done with domes and atmosphere control. Look at us. We *never* go outside. Why isn't that enough? Why tamper with people?"

Dr. Margaret exhaled impatiently. "You have no interest in the problem itself, then. You see nothing to be gained from the simple increase of human knowledge and the concomitant extension of human control. Really, Laura, you do exasperate me. You have a fine mind—I saw to that. If only I could convince you to use it."

"I like to work with the patients," said Laura. "Why can't Raina do the lab work?"

Dr. Margaret looked at Laura sharply. Laura was pulling her hair across her face and examining it with pleasure. It is very beautiful hair, Elaine tells me. "I'm thinking of doing just the opposite," said Dr. Margaret. "I'm wondering if Raina couldn't begin to handle a caseload."

In spite of being the only hospital in the sector we are never full. The different planets have their own first aid stations, and most people handle their own low-level care. The only exceptions are the innoculations. We do them, because Dr. Margaret feels the immunizing agents might pose a danger if they were carelessly allowed into the environment.

Elaine told me there had once been a mining accident and they had had more than a hundred patients at once, but I have seen nothing like that. I had never been needed for patient care and had rarely gone onto the ward.

But shortly after this one of Laura's patients was reassigned to me. He was a young male, might even have been younger than I am if I had known a way to count years for myself, an aging in the body without the usual passage of time. He was a geologist from the outermost station. Dr. Margaret came to my room to inform me of the reassignment. She entered before I had risen, entered without knocking although I believe she invariably knocks for admittance into Elaine or Laura's room. She looked tired. Laura had recently cut her hair for her—very short. She had slept on it and not combed it, pieces stuck up about the ears.

She was characteristically abrupt. "Raina, we are very close here, closer than most families, because we work together and are so isolated. There is no need for any of us to have secrets from the others."

It was my own thought. It gave me a peculiar feeling to hear someone else express it. It was sweet, this unexpected matching of something inside me to something outside. Very sweet. Then Dr. Margaret handed me a piece of paper. On it she had written two chains of prime numbers. "Here are the access codes that Elaine and Laura use. If you should see a message come in for either of them, I want you to read it and to tell me about it. Memorize the access."

Always underestimating me. Having seen the num-

bers once I would never forget them. I handed the paper
back. Dr. Margaret turned to leave the room, stopping
briefly at the door. "I almost forgot what I came down for.
You'll see you have a patient when you punch up your
duties. An interesting case. Keep me informed." She left
and I saw her neck receding from me, startlingly white
where the hair had been cut away.

The geologist turned out to be one of those rare
individuals who could not tolerate the innoculation.
Instead the introduction of passive immunities had
caused an alarming agglutination of the red blood cells.
He had required replacement of the entire blood supply;
Laura had handled that and seen that he had no adverse
reaction to the foreign blood. It was left to me to see if he
could now tolerate and use the immunizing agents, a
slow, tedious process, most of which could still be done
in the lab. "Every single person is different," Dr.
Margaret told me enthusiastically. "That's what makes
medicine so fascinating. Just when you think you've got
it all figured out, someone comes along who reacts
differently."

The geologist persisted in calling for me. He
couldn't wiggle his toes, he claimed. He had a headache.
"I'm really quite busy," I told him, but he ignored this.
Whenever I was in the room, he stared at me. Once,
when I was withdrawing blood, I suddenly felt his hands
attach themselves to my waist and begin to move
upward. I gave the needle an extra push and he released
me.

"Ouch," he said, but he was laughing.

"Don't do that again." How did I feel? Before I
could decide, choose, and identify one of the feelings
inside me, I turned, and saw Dr. Margaret watching
from the doorway. I could see that she was pleased.
"Bravo, Raina," she said. "I never thought you'd be so
good with people."

I wondered what she meant, what anyone would
mean if they said that. Did it mean I pleased the people
around me? Did it mean I controlled them? Should I be
trying to do either? These were new thoughts to me.

Two weeks later Laura came to my room at night. I

could smell her coming—her shampoo floated through the door just ahead of her. Such a gentle smell.

Before it had even registered, Laura appeared. Her face was red about her eyes and I noticed suddenly that she had found a way to thin her eyebrows. She walked through the doorway and straight up to me, raising her hand. I heard and felt it hit my face. "You're even worse than Gwen," she said in a low voice that shook. "What do you know about loyalty? What do you care about love? You're Mother's perfect little daughter, aren't you?" She raised her hand to hit me a second time, but I had no trouble catching it.

"Don't do that again," I warned her. And then said, "I don't want you in my room unless I've asked you." I tried to sound firm, but I felt sick inside, shredded. I can't bear disharmony. "Please go," I told her and, to my surprise, she did. She was crying and left the room almost doubled over. The last I saw of her was the exaggerated curve of her back.

Laura and Elaine argue with each other constantly, but it's different, somehow, from the way they argue with me. I never argue with anyone. It hurts to do it. Since Dr. Margaret oversees our dinners, they are peaceful and professionally oriented. Breakfast is often one long quarrel.

Laura tells Elaine she eats too much. "I say this because I'm your sister and I love you," she says, ostentatiously heaping her own plate.

Elaine tells Laura she frightens men away with the desperation in her approach. "It embarrasses me just to watch the way you throw yourself at them. I'm not saying this to hurt you. I only want to help."

They're happiest when they unite against me. I make all their differences disappear because I am so much more different. At breakfast yesterday, Laura was combing her hair. She was wearing yellow coveralls and trying to attach a clip, shaped like a bird, to the twist of her hair.

Elaine watched with annoyance, irritated because she thinks this preening at the table is unhygienic. But what she said was "Laura, do you really have the time to just be sitting here? Shouldn't you be in the lab? All the temperatures on those cultures need to be changed."

"It's not my day to work in the lab. I did it yesterday, *Elaine*."

"Yesterday you were paying me back for working twice last week. You went out on call, remember?"

"I already paid that back. You're so dim. You think you can boss me around just because you're bigger." Laura smiled nastily. "Of course, you're bigger than just about anyone, aren't you?"

"Shut up, Laura. Why should I do your work on top of mine?"

"It's Laura's lab day," I said. I remembered Laura pleading to go on call in Elaine's place, offering to take the extra duty. I hoped to settle the dispute which, as always, was upsetting me. But I only annoyed them. They won't admit my memory is better than theirs. They both looked at me at once.

"Why don't you take the lab today, Raina? You like lab work." Elaine peeled the wax covering off an imported fruit.

"I think that's fairest," Laura agreed. "When we're not sure and all. Don't you, Elaine?"

"I really do."

"I'm supposed to help with the boosters," I said. "We've got a whole transport coming in from Athens 4."

"Then you'd better hurry," Elaine advised. I put down my knife, my breakfast unfinished. "Hurry up, Raina!"

I almost told her that I didn't have time. I looked at her and started to form the words and then didn't. I gathered up my dishes instead and as I was leaving the table I heard Laura whisper something to Elaine. "I thought for a moment she was going to argue with you," she said.

I looked back. Elaine and Laura were sitting with their heads very close together—the dark hair and the red hair almost touching. "No," Elaine answered. "Passivity is part of the program," then I was through the door, hurrying to the lab. I could have argued with her

though, could have chosen the words that would have
been like a piece of myself, held outside me for Elaine
and Laura to look at. Hadn't I told Laura to get out of my
room? Hadn't I told my geologist patient not to touch
me? Hadn't anyone noticed these things?

I wondered if they had noticed how much of the
hospital work I was now doing. Without extending my
hours, I had become increasingly efficient. I now did
more than any of them, even Dr. Margaret. I didn't mind
this. At least when I had done something myself, I knew
it had been done well. Elaine is clumsy and Laura is
forgetful. Each of them has contaminated entire experiments. And Dr. Margaret? Strange, with her reputation,
but I'm beginning to think that she is unimaginative.
Her approach to immunology is strictly a defensive one.
I'm beginning to wonder if we have to be so conserva-
tive. Not that it was up to me.

When I had finished Laura's lab work, I hurried to
the patient hall. It was full and I was late. Dr. Margaret
gave me an irritated glance. "Laura came in to help out
when you didn't show," she said in an undertone the
patients wouldn't hear. "I think you'd be ashamed to
have her doing your work."

I began to punch up the records for the individual
patients and came upon an anomaly which I called to Dr.
Margaret's attention. There was a little boy in the Athens
group on whom we had no record. He said he had been
innoculated by his mother. It shouldn't have been
possible, but a blood test bore him out. He wore yellow
coveralls and red boots and had shiny black hair. Elaine,
Laura, and Dr. Margaret fussed over him and kept all
the other patients waiting. "Isn't he sweet?" they cooed.
"Isn't he the sweetest thing?"

Dr. Margaret gave him the booster personally and a
candy for being so brave. We stood together inside,
listening to the ship leave. "You could still send a
message to Gwen," said Elaine. "Please, Mother."

But Laura said, "No." I saw with surprise that she
was crying; I hadn't heard it over the transport engine,
but now she was having trouble speaking, her words lost
in great, gusting sobs. "She doesn't want us to have

anything. She could have come here for the delivery. She knows how seldom we get babies." She said something else that was lost in her crying, then became audible again. "She could at least have informed us. We are the doctors, here, after all. Births and deaths all routinely logged. She could have let us share in this, but she didn't. She only sent him now to show us what we're missing."

Dr. Margaret spoke quietly. "Perhaps it's time for one of you to have a baby. I could arrange it. During the pregnancy we could get more help for the hospital like we got Raina."

"Another Raina," said Laura. "No thanks." She looked at me bitterly and left the hall.

Dr. Margaret put her arm around Elaine. "I loved her, you know. You know I did."

"Another Raina." Those were Laura's words and I remember them now as I remember everything else in this hospital, exactly, accurately. Why didn't I hear them? How could I listen so carefully and hear so little?

This morning I heard them again, as I sat at the console, reading in a patient history and was interrupted by a message coming over the screen—a printed message, which meant it came from somewhere outside the sector. I couldn't access it with my own code, so I realized it was a secret message—something for Elaine, or Laura, or Dr. Margaret. A secret message for anyone but me. "There is no need for any of us to have secrets from the others," I told myself, and I punched in Laura's access.

The message came across the screen slowly. It was from a company called "Help Wanted." It read:

Regret to inform you RAINA has been found to have a flawed personality structure and may be dangerous. Incidents in other sectors force recall of all units. Respond. . . .

I sat at the console a long time, looking at those words. "All units," I read. "Another Raina," I remembered. I could only make it mean one thing. I began to type the response.

> RAINA is like one of the family. We cannot think of . . .

then I erased it and began again.

> Message received. Situation under control. Appropriate steps being taken.

And I sent it.

It was past time for me to be in the lab. I hurried there, anxious not to show Dr. Margaret another example of tardiness, afraid I might have to create an explanation for it. But the lab was empty. I began to update the logs and Dr. Margaret came in. She did not speak to me and I knew that if I didn't have to fabricate anything, if it was only a matter of withholding, then I could keep a secret. Dr. Margaret had taught me that herself, she and Elaine.

Dr. Margaret punched in a model of a new experiment she was designing and began to explain it to me. I concentrated on her instructions, pushing my secret down deeper inside me. I couldn't think about it now. I had to be alone. "It's a very cautious approach," I told Dr. Margaret. I hadn't even known I was going to say it. It was not a smart thing to say. I had not offered an opinion before and this one made her look up from the screen to my face with surprise and displeasure.

"I think that's best," she said, and I felt that queer, unpleasant feeling inside me that meant I didn't agree. "You have a different idea?" Dr. Margaret asked coldly. "You have a better idea?"

"Your work is all parasite-specific," I said. "When the infecting organism changes, the agent is no longer effective. You've simply perfected the disease."

"I have had some small success with my methods." Dr. Margaret's voice was edged with sarcasm. "I've also seen what more radical approaches can come to—'The operation was a success, but the patient died.' That's quite an old joke, really, but I bet you've never heard it before." She turned away from me back to the screen, her back stiff with anger. "Just do the experiments I design." Soon she left for the patient ward.

My hands were shaking, but the sickened feeling inside me began to fade and was replaced with a kind of exultation. I had disagreed with Dr. Margaret and I had said so. How strong I was becoming. Stronger even than Laura. Strong enough.

I changed the temperatures on the cultures and saw what I would have to do. I did not make this decision easily. Some of the disharmony I had lived with had even moved inside of me so that I was all in parts—seeing what was required, yet still reluctant. I went to the lab shelves and selected a fatal disease, something airborne and quick. If Dr. Margaret hadn't been so limited in her vision she might have discovered an innoculation against it. Then I wouldn't have this option. It is her own weakness, after all, that condemns her. I left the disease still frozen and harmless in the lab until I could make my other arrangements. Before I defrost it, I must have a way out.

For I am not Gwen. Dr. Margaret would not be hurt by my defection, she would be outraged. She would come after me with all her influence and all her money and I would be destroyed. I thought all this as I sat in the lab among the glove boxes and test tubes. I laid my cheek on the black surface of the table and then lifted it up slightly. At a certain angle, the tabletop was so polished I could see a vague outline of my face. I covered it with my hand, pushing down the part of me which objected.

Then I went on with my work. I set up Dr. Margaret's experiment. I went to the ward to look at my patients. I saw the geologist last of all. "You'll be released soon," I told him. "Two or three days at the most."

He turned on his side, rested his head in the cup of his palm. His eyes and hair were an identical shade of brown; the hospital light reflected off them both. "So I'm cured," he said. "You've cured me of everything." His smile was broad and affected every part of his face.

I leaned toward him, lowering my voice. "Jim," I said. "Will you take me with you?"

His eyes opened in surprise. I spoke again, tremblingly. "Even if I need to leave the sector? Would you help me?" It was my first attempt to persuade anyone to do anything for me. I reached out and moved a piece of his hair back from his forehead. It was so easy. I am good with people.

Jim thought he could secure a vehicle within the two or three days I was willing to spare. Fuel, he said, would be the bigger problem, but he knew a man on Athens. . . . We agreed that I would use the time to erase him and myself from the data banks. I had planned to do this anyway, but he was quite insistent on the point. I wondered for the first time if he might not have some secrets of his own.

There is so much I do not know. I have no memory of the time I spent outside the sector. In my own mind I have never even left the hospital. When I begin to think this way, I calm myself with what I *do* know: I can keep a secret; I am strong; I am good with people; I know nothing of loyalty and do not care about love. It is enough.

Now it is time for dinner. I will go in and sit and listen to the conversation. I will respond when I am spoken to and will otherwise say nothing.

I realize now that all of us have memories beyond our ability to retrieve them, memories we cannot remember. My life is all memory now, so much so that I can no longer distinguish between a recollection and a premonition. My past is my destination, after all. I am returning to what I left behind, to my family, to my sisters, endangered as I am now endangered, fighting as I am now fighting.

If I must sacrifice the flawed personality structures with whom I have worked—Dr. Margaret and her need to control, Elaine and her need to subvert, Laura and her need to escape—then I will do this for my sisters. I know they will be worth the sacrifice. They will, after all, be just like me.

And if they have been taught as I have been taught, then we will find each other. I do not doubt it—it has the solidity of memory. One day, in the darkness, I will whisper my name to someone else. One day, somewhere, I will look at someone else and see my own face.

OTHER PLANES

It was a special occasion, a farewell lunch, so Katy ordered white wine. The stem of her glass was icy; she tightened her fingers on it to drink, looking across the rim at Sonya, whose glass was raised. "This time tomorrow," Katy said and held out her wine until the two glasses touched.

This time tomorrow Sonya would be on a plane to Brussels. Katy paused to wonder just how many lunches she had bought saying good-bye to Sonya. There had been one when Sonya had gone on assignment to Paris; another when she had vacationed in Indonesia. Sonya had moved to New York and come back, married in Boston and divorced in Mexico. Now she was on her way to Europe and a second marriage. This time tomorrow Katy would be where she always was—left behind.

Katy sipped her wine slowly, pushing the short hair around her face back with her free hand. The waiter came and stood beside Sonya, who closed her menu and handed it to him. "I'll just have a small, green salad," she said.

He looked at Katy. "That sounds good. I'll have that, too." Katy's tone was virtuous and Sonya smiled at her. The waiter left behind a basket of hot bread. Sonya passed it to Katy, who tore off a slice, buttering it generously. "Are you all packed?" Katy asked.

Sonya sat back in her chair and laughed. "Katy," she said. "You know me better than that." Her soft, blue blouse was clearly silk and her dark hair was swept back

with combs the color of her fingernails. There was
something regal about Sonya. Katy felt she had spent her
whole life trying not to be jealous of it.

Of course it wasn't really her whole life. It was
. . . "How long have we been friends?" she asked.

"Forever," Sonya answered. "Let's see, when we
met I was dating Tony, so I was a high school junior and
you were what? Ninth grade? Yes. 1970."

"A long time ago," Katy said sentimentally. "Hard to
remember so far back," although, in fact, she remembered perfectly. She remembered that she wore braces
for four years, that she was always fifteen to twenty
pounds heavier than she wanted to be, that whatever
clothes she wore always seemed to be wrong—wrong for
her figure, wrong for the occasion. An adolescence much
like everyone else's, she now supposed. With the
possible exception of Sonya.

"You were such an innocent," Sonya told her.
"Remember how we used to talk about sex? You knew
nothing."

Katy had taken a bite of her bread and was forced to
swallow it quickly. "I was very grateful to you. My
mother was mystifying on the subject and I couldn't
understand the books, even the ones with illustrations.
You were the only one who tried to explain. Of course,
you weren't entirely accurate."

Sonya smiled, but her voice was unamused. "You're
kidding," she said. "What part did I have wrong?"

"I think your most dramatic mistake was your
definition of the word 'cherry.' You said it was what
happened when a girl who was too young to have a baby
had sex. You gave me the lurid notion that it was
something *like* a baby, something which was born, but
was incomplete somehow. A lump."

Sonya shook her head. "It sounds like I had the
right idea and you just misunderstood. Anyway, I must
have done all right with the essentials. You've got Jamie,
after all. How is the little guy?"

"He's great," said Katy. "He's wonderful. Except
some kid at school told him the plot of *Friday the 13th*.
Now he's having nightmares. He's easily freaked. Last

night I woke up because I heard him running top speed down the hall. He burst into our room and said, 'Can I sleep with you guys?' But casually, you know. Like he was just out for a stroll and thought he'd drop by. Not like something chased him out of his own room."

"What sort of nightmares?" Sonya asked.

"Witches, ghosts, big spiders. The classics." Katy reached for her wine glass. She looked at her fingers, magnified by the glass's curve and the pale liquid.

Sonya had leaned forward again. Her voice was suddenly animated. "I saw a ghost once," she said. "Did I ever tell you that?"

Katy did not respond. Of course Sonya had seen a ghost. Sonya had done everything.

"Did I?" Sonya persisted.

"No."

"It was at Mike Fletcher's ski cabin. You remember Mike? Stockbroker. You introduced us—I think you dated him first. Well, he took me up to his cabin and one morning he went out hiking and I was all alone. I went into the kitchen to get a cup of coffee and there was this man—heavy, with a day's beard. Wearing a plaid, flannel shirt like a Pendleton only not so nice. I was so scared I couldn't move. I just stared at him, thinking, 'I'm here alone with a strange man.' *Then* I noticed I could see through him. I could see everything on the other side of him. I got out of there fast, believe me."

The waiter arrived with their salads. "I hope you enjoy your lunch," he said. His words were directed to Sonya. Katy thought he didn't give a damn if she enjoyed *her* lunch and then repressed the thought. She was being ridiculous. Sonya sipped her wine and waited until he had gone to finish her story.

"When I'd calmed down and had a chance to think I said to myself, 'What are you afraid of?' The thing about ghosts is that they really can't hurt you. You should tell Jamie that. They exist in another plane and they can't break through to you."

Katy picked up the iced fork and began to eat. The lettuce leaves were too large to fit comfortably into her mouth. She tried to cut one with the edge of her fork.

Sonya continued. "I marched right back into that kitchen and said, 'You don't belong here and you're scaring me. You have to go back.' That's another thing you can tell Jamie. A ghost has to go when you tell it to." Sonya put a delicate tomato slice into her mouth. "I told Mike about it and he thought I was hilarious. But two weeks later he was telling his mother and she said that a man had hanged himself in that kitchen fifty years ago and I'd described him exactly. But exactly."

Katy didn't want to think about Mike. What did it matter? She had Kevin and she had Jamie and Mike had been arrogant and self-centered. And boring. She really hadn't liked him that much. Neither had Sonya.

The wine glistened in Katy's glass. She slid her fingers down the cold, wet stem. "I saw a ghost once," she said. "When I was very little. About Jamie's age. I'd completely forgotten. You just made me think of it."

"Tell me about it." Sonya's voice was skeptical, amused. It irritated Katy. Why was her relationship with Sonya so difficult, Katy wondered, and immediately answered herself. It was her own fault. You couldn't blame Sonya for being bright, successful, and attractive. You couldn't blame Sonya for the things those qualities brought her. If Katy was uncomfortable, that was Katy's problem. Katy was irritated because, really, in her heart, she felt guilty. She didn't want to be the sort of person who would let envy ruin an old friendship. It was not to her credit that she had to work so hard to prevent this.

"I'll try to tell you," she said. "But it was so long ago. I'm not sure how much I'll remember. We were in New Jersey. Teaneck. Just for the summer. My dad was teaching the summer session and we lived in some other professor's house—he was in Europe. At least, that's how I think it was, though the house was awfully palatial to belong to a professor. I think there were three or four stories. And acres of land and a circular driveway that went all around the house. My dad taught me to ride a bike in that driveway."

"That's sweet," said Sonya. "But get to the ghost."

"Well, there was a barn, too. With horsestalls and hay, but no livestock. It smelled horsey, though. It was used for storage. The professor collected antiques. He had paintings and furniture out there covered with sheets. He even had a suit of armor. Those things are so eerie anyway, the way they stand there all stiff and empty. You know, I just realized all that stuff was probably out there because of me. Don't you think? It was too valuable to really be kept in a barn. The professor probably just moved it all out of the house temporarily to protect it from the six-year-old child who was coming to spend the summer."

Katy took a bite of her salad. With Sonya watching she chewed awkwardly. "It was a very lonely summer for me," she said. "I'd left all my friends back home and I never made new ones. I spent a lot of time just sort of wandering. Around the house, around the yard, around the barn. I was frightened of the barn because the light was so patchy. There were bright spots and dark spots— it made it even harder to see than if the whole thing had been dark. But I was attracted to the barn, too. Because of all the stuff. One day I went into it and there was a woman there. Very pretty. Beautiful. At least that's what I thought at the time. You know how children always think anyone dressed up is beautiful. She had on a backless sundress, tight at the waist, like they wore in the late fifties, early sixties. And she was wearing a lot of perfume, but I could still smell the hay. She surprised me because she was standing in a shaded corner near the stalls but she didn't frighten me."

"You remember it very well," Sonya pointed out. "For something you haven't thought about in years."

"I remember that she knew my name," Katy added. "She said that I was pretty and to please not tell anyone that I'd seen her. Then she slipped away toward the back of the barn." Katy tore off another slice of bread. It was warm in her hand and she tucked the cloth napkin around the others. "I didn't think right away that she was a ghost. It didn't occur to me until days later that she must have been."

"And did you tell anyone about her?" Sonya asked.
"No."

Sonya stabbed a piece of lettuce with her fork.
"Your father was having an affair," she said.

"What?"

"Come on, Katy, this is a little innocent even for
you. Why do you insist this woman was a ghost? Nothing
about your story suggests she wasn't a perfectly ordinary
person. She was dressed appropriately for the times. She
left in an ordinary way. You couldn't see through her the
way I could with my ghost." Sonya put down her fork
and turned her face away from Katy just slightly. The
dim restaurant light glinted off the combs in her hair.
"College professors are the worst," she said. "I was
propositioned by four of mine."

She picked up her wine glass in both hands and
leaned back in her chair. Katy refused to meet her eyes,
but she could feel Sonya looking at her and she picked
up the heavy red napkin to hide the trembling at the
corners of her mouth. When Sonya spoke again, her
voice had softened. "You never told anyone so I think
you knew the truth all along, consciously or subcon-
sciously." Sonya lifted her fork, then set it back down,
tines resting on the plate, silver handle on the table-
cloth. "I have to go to the restroom."

She was off to have a cigarette. Katy knew that.
Sonya knew it too, she thought, consciously or subcon-
sciously. Or perhaps she had simply seen that Katy
needed a moment alone. That was the problem with
Sonya. There was always the generous explanation so
that you never knew if she meant to hurt you or if it was
just something that happened. You just knew you always
ended up hurt. Katy's eyes filled with tears and she shut
them tightly to force them back inside again.

With her eyes closed she tried to visualize her
father as a young man. She couldn't do it, only a fuzzy
vision of him the way he'd been at the end, wasting away
with his broken-stick elbows and hospital pallor. The
wine she'd drunk made her head begin to spin and this
brought another impression—not an image, but a physical memory, a sensation. She was walking between her
parents and they were holding her hands. Every third
step they were swinging her up into air. "One, two,

three," they would say, and she was flying, she was falling, but always she was supported and protected by their hands.

Katy finished her wine in a single swallow. She motioned for the waiter and paid the bill—two small green salads, two glasses of white wine. "My friend is coming back," she said, "so don't take her dishes. And would you apologize to her for me? Tell her I had to go." She counted out a tip from her change and put it by the wine glass. And then she left Sonya behind. Katy walked out of the dark restaurant into the bright afternoon. She felt dizzy so she left the car and kept on walking. She walked all the way home and her gentle ghosts followed her.

THE GATE OF GHOSTS

"The first time I heard about China," Margaret said, "when I was a very little girl like you, I imagined it to be full of breakable objects." As she spoke she poured a stream of milk onto Jessica's Cheerios from a blue plastic cup with Jessica's name on it.

Elliot was late for class. He put his own breakfast dishes into the dishwasher, swallowing the last of his coffee hurriedly. "Very logical," he said. "One only wonders what your first images of Turkey must have been."

"I probably wouldn't even remember this," said Margaret. "Except for the shock I got years later when I read *The Wizard of Oz*. Dorothy climbs over a great wall into a world where all the people are made of porcelain. It was just like my China."

"I don't want any cereal," Jessica said. She tilted her face upward so that the dark hair around it fell back and exposed its white outline, round along the forehead, but with a sharp pointed chin. The hair was not Chinese, but close, a mixture of Margaret's coarser brown and Elliot's shiny black.

"Could you have told me that before I poured the milk?" Margaret asked.

"Before I wanted cereal." Jessica averted her face and looked at Margaret from the corners of her eyes. "Between I changed my mind."

"That's just too bad," said Elliot. " 'Cause now it's made and you have to eat it." He slid the knot of his tie upward and ignored Jessica's frown. "I may be late getting home," he told Margaret. "Or not. I'll call you." He returned to the table to give Jessica a kiss, but she moved her cheek away at the last moment. He petted her hair instead. "Have a good time at nursery school, moi-moi," he told her. "And eat that cereal. Children are starving in China." He looked at Margaret. "Don't you eat it for her," he said and left in a sequence of familiar sounds: footsteps, the car keys in his hand, the door, the car motor.

Jessica pushed her Cheerios away. Margaret pushed them back. "Lots of people have imaginary worlds," Margaret said.

"Can I have juice, too?" asked Jessica. "And toast with jam?"

"Eat your cereal while I make it," said Margaret. "Before it gets soggy." Jessica began to stir the Cheerios. She moved the spoon faster and faster; milk spilled out of the side of the bowl. Margaret had just finished spreading jam on the toast when she heard a car horn in their driveway. "Oh, no," she said. "That can't be Mrs. Yates. Not yet." She looked out the kitchen window. Mrs. Yates waved to her from the driver's seat of the green station wagon. "Your carpool is here," Margaret told Jessica. "Run and get your shoes, sweetheart."

Jessica ran for the bedroom and did not return. Margaret called to her twice and finally went after her. Jessica was jumping on the bed. "When I go real high," she said to her mother, "I can see over the fence. I can see Charlie." Charlie was the red setter who lived next door.

"Your shoes?" Margaret asked.

"Lost."

Margaret lifted the mound of bedspread which was growing at the foot of Jessica's bed and found one blue sneaker with Big Bird's picture on it. She felt under the bed until she located the other.

"Were they there?" Jessica asked in amazement. "All the time?" She dropped to her seat and let Margaret stuff her feet into the shoes and tie the knots double.

"Now run," said Margaret. "Mrs. Yates is waiting,"

and on the way out the door she handed Jessica the toast to eat in the car. She stood and watched while Mrs. Yates fastened Jessica's seatbelt and then went back inside. She moved the bowl of Cheerios out of its puddle of milk to her own place and ate the withered cereal without tasting it. The only noise in the house came from the furnace—a steady hum like distant freeway traffic. And then, outside the house, very far away, a siren. Margaret always noticed sirens and she was particularly alert to them whenever Jessica was away. Nursery school had been Elliot's idea.

"She needs friends and you need a break from her," he'd said. He'd insisted. Jessica was making the adjustment more easily than Margaret was.

"She's still a bit quiet with the other children," the teacher told Margaret. "But, of course, she came in late. We have to give it a little time. And she seems completely comfortable with me. She has a wonderful imagination. She was telling me yesterday about some sort of kid's world she visits."

"Yes," said Margaret. "We hear about it frequently. Please watch her closely on the jungle gym. She's not always sensible in what she tries to do."

"Her coordination is excellent," the teacher protested. "Actually, her coordination is exceptional. Look at this." He went to his desk for a folder with Jessica's name on it, fished through it, withdrawing a small construction-paper rabbit. "Here's this week's scissors project. You see the control Jessica has." The teacher was young with no children of his own. He looked at Margaret's face curiously. "You mustn't worry about her," he said.

It was a sentence Margaret had been hearing all of Jessica's life. "Don't worry so," the pediatrician had told her the very day Jessica was born. Margaret held the baby awkwardly, feeling completely inadequate. Jessica was so small, smaller than she'd imagined. And fragile. How thin the bone was which protected the brain. It could be crushed in a moment's carelessness. The lungs could deflate and then not fill. And what kept the human heart working, after all? Didn't some hearts fight for life

harder than others? Wasn't that what was meant by the
will to live? What kind of a heart did this baby have?

The doctor had none of these doubts. "A perfectly,
healthy baby girl," he said. "Ten on the Apgar. Alert.
Active." He smiled so that Margaret saw the white stain
of an expensive filling on one of his canine teeth. "We
should be so perfect. Do you know, at this age, if she lost
a finger at the knuckle her recuperative powers are so
strong she could regenerate a new tip?" He patted
Margaret on the shoulder. "Don't worry."

"You're holding her back," Elliot said, months later,
critical of the way Margaret kept returning Jessica to the
sitting position whenever she pushed her legs to stand.

"I just don't want her to fall," Margaret answered.
She carried Jessica a great deal, put latches on their
cupboards, lids on their plugs, inspected all toys for
small, loose parts that might cause choking. She did
what she could, but the biggest danger was something
inside Jessica, herself. Jessica was willful and too in-
trepid; it was a constant battle between them. When
Margaret found Jessica piling toys inside her crib and
climbing to the top of the bars, she removed the crib
mattress and made a new bed for Jessica on the floor. She
had just finished when she heard a delighted crowing in
the kitchen. Hurrying in that direction, she found that
Jessica was now able to climb up onto the kitchen chairs.
"She can't be out of my sight for a minute," she
complained to Elliot, who was letting his daughter twist
his hair up in her small fists.

"But she never falls," he pointed out. He untangled
Jessica, tossing her casually above his head, kissing her
when his hands snatched her back from the air. Jessica
laughed. Margaret looked away.

"She never falls because I'm always there," Margaret said quietly. "I'm always there to catch her. I have
to be."

"Don't worry so much," said Elliot. "Please."

Only one other person saw in Jessica what Margaret
saw there. Though critical of Margaret's lack of discipline—by the age of four no one could deny that Jessica
was thoroughly spoiled—Elliot's mother Mei kept the

same careful, frightened watch over Jessica that Margaret did. Elliot said once to Margaret that Mei had fed Margaret's natural fears so that they never disappeared as they should have. "You support each other," he said. "And it gets out of hand." He must have said this to Mei, too, so that she never spoke to Margaret of her own anxieties, but muttered occasionally to Elliot under her breath or in Chinese. When she had gone home, Margaret would press Elliot for translations. "Kui khi," Mei would say frequently and with significant emphasis and Elliot said it meant merely difficult. A difficult child.

Margaret read the paper. "A's Play to an Empty House," it said. She made Jessica's bed and changed the sheets on hers and Elliot's. She set out a chicken to defrost. She waited for Jessica to come home.

Two hours later Mrs. Yates walked Jessica to the door. Jessica shed her shoes at once and leapt from the linoleum entryway to the green and blue flowered couch, bouncing from foot to foot down the length of it and falling as if exhausted onto the last cushion. Margaret thanked Mrs. Yates and closed the door. "That's no way to enter a house," she scolded.

Jessica smiled and her eyes narrowed to dark slits. "Did you miss me?" she asked artfully. "I always miss you." She gave Margaret a hug so that Margaret could feel her heartbeat, strong and fast. Margaret held her a second too long. Jessica wiggled. "I painted," she said. She was still holding four wet pieces of paper in her hand. She unfolded them on the couch. They were watercolors, done fuzzily in shades of pink and purple.

"Lovely," said Margaret. "What are they, darling?"

"The other place. Do you think it's pretty?"

Margaret looked at the paintings more closely. She could almost imagine a landscape behind them, here a body of water, there a cliff, a stormcloud. But, of course, indefinite shapes like these were in the very nature of watercolors. Some of the purple paint had been applied very thickly. It dripped on the cushion. Margaret picked the paintings up. "Your teacher says you've been telling him about your place."

"He's too busy to listen. But sometimes I tell him. When I've just been."

"Do you go when you're at nursery school?"

"It's not at nursery school." Jessica's tone was a copy of Elliot's, patient, logical. "I can't be there and at nursery school at the same time."

"Then when do you go?"

"Between times."

"Between nursery school?"

"No, between all times."

Margaret looked at the paintings again. "I love the colors. It does look pretty. Could I go there?"

Jessica shook her head extravagantly. The dark hair flew against her cheeks and flew away again. "You don't," she said. "So I guess you can't."

"Can you go anytime you want?"

"Yes."

Margaret put the paintings flat on the kitchen table. "I bet you're hungry," she said to Jessica. She opened a cupboard and brought out the peanut butter. "Shall I make you a sandwich?" Jessica dragged a chair from the table to the counter and stood on it to help. "Did you remember Daddy and I are going out tonight?" Margaret asked her. "Paw-paw will come and stay with you."

"Good," said Jessica.

"But don't talk to her about your other place, okay? It just confuses her."

"She knows a lot about other places," Jessica argued. "She's always telling me about China."

"She's never been though," Margaret told her. "She lived in Taiwan when she was little, but never in China. She moved here when she was about your age, so really this is her home. And anyway, China today is all different from what she tells you."

"She says that in China our name would be Ling. Did you know that? She said our name was always Ling until we came to this country and then when Daddy's other grandpa said that, no one understood him. They thought he said Leen. So Leen is our American name, but if we ever went back to China it would still be Ling."

"Does it make you feel funny?" Margaret asked. "To have different names in different places?"

"No." Jessica picked up the sandwich and took a large bite without detaching the bread. She removed the sandwich from her mouth, looking at the marks her teeth had made with evident pride. "I'm used to it."

"When you're in the other place, are you Chinese?"

Jessica shook her head. "Everything is different. Am I Chinese here?" She didn't wait for Margaret to answer. She ran to the back bedroom for the television and "Sesame Street," stopping only long enough to abandon her socks in the hall. Margaret heard another siren, but the sound affected her differently when she knew where Jessica was. Someone who needs help is getting it, she thought, picking up the socks. It was a civilized sound; it was a civilized world. Sometimes, a life depended on this.

When she was just Jessica's age, just four, Margaret had drowned. She had fallen into the Wabash River, downstream from her father, who was fishing, and the current had carried her quickly away from him. The world had divided itself sharply in two: a place where she could breathe and a place where she could not. She did not know how to swim and the river was irresistible; still, she had managed, for a time, to stay in the world she knew. She had managed to keep her face, at least, above the water, until she was tired and grew confused about which world was which. Eventually she had let herself be taken into the new world, a world with colors she had never seen before, blurred images and a pain in her chest she felt less and less the deeper she went.

The fundamental aspect of this new world was movement. When she was older, Margaret learned that people were always in motion, that as the earth turned it spun its inhabitants with it at the speed of a jet plane. It made her remember the one time this velocity had manifested itself to her, when her body had stopped resisting, when she fell out of one world and into another. And she remembered that it was beautiful. So that later when she separated herself from the river, when she emptied the river out of her and came back, her feelings were mixed. She came to the sound of her father's voice. And this is what she remembered most clearly—that she had a choice. Coming back was a decision she made. She could have stayed. She could easily have stayed.

A policeman had been pushing on her with his hands. Her eyes had opened on his face, and then behind him, the face of her father, and she hardly recognized it at first, it was so contorted with fear. They told her later that a third man had pulled her out. He had come into the water fully clothed and he had lost his shoes. While Margaret was lying on the rocks of the riverbank, being very sick, he had disappeared. They could never thank him enough, Margaret's father had said and, in fact, they could never find him to thank him at all.

In Margaret's simple childhood there had been no need for imaginary friends or imaginary places. She knew such things could be healthy and innocent; still it frightened her when Jessica spoke of the other place. She wanted to forbid Jessica to go there. The only other place Margaret had ever known was seductive and deadly. You returned from it only through the fortuitous hand of a man you never saw and your love for your father. Who would bring Jessica back to her? How much did Jessica love her? If it came to a choice, would Jessica come back? Always?

Perhaps Mei understood Jessica better. Mei, herself, believed this was true. Even before she had come to this country, and she had come as a very small girl, there had always been another place—China, the China her parents remembered, the China they imagined, the China they fled. Mei had been told dozens of stories—how their neighbor Chang had to beg for money to bury his mother, how the family across the courtyard had bought the Fifth Rank and the Blue Feather for their son when he failed his examinations and how even this did not satisfy him, how the widow Yen's son sold their pig for opium and told her the pig had been stolen. Mei's family lived in Taiwan and then in Oakland and they talked about China as if it were home.

And China sent them messages. Famine, said China. Send money. War, said China. Bombs. Revolution. And then the messages stopped coming for a while and resumed again when Mei was a grown woman with a son of her own. The new messages were letters from relatives who swore they would be jailed if more money was not sent. The new messages were third-, fourth-, fifth-hand reports of bodies seen floating in the Yangtze with their hands tied together behind their backs and their faces eaten away by fish. These messages tore Mei's parents in two.

But Mei had developed her own methods of coping with other places and avoiding the sense of division. Mei's approach was inclusive instead. In the home was China and Mei believed in the new China, where professors were driven through the streets with sticks like pigs, but children were fed and medical care was available to all. Mei believed in the old China, where dead ancestors could advise you through a medium on the most propitious placement of your house or the best day on which to marry. And Mei spoke English with no trace of an accent and believed in the United States as well, in innoculating your children against polio and sending them to college, where they would study chemistry or physics but not drama or sociology. This was the world outside the home. And Mei, who was raised a Catholic, believed in the church, too. Elliot had once teased her by saying you never knew what to expect with Mei. Did he have a fever? She might stand an egg on end in a bowl of raw rice while speaking his name. She might give him aspirin and take him to the doctor. She would probably do both.

"How pretty your mother looked tonight." said Mei to Jessica. They were eating dinner together. Elliot and Margaret had gone to a faculty party. "The wine color is good on her." Mei was especially pleased because Margaret had been wearing the necklace Mei had given her, a piece of jade carved in the shape of a pear on a very fine chain. A family necklace.

"I look like her," said Jessica.

Mei smiled. "You have her hair," she conceded. "But you look more like me. When I was little. Same eyes. Same skin." Jessica examined her grandmother frankly. Mei saw disbelief in her face and also saw that Jessica was not flattered. "When you come to my house, I'll show you some pictures," Mei said. "You'll see."

"We have a picture of you," Jessica reminded her. "In the hall." Newly wed, dressed in western finery, Mei and her husband had gone to San Francisco to have the picture taken. Mei had worn a stole and pearls; her expression in the photograph was a sophisticated one. She could see why Jessica would question the resemblance, based on this evidence. Certainly, she thought, Jessica's taste in clothes was more flamboyant. "Don't try to look at her directly this evening," Elliot had warned Mei before he left. "Put a pinhole in a piece of cardboard." Jessica was wearing pants with large orange blossoms on them. Her shirt was a blue and red plaid. Her feet were bare, but she wore a sling around her neck fashioned from a red bandanna to support an uninjured arm. She had made Margaret do her hair in three pigtails. She was eating broccoli with her fingers.

"Use your fork," said Mei, who had chopsticks herself.

Jessica smiled at her grandmother and put a piece of broccoli on her fork with her fingers.

"I used to spank my children with a wooden spoon when they wouldn't eat nicely," Mei told her.

"I'm not your little girl, Paw-paw," said Jessica.

"Does your mother let you eat with your fingers?" Mei could believe this.

"I'm not her little girl either. Not always."

"Whose little girl are you then?"

"Nobody's. When I'm in the other place I do anything I want." Jessica turned her fork over so that the broccoli fell back onto her plate.

"You're not in the other place now," said Mei. She took a drink of water. "Lots of children have imaginary places," she added.

"I never see them there."

"Eat your broccoli with your fork," offered Mei, "and I'll tell you a story while you're doing it."

"About China," said Jessica.

"About China long ago," Mei agreed. She waited until Jessica had speared a piece of broccoli and put it into her mouth before beginning the story. "Long, long ago," she said, "in China, there was a fisherman. He worked very hard. In the good weather he was always on the sea and in the bad weather there were always nets to mend and the boat to be worked on. He was never rich, but he was never poor."

"He had a little girl," suggested Jessica, chewing noisily.

"He had a daughter," Mei agreed. "And he loved her very much, although she was a great deal of trouble. She was not a good little girl; she was kui khi—quarrelsome, demanding, always falling down and tearing her clothes."

"She should wear pants," Jessica said, "and not dresses. When I fall down and I'm wearing a dress my knees get scrapes."

"Her knees were always scraped," Mei said. "And she worried her father very much because he couldn't watch out for her the way he thought he should and still work at his fishing. He had no wife, you see. He had to leave her alone so that they could eat and then when he came in from the sea there was always some new trouble she had found." She paused to force Jessica to eat another piece of broccoli. "She was a great worry to him. Then he had a greater worry. The fish stopped coming. He worked as hard as he ever had and he worked as long or longer, but there were no fish. The few strings of money he had saved had to be spent on food and on the nets and then there was nothing. The fisherman couldn't understand it. Other fishermen were still catching as usual.

"He went to a fortune-teller, though he had to sell his heavy coat to pay for it. The fortune-teller told him his little girl had an adopted daughter's fate. He said she stood at the gate of ghosts. He said she was not only kui khi, but also kui mia."

"What does that mean?" Jessica asked.

"Not all kui khi children are kui mia," said Mei, "but all kui mia children are kui khi. A kui khi child is expensive and hard to raise, but a kui mia child is dangerous not only to herself, but to her parents, as well. She has a dangerous fate and the dangers which gather about her may destroy her family, too. This is what was happening to the fisherman. The fortune-teller told him to give his daughter away."

"Did he?" asked Jessica in horror.

"He didn't know what to do. He loved his little girl more than anything in this world. He couldn't bear to think of being without her. But if he kept her she would starve along with him. He came home and cried late into the night, asking his ancestors for help and guidance. And his little girl heard him. Now she was noisy and stubborn, but she was not selfish. She heard how unhappy her father was and she heard that it was because of her. She decided to run away. In the dark, in the cold, she left the house and ran down to the ocean. She told the spirit of the sea that her father was hungry and poor and that he must have fish. She offered to trade herself for the fish; she left her shoes on the sand and ran out into the water until it covered her entirely."

"Did she die?" Jessica asked. She had forgotten to eat. Mei picked up the last piece of broccoli with her chopsticks and fed it to Jessica.

"Her father believed she had. He found her shoes by the water the next morning and his unhappiness collected in his eyes and blinded him. He pushed his boat out into the water and fish leapt into it, without bait, without nets, but the fisherman didn't care. When he was on deep water, he overturned the boat to join his daughter. His clothes grew heavy in the waves and pulled him down. He prepared to die. But what do you think?"

"He didn't," said Jessica.

"No. The water spirits were so touched by his love for his daughter, as touched as they had been by her sacrifice, that they gave him gills. They turned him and his daughter into beautiful fish which hid the little girl from her fate. She and her father stayed together under the water and lived long and happy lives in the weeds and the waves. Of course, having been human, they were too clever to ever be caught."

"I'd like to be a fish," said Jessica.

"It's a carefree life," Mei agreed. "Except for bigger fish. No ice cream, of course. No 'Sesame Street.' Lots of baths."

Jessica made a face. "You have to be suited to the underwater life," Mei added. "The fisherman and his daughter, they had to be changed first."

"So they could breathe," said Jessica.

"So they could be happy. For them, the upper world was hard work, trouble, and separation. For you it's the park and being the only four-year-old who can pump herself on the swings. It's school and getting to paint. It's all the people who love you—your mother and your father and me. You better stay here, I think."

"Sometimes," Jessica said. "Sometimes I will."

Mei put Jessica to bed with many trips to the bathroom and sips of water and the light on in the closet and off in the room and then off in the closet and on in the hall and a long discussion of which stuffed animal should sleep with Jesssica tonight, a discussion during the course of which Jessica changed her mind several times. It was a tedious process and Mei was glad not to have to do it routinely. Perhaps a half an hour after the last request, Mei heard Jessica scream.

She ran to the bedroom and put her arms around Jessica, who was sitting up, crying. Jessica's heart was beating like a bird's. It was flying away. Jessica felt cold.

A child could be so badly frightened her soul leapt out of her body. It might return to her immediately. Or a ghost might take it. This had happened to a little neighbor boy in Taiwan. Mei did not remember the boy or the incident, only the adults talking about it. The boy had been frightened by fireworks. His parents had gone to a Taoist priest, who communed with the spirit world and tried to bargain for the boy's soul. The parents had also gone to a Western-style physician. Both had charged a great deal of money. Neither had helped. Eventually, the little boy had died. Mei held Jessica and rubbed her arms to warm her. She called Jessica's soul back and it came. "Paw-paw," said Jessica, still crying. "I was scared."

"It was a dream," said Mei.

"No."

To return so soon afterward, even if only in memory, was dangerous. "Don't talk about it," Mei warned her. "Not yet." She carried Jessica in her arms out to the couch, where she sat, holding Jessica and rocking her. Jessica went to sleep and still Mei held on.

Hours later Margaret and Elliot returned. "Why isn't Jessica in bed?" Margaret asked. "Has she been giving you a hard time, Paw-paw?" Elliot took the little girl from his mother. Jessica was limp in his arms. Her head fell back; her mouth opened. Elliot carried her down the hall and into her room.

"She was frightened," said Mei. "Badly frightened."

"By what?"

Mei looked at her hands, resting in her empty lap, and did not answer.

"By what?" Margaret repeated.

"A nightmare?" asked Elliot. He had returned to the doorway. "I used to have nightmares when I was little. Do you remember, Mother? Night after night sometimes."

"I remember," said Mei. "This was not a nightmare." She looked at Elliot. He was backlit by the light of the hall. He was a shadow. Mei spoke to the shadow of her son. "Kui mia," she said.

"What does that mean?" asked Margaret.

"Spoiled," said Elliot quickly. "It means spoiled."

"No," said Mei. She could not see Elliot's face and she didn't care anyway. So he had a Ph.D. in genetics and a Caucasian wife. Did this mean that he knew about other worlds? Mei understood Elliot's world quite well. She had worked in it all of her adult life; she had her own kind of faith in it. But she saw what Elliot would not admit—that it had limitations. The doctor told you that if you could get your husband to give up smoking he might live to be a hundred and then rapped his knuckles three times on his desktop. "Knock wood," he said to you. Your daughter took a job with a large computer company. She took you to see the new office building the company had built for its California branch and there was no thirteenth floor. The space shuttle went up nine times and it worked perfectly until the moment it exploded and sent seven people to God.

Your home and your family especially were another world. The closer you got to your own heart, the less rational the rules. For your family you didn't choose one world over another. For your family you did everything, everything you could. Mei knew Elliot would not see this. She looked at Elliot and she spoke to Margaret. "It means threatened," Mei said. "It means vulnerable. The kui mia child has a dangerous fate." She could feel Margaret looking at her. They made a sort of triangle; she looking at Elliot, Elliot looking at Margaret, Margaret looking at her.

"Let's talk about it in the morning," said Elliot. "I better take you home now, mother." He reached into his pocket for the car keys, slid the ring over his finger.

"There are things you can do," said Mei. "You should see a fortune-teller. I would pay."

"And I can tell you now the kind of advice we'd get," said Elliot. "Don't take the child to weddings. Let her drink only powdered milk. Lessen her attachments—have her call her mother 'Aunt' and her father 'Uncle.' Monstrous irrelevancies which would be bound to upset and confuse Jessica. Jessica is a bright and beautiful and normal little girl, but if I allowed this then I think she *would* begin to have problems. I'm sorry, Mother. I really am sorry. I can't do it."

Mei looked at Margaret, who was holding the pendant of her necklace between her fingertips and twisting it. Margaret had told her many times when she was pregnant with Jessica that she planned to return to work after the baby came. And then Jessica arrived and the subject had been dropped. Mei had never questioned Margaret about it, because she understood it perfectly. With a different baby Margaret would have

gone back to work as she'd planned. But you don't leave
a kui mia child in day care.

"I will see a fortune-teller myself," said Mei. Elliot
rattled his car keys and Mei stood up. "There can be no
harm in that. I will tell you what the advice is and then
you can decide if you will take it or not." She went to the
door where she had left her shoes and slid her feet into
them. She spoke once more to Margaret. "The child
must be protected," she said. "Her other place is the
spirit world."

"Her other place is death," said Margaret quietly,
her face taut and white. She let the pendant go; it swung
heavily at her neck.

"Lots of children have imaginary worlds," said
Elliot. "I think you're worrying over nothing."

Jessica woke in the morning when the sunlight slid
off the bedroom wall and onto her face. The house was
quiet; the door to her bedroom was shut. She didn't like
that. She couldn't go to sleep at night without the hall
light, but her parents always turned the light out and
shut the door when they went to bed because the fire
department had told them sleeping with the door shut
was safer. It didn't feel safer to Jessica.

There was a lump in her back which turned out to
be Beatrice, the stuffed gray mouse with pearly eyes that
Jessica had slept with. Jessica pulled Beatrice out from
underneath her and dropped her to the floor. She lay still
a few more minutes trying to guess if her parents were
awake. They tiptoed about the house when they thought
Jessica was sleeping. They spoke in hushed voices and
opened doors slowly. But Jessica heard them anyway.
This morning there was nothing.

Jessica got up and put her sling on, round her neck,
over her pajamas. She opened the door and went across
the hall to her parents' bedroom. She found her mother
sitting back on her heels on the floor by the closet.
"What are you doing?" asked Jessica.

"Good morning, sleepy-head," said her mother. She
leaned forward and swept a flat palm over the rug. "I'm
looking for my necklace. I dropped it last night when I

was getting undressed and then it was too dark to find it."

"I'll help look," said Jessica. She crawled slowly about in front of the closet, her face close to the pile. It soon bored her. "I'm hungry," she hinted. "Starving."

Her mother stood up. "Well, I'll make you breakfast then. You go get dressed. We can find it later. What would you like to eat?"

"Cheerios," said Jessica. "From the new box." The new boxes contained prizes, small bugs with lots of legs that stuck wherever you put them and glowed in the dark. Jessica had seen them on television. There were pink ones and green ones and yellow ones and Jessica wanted at least one of every color; she knew she would have to eat several boxes of cereal to make this happen.

She returned to her own room and her own closet. The window was open. She could smell something nice—the neighbors' flowers, the ones that looked like the brush her mother used to use to wash out her baby bottle, the ones that were purple, the ones with all the bees. Charlie had gotten stung last week and howled and howled. Jessica jumped on her bed twice to see if Charlie was in the yard. He was sleeping, stretched out on the patio in the shade.

"Good morning, Charlie," Jessica called and then dropped to the bed and out of sight before he could locate her. She waited until he might have gone back to sleep. Then she did it again, this time kicking her feet out from under her so that she landed on the bed on her back. She lay for a moment smiling.

"Your Cheerios are ready," her mother called. "I'm pouring the milk." Jessica bounced off the bed, grabbing the clothes she had worn the night before. She dressed as quickly as she could. The pants were turned inside out, but she left them that way in the interest of speed. She found socks. She put them both on the same foot, one on top of the other.

"How about wearing two socks?" her mother said when she saw her.

"I am," said Jessica.

Her mother didn't pursue it as Jessica had hoped she would. "Sit down," she said instead.

There was something about her mother's face Jessica didn't like this morning. Her mother looked tired and rubbed the sides of her head as though they hurt. "Where's Daddy?" asked Jessica.

"Jogging."

"Are you crying? About your necklace? Was it your very favorite, favorite one? You can get another."

"No, I'm not crying," her mother assured her. "I'm sure the necklace will turn up. How far could it have gotten all on its own?"

"Maybe it fell between?" Jessica suggested.

"Between what?"

"Between now. To the other place."

Jessica's mother looked at Jessica's face. Jessica smiled and her mother reached out and petted her hair. It was tangled and her mother's fingers caught in it and pulled a little. "Ouch," Jessica said, just as a warning.

"It *was* my favorite necklace," her mother said. "Because Paw-paw gave it to me when you were born. I'm supposed to give it to you someday. So it always made me think of you and of the day you came. A new necklace wouldn't do that. Does that seem silly?"

Jessica shook her head.

"My mother had a watch. It was a man's watch and very expensive, but it wouldn't work at all because someone had worn it in swimming and it wasn't waterproof. The man who owned it first just left it when he saw it was ruined. But my father picked it up and gave it to my mother and she kept it all her life."

"*That* seems silly," said Jessica. She felt more interest in the necklace now that she knew it was to be hers someday and also a slight irritation with her mother, whose carelessness had lost it. She wanted to go and look for it some more and her irritation increased when her mother insisted she stay and eat her Cheerios first. Jessica took a large spoonful, chasing and catching many of the floating circles. She chewed and wondered if her mother would let her dump the box out into a bowl to find the prize if she was very careful and put all the Cheerios back without spilling.

"Do you go to your other place when you're unhappy here?" her mother asked and Jessica had to swallow some of the cereal in order to answer.

"No. I just go when I feel like it."

"Do you feel that you're different from other children?"

"How?" Jessica asked.

"I don't know. Do you feel that you look different or like different things or that other kids don't like you? Your teacher says you're very quiet at school. That doesn't sound like you."

"Everybody's special in their own way." Jessica had learned that from Mr. Rogers. She said it with appropriate authority.

"But sometimes being different, even being special, can be hard. Sometimes it makes people feel bad. Do you ever feel like that?"

"No," said Jessica. She paddled her spoon in the cereal bowl and watched the Cheerios move on the currents she made. With Paw-paw a meal was over when your plate was empty. With her mother it was more a matter of how much time you had spent sitting still. Soon her mother would be satisfied and would let her go and look for the necklace. The Cheerios were already soggy and there was really no need to eat them. "Am I different?" Jessica asked.

"You have the other place. That's different."

"Lots of children have imaginary worlds," Jessica reminded her. Even though she didn't know exactly what was meant by an imaginary world. She thought it might be like on television when children begin by pretending that they're on a boat in the ocean and then they really are and their clothes have changed and their stuffed animals can talk. Which wasn't really much like the other place. The other place wasn't something you would pretend.

"Paw-paw said that something frightened you last night," her mother told her. Her mother was speaking slowly and carefully. Her mother wanted her to remember what Jessica had been trying to forget.

"Can I have toast?" Jessica asked.

"What frightened you?"

Jessica dropped her spoon and pushed the cereal bowl away. "I'm not going to eat anymore." It was a deliberate attempt to change the subject; it was supposed to make her mother mad.

"What frightened you, Jessica?"

Jessica pushed the spoon off the table with her elbow. It bounced with a tinny sound on the floor. She slid lower and lower in her seat until her mother disappeared below the horizon of the tabletop. Jessica slipped off the chair entirely and sat by the spoon underneath the table. The woodgrain was rough from this angle. It felt like being in a box. "I don't want to talk about it," Jessica told her mother's shoes. They were gray sneakers with pink stars—kids' shoes except that they were so big.

Her mother slid forward; her knees came closer to Jessica's face and then back again and her mother was sitting on the floor under the table beside her, cross-legged. Her mother had to hunch a little bit to fit. "I really need you to tell me about it, sweetheart," she said. "I really need to know what happened."

Jessica looked away. "I went to the other place," she said. "And then I couldn't get back. I thought I'd never see you or Daddy or Paw-paw again. That never happened to me before." Jessica was doing her best to talk about it without really remembering. She didn't want to feel it again. "I was scared," she said, just as a fact. "Finally I heard Paw-paw calling me and then I knew where she was and I could get back out. Paw-paw let me sleep on the couch."

Her mother took Jessica's face in her hands; she pressed a little too hard. Jessica let her mouth go all funny, like a fish's, but her mother didn't laugh.

"You must never go again," her mother said.

"It's never been like that before."

"Still. It's too risky. What if Paw-paw hadn't found

you? I couldn't bear it. Please, Jessica. Promise me you won't go back."

Her mother was staring at her, all unhappy. It made Jessica uncomfortable. "Okay," she said. "I won't."

"Promise me."

"Promise." Did she mean it, Jessica wondered. No, she decided. She just would never go back at night. Any world was scary at night. "Can I go look for my necklace now?" Jessica's mother released her with obvious reluctance. Jessica took it as an answer. She crawled between the chairs and stood up. Her mother didn't move. "I'll put my shoes on first," said Jessica. It was a conciliatory gesture. She ran down the hall and into her room. The curtains waved at her when she opened the door. She slammed it to make them wave again. Her knee itched around the scab she had gotten two days ago at the park when she jumped off the swing while she was still swinging. Jessica rolled up the leg of her pants and picked the scab off. There was blood. She should go show her mother. Her mother would want to know. But her mother was already sad. Jessica decided to find the necklace first. Then her mother would be happy and Jessica would get a Band-Aid. Jessica went to her mother and father's room.

The rug was empty. In Jessica's room the rug had puzzle pieces on it and books and dirty socks and Legos and papers from nursery school and a shell from the beach that you couldn't really hear the ocean in no matter what they said and a teddy bear with one eye glued shut in a permanent wink and kite string, but no kite, it had gone up in the sky and was lost. It would be hard to find a necklace in Jessica's room. It should be easy here.

Jessica lay on her stomach and looked. She pressed her chin into the rug; the pile was like grass. There was a whole different world in the rug, now that she was close enough to see it. Perhaps bugs lived there or odors like it said in the commercials. Small creatures making their homes at the roots of the pile so the rug towered over their heads and Jessica never saw them. Creatures that were sucked up in the vacuum, that would be horrible.

She couldn't find the necklace. She looked around the closet and by the bed and at the door to her parents' bathroom, a bathroom with no bathtub in it like hers had, but just a shower and a toilet. There was only one other place Jessica could think of to look. She squeezed through into it.

Today it was filled with wind, so hard, so fast, it lifted her right off her feet. Jessica laughed when she realized she was flying. The wind lifted her hair from her neck and held it in the air over her head. It turned her around and around, higher and higher. The shapes of the landscape changed as Jessica moved faster—straight lines curved into fans, closed walls opened like windows. And then Jessica was moving too fast to see shapes at all; they changed into rings of color which encircled her; objects which had had places before now became endless bands, their beginnings and ends fused together. Jessica made no attempt to control her height or her speed; she let herself go completely limp and went wherever she was taken.

She thought she heard her mother calling her. Jessica ignored it. Her mother would still be calling her whenever Jessica chose to return. She had learned that these trips took no time at all. They happened between time, no matter how long she felt she had stayed. Except for last night. The thought came to Jessica suddenly, making her frown. Last night Paw-paw had missed her and come looking. Jessica extended her arms, hands wide open facing backward to see if that slowed her spinning. Instead the wind slapped against them, turning her even faster. She was moving so fast now that it was hard to breathe and there was a pressure against her eyes so she closed them. Colors happened inside her head like fireworks, the colors you see when you press your fingers against your eyelids and leave them there. Colors in lines like snakes and bursts like stars and drips like paint. Jessica pulled her arms in and the spinning slowed so that she could get her breath.

Her mother called again; the voice came from below her. The second call made Jessica realize that time was passing. If her mother found her, like Paw-paw, then her mother would know she had not kept her promise. Jessica opened her eyes and tried to return. She put her arms straight up over her head and fell toward her mother's voice. The wind caught her up again. She arched and straightened and fell. And was carried up. It was like a swing, up and down, up and down. Jessica worked harder. She made a little progress, but only slowly. She remembered the last time. She began to be frightened. Her mother was closer now and she wanted to beat her mother to the place between the worlds, to the door, but the flying was so effortless and the returning so tiring. She gave it up and felt herself being lifted away.

"Jessica," her mother called. It was a scream that the wind carried all around her like the colors. The scream dissolved into continuous sound. It was joined by another scream which went on and on. Jessica twisted in the wind and tried again to fall. She tried as hard as she could. She was crying now and the wind was so quick that the tears never even touched her cheeks but were blown away right out of her eyes. Her heart pounded on the wall of her chest. She wanted her mother. She wanted to go home. And suddenly the spinning slowed. The tears streaked her face. The wind began to fade and Jessica could do whatever she liked. She turned a cartwheel in the air, very slowly, arms and legs straight like a star, since this was something she could not manage in the other world. She closed her eyes. She opened them and she was lying in her mother's lap.

Her mother's face was something awful, the strangest color, and Jessica knew it was because of her, so she looked quickly away to pretend she hadn't seen it. "Don't be mad," she said. The words came out like hiccoughs because of the crying. "I was scared." Her mother held her so tightly her heart beat into Jessica's body as if it were Jessica's own. Jessica relaxed. "I was looking for your necklace," she told her mother. "But it's not there either. Maybe some other place." Her mother did not answer. Jessica guessed she was mad about the broken promise. Jessica guessed that she was going to want to talk and talk about it again the way grown-ups never could let go of things until they repeated them-selves and made you repeat yourself. Jessica, who did not want to think anymore about how frightened she had been, but knew she would be made to, felt very cross, herself. "I came back," she pointed out sulkily.

Her mother's grip on her tightened. "Jessica," her mother said in a hoarse, funny voice. "Jessica."

Jessica looked past her mother toward the window. It was *raining* outside and Jessica hadn't even noticed. Her father would be home soon and he would stand in the kitchen and shake the water out of his hair like a dog. It cheered Jessica up to think about it. She slipped her arms around her mother's neck and fastened her hands tightly over the opposite elbows. She would not let go. Not ever. When her mother stood up, and for the rest of her mother's life, Jessica decided, she would be there, hanging from her mother's neck like a stone.

THE BOG PEOPLE

It will be the women who come for me. What is between us is between women. They will come, cold and sober as stones, and they will commit their gentle hands to harshness, because they will want me to understand. It was a sin of the body, their hands will tell me. And so it is the body that must pay.

Men will come too, some of the men, but only for the sport in it. The men will have been drinking. They will stand outside, laughing and telling jokes the women should not hear and so will not hear. The men will be flushed and sweating from the jokes and the beer. They will watch, but they will not interfere. They never interfere when it is a matter for women.

The women came before, for Mary Katherine when she married Donald Ban Devins. They crowded here into our small bedroom where she stood before the dresser mirror in her white slip, waiting for them. They wound her hair around white flowers, lifted her wedding dress carefully over the hair, slipped the tiny buttons on the back into their small holes. Only a woman's hands are careful enough for these things.

"You will be next," they said to me, laughing as I stood in my stiff apricot dress, clutching my bouquet with both hands. "Next time it will be your turn." And they shooed me from the room because Mary Katherine and I had no mother and there were things she needed to be told. Things so terrible that if she had known them before, known them *in time*, she would never have

151

agreed to marry Donald, a wordless man whose ears stuck out from his head and were red and not very clean. Not if she had to stay in the factory for the rest of her life.

Things no one wanted me to hear, so I went downstairs and sat with Father Hume, trying not to crease my dress, because it was rented, like Mary Katherine's, and already the hem was soiled where I had forgotten to lift it. Father Hume talked to me about the Bog People. He is an educated man and he told me how in the Jutland, sometimes, in Denmark, or in Ireland a man is digging for turf in the bog when his spade hits a body. The body is hundreds of years old, but the bog will have mummified it so that it is preserved almost perfectly—discolored, but not decayed. And these bodies bear the marks of ritual murder. Their throats have been slit or they have been strangled or their heads have been cut from their bodies entirely. They surface like memories. Father Hume had names for these bodies: the Tollund Man, the Windeby Girl, and the one they think is Queen Gunhild who left Norway a thousand years ago because King Harald of Denmark promised to marry her, but he drowned her in the bog instead.

Mary Katherine came out in her wedding dress and danced as if it were the last night of her life. She danced with one man after another, holding them all close against her body while she danced, but it was all right because it was her wedding day and she would never be holding another man but Donald again.

Then she danced with me. She smelled of beer and some of her hair had come loose, not so she looked messy or drunk, though. Just a little hair, curling around her face. She danced with me because I was not coming to live with her and Donald. A young, newly married couple could not be expected to care for a fourteen-year-old girl. Mary Katherine held me as tightly as she had held the men and I could feel her breasts against me just as they must have. "You look so beautiful," she whispered, "in that dress," although I knew it wasn't true. I had seen myself in the green-tinged mirror in our bedroom. The sleeves of my dress were belled and made my arms look like sticks. The darts over the chest were too big, so the dress collapsed against me in a way that embarrassed me. I held my flowers over my chest so that no one would see, but I was glad I was not marrying Donald Ban Devins.

The women came again, but it was not for me. They came for Elizabeth who lived next door and had decided to marry God. They held her hair in their hands and cried because it would all be cut off and because God had made Elizabeth so much more beautiful than he needed to. They took the worldly things from her, her jewelry, her clothes, and the more they took the more bare and beautiful Elizabeth became. "You could be a nun," they said to me. "God doesn't care how beautiful you are. God thinks that goodness is beautiful."

Elizabeth's mother cried the hardest of all, although she had always wanted to give Elizabeth to God. She sat in the gray light of her television set and cried until she was red in the face and the tears pooled in the lines of her skin. "Because of *them*," she sobbed, "the boys are growing up very rough and wild and the girls are afraid to leave the house. Look at her. So beautiful. And afraid to leave the house."

"I'm not marrying God because I'm afraid, Mama," said Elizabeth, and since she was practically a nun already, everyone believed her.

Elizabeth never liked me, but she gave me a gold ring with a red stone and when I went home where no one could see I slipped it on slowly and pretended my right hand belonged to someone else; that someone else was giving me the ring. But I was glad I was not marrying God since I was neither good nor beautiful. I knew I was not the first because, given a choice, I would rather have been the second. God could have made me beautiful, but He didn't. How was I supposed to feel about that?

My father came home for Christmas and a cold black Christmas it was. There were no lights on the houses or the streets since the streets belonged to them now and maybe the houses did, too. The strangers, my father called them, although they been here longer than anyone could remember. We killed them when we could and they multiplied and now the streets and shops were filled with their sharp alien faces which matched the sharp unmusical sounds of their speech. It rained steadily, clearing the air of the dirt of the factory, mixing with the oil of the transports on the asphalt. My father stayed in and his friends came to visit, not in large groups which would have been provocative, but a few at a time. If there had been work, my father could have lived with me, but there wasn't. This meant that I had no father as well as no mother and the women were always sorry for me because my mother was in heaven and never seemed to notice that my father was overseas.

Mary Katherine was pregnant and looked strange for she gained no weight anywhere, but her belly swelled like a tumor instead of a baby and she craved starch and charcoal. She was detained for two hours when she was stopped, carrying an egg timer in her purse. It was broken; she was taking it to Heatley's to be repaired; she told them so, but they thought it was the timing device for a bomb. They questioned her and searched her and kept her standing for two hours until she fainted off her feet.

When Donald heard he slapped Mary Katherine twice, once with his knuckles and then coming back with the palm of his hand so that on one cheek she showed the imprint of his ring and on the other of his fingers. He slapped her for being so stupid as to carry an egg timer in her purse. It started her labor so the women came for her again. No one said anything about the marks on Mary Katherine's face. They all knew the boys were growing up like soldiers, hard and mean. Mothers made killers of their sons and they did it for God and they did it for the dead and they did it for us all. Even though they knew there would be no way to channel all that meanness. Men who were raised to kill were bound to be brutal to the women as well. Mary Katherine was in labor for twenty hours and the doctor sent me away with Donald and my father so I wouldn't see it. When it was over, Mary Katherine had given birth to a soldier.

The day after Christmas my father took a boat-train

out, and a bomb, hidden in a garbage can in Cathedral Square, tore seven of them apart as if they'd been paper.

They responded with a new weapon, like nothing we had ever seen before, like things we had only heard of, so that we called it the Eye after the Eye of Balor. It was as large as a closet and it took four of them to move it and aim it and set it off just as it took four men to open Balor's Eye. It could turn a stone building to rubble, so for a long time, for two years, there were no more snipers and no more bombs. The effectiveness of the Eye showed on more women's faces than just Mary Katherine's.

It filled us with horror, but there was a satisfaction there, too. When they had come, a hundred years ago, they had come to show us civilization. They were higher than we were; they said it and to prove it they refused to match us, quite, blow for blow, body for body. There were limits, they told us, to what civilized creatures would do. All pretense of civilization was ended now with the Eye and it made them both complacent and embarrassed just as it made us terrified and pleased. Because of the Eye they intruded more into our private lives, stopping us at our markets, at our theaters, at our jobs, coming into our homes on any suspicion. They took us to their base for questioning though they had always used our own police stations before. They stamped the word *Dissident* on my father's file and no one could tell us why, but it meant my father could never come back, not even to visit. They intruded everywhere, into matters which concerned the men and matters which concerned the women. "It's like we live in glass houses," Mary Katherine complained. She was teaching her son to throw stones.

Someone else's son threw a bomb into a transport truck on a meatless Friday and killed thirteen of them. Other bombings followed again, and shootings, and the Eye made large sections of the city completely disappear.

I met him on a Tuesday coming home from Mac-Auley's Market, groceries in my arms. He stopped me to search the stringed bag. "Stay away from the Hub tomorrow," he told me. "We don't want civilian casualities."

I called him a liar. How many civilians had already been killed without them caring? How many of us died, innocent or not, every time they opened the Eye. "If you're not frightened of my eggs," I said, "if you don't think I'm going to stone you with potatoes, then may I have my bag back?" I was cold as I could be, so angry with him and his great concern for our civilians. But he was staring at me. He did not return the bag.

"I'll see you home," he said, not asking, just telling me. "The streets aren't safe," and it made me laugh suddenly because I knew and he must have known I would be safer without him. He was pretending that he could protect me, pretending that he could be a man and I could be a woman and this made me very soft toward him, all the more so since it wasn't true. I was the one protecting him by going along with the pretense. This was the first sin. "There are sins of the mind," Father Hume told me, "and sins of the body," and this was a sin of the mind, a lie I told, but all the rest were sins of the body. All the ones which came later.

My mother's name was Undine, like the water sprite who must seduce a man and bear his child before she can be human. My mother became so human she died giving birth to me, died in this same bed where I am lying, soaking the sheets with my sweat. Because of my mother, my father was secretly glad to have to work in foreign places where he did not eat his breakfast looking at my face. "Mother was mad for him," Mary Katherine told me. "Always touching him. Holding his hand, pulling his hair, and laughing at him." And it was confused in my mind as to who had killed my mother— was it him or was it me or was it the doctor who came for the birth or the women who cared for her after? All I knew was that it was a sin of the body and the body was probably mine.

So when I met him he was lonely, but I needed him more. Needed him wanting my body as if the want could heal me somehow. His eyes were brown and his voice was quiet and he was loving, gentle with me and careful.

He could pull me together inside, in the very center of my body, and explode me there just by touching me repeatedly and this was something no woman had ever told me about. I said I would meet him in places we pretended were hidden, places at the edges of the city. I took the sacrament from Father Hume without confessing and the sin grew. I ate the body of Christ and made it part of the sin. I didn't care. Hadn't my mother died for love? I didn't care. I only cared that I ached when we couldn't meet, that no one else had ever wanted me and I repeated in my mind the beautiful things he said to me in his unmusical, alien voice.

Mary, Mother of God, pray for me. When I hear the men coming then the women will be leading them.

Finally I brought him here, into my house. It was the Burke girl who found us and herself only twelve years old. She kept her mouth shut about it five whole days until the Eye took her little brother and Mad David Connelly and Donald Ban Devins too, all at once. Melted their bones so there was nothing even to bury. But maybe she confessed it, because Father Hume's sermon on Sunday was about the Bog People again and when he talked about the Windeby Girl he looked straight at me.

Most of the bog bodies are male, bridegrooms to the bog. They were fed a meal of grain; they were tortured and they were sacrificed. The Windeby girl was very young. Her lower abdomen had decayed, but her upper body was preserved and she was not tortured before death, but the hair on the left side of her head had been shaved off and her eyes were blindfolded. She was pinned into the bog with birch branches and a large stone to hold her light body down. And Father Hume says, and he understands exactly what he is saying, that these bodies prove our early ancestors were civilized. Because they had human sacrifice and therefore religion. Father Hume will not be among those who come for me tonight. He will stay in his home pretending not to know that the women are gathering.

The Windeby girl may have been murdered as a punishment or it may have been an honor, but I think it

was the first because of her hair. When the saintly Queen
Anne died, her hair continued to grow. A hundred years
later they opened her coffin and her hair had grown to
her feet, still the same golden color and fragrant. This
was a sign of her holiness and they cut away locks of it
and sold them on the streets. So that everyone could
own a piece of the holy woman's body. Sometimes in
pawnshops they still sell necklaces with golden hair
coiled inside and say that the hair is Queen Anne's. The
Windeby Girl had no hair although she had been given
many centuries in which to grow it back.

Holy Mary, Mother of God, I am here in my glass
house which is my body. Pray for me.

Pray for me. I have seen our own rituals.

It will be the women who come. They will come as
they came for Mary Katherine, just that way. Loving and
vengeful while I stand here before the green mirror in
my bedroom, my face on the surface colored with green
as though I looked up at them from beneath the water of
a lake. The women will undress me and they will cut my
hair, pulling it roughly. The hair must be cut in case a
word or a kiss has caught in it. There will be tar for my
body and I will wear it for days, hot tar because my body
has burned and now must be purified. They will scald
away the skin where he has touched me, but they will
know and I will know that I can never pay enough, that
nothing, nothing they do will ever remove his touch
from my body.

WILD BOYS:
Variations on a Theme

The village of Brenleah was surrounded on three sides by forest, like the shadow of a great hand, cupped and trying to close. It could be warded off with steel in the spring and fire in the fall, but it always returned, sending its roots into the fields, its branches against the fences. The villagers called it the king's forest, but this was a hubris about which the forest itself knew nothing.

The fourth side of Brenleah was open to the road. My father said that the road began at the capital, carved into the very stone of the earth. By the time it reached Brenleah it was merely dirt. We were, after all, only a little ending and one of many. "The road," my father told me once, "is the great story," but all great stories have small branchings which seem important and complete to those who live them. One man's ending is another's beginning, and this is always true. This is what my father taught me. Of all the men in Brenleah only my father, given the two enemies, the forest and the road, feared the road more.

The sign on the freeway exit said, "You are now entering Villanueva, a planned community." Wystan had been five years old when his family first moved in. Then there had been two adjoining vacant lots on his own street and a large, untilled field a little more than a block away. But the plan had called for the lots to become

159

townhouses and the field a park with a drinking fountain, a blue port-a-potty, and two slightly shaded picnic tables made of concrete instead of wood. There was nowhere left to play, except for the creek which was on private property, even if Wystan had someone to play with, which he generally didn't.

He was down at the bike path after a spring rain looking for toads. You hardly had to look, they bloomed in such profusion. No matter how parched the summer, how frozen the winter, they popped from the mud in the thousands after the first rains. Wystan loved the toads, wet brown jewels the size of human fingernails. You could cup your left hand over them like a roof, tickle them with your right, and they would leap into your raised palm.

Their season was brief. They ate no one's plants and bit no one's arm, so the Villanueva planners ignored them, unlike the moon-green caterpillars and summer mosquitoes, each of which had individual abatement programs, subplans of the master plan, devoted only to them. The boys who lived in Wystan's neighborhood had their own plans for the toads. They were motivated by the sheer volume; you don't value something so abundant. The boys were experiencing a toad-glut.

They built pyramids out of toads and tried to run them over with their bicycles. A single toad was hard to hit; a pile of toads improved the cyclist's odds. The corpses of a dozen successful runs were already smashed into the asphalt. Wystan's heart flattened in sympathy. He became a toad-rescuer, scooping up uninjured toads, transporting them to the safety of the grass. He did this with such stealth and cunning he had completed five successful missions before he was noticed.

He was kneeling, cupping his hand around the sixth toad when Enrique's tire skidded into his wrist. Enrique was eleven, Wystan's own age, but better at sports. "Get out of my way, Wissy," he said angrily, taking a quick offense in case Wystan was hurt and would start to cry. Wystan wasn't. He closed his hand around his toad and stood up.

"Wussy," said Jason. He was two years older and the

sort of boy who would go for your head in dodge ball even if only a hit below the waist counted. Jason was stringing toads together into a toad necklace. He had seven so far. He held his work against his little brother Matthew's chest and stood back to examine it critically. Fourteen long back legs twitched over the words "E.T. Welcome Him." "More," Jason decided. "Give me yours." He didn't even glance in Wystan's direction, but Wystan knew the sentence was directed at him.

"I don't have any," he said, his voice high and unconvincing. He cupped his hand tighter to minimize the size of his fist.

Jason's face expressed surprise. "Sure you do, Wuss." He was all friendliness, too much older, too much bigger than Wystan to need to resort to a threatening tone. "Open up your hand."

Wystan didn't move. The toad squirmed inside his fist. Jason took a step toward him. "Open your hand," he repeated quietly. Wystan decided to die for his toad. His feet made the decision, taking his head completely by surprise. His feet turned and pounded away in the direction of the creek; he ducked through the wire fence which separated the bike path from the large lots and houses behind it, estates which predated Villanueva and were owned by doctors. He felt the toad's heart beating inside his palm. It would be safe in the water, he thought. Now, where was he going to be safe?

Then there came a time when I lived in the king's forests and ate what I could steal from the bushes and the streams like an outlaw. I suppose that I was often cold, often hungry. I remember these things as facts, but they are faded, soft in my memory, like an old tapestry seen in firelight. My father led me into this life, a life for which he, himself, was particularly ill-suited. But my father had always seemed ill-suited to ordinary life as well.

My mother raised poultry, gardened, cooked, and sewed. We lived in her village. My father had come to Brenleah as a stranger the year I was born, and although his life in the village never struck me as anything remarkable or extraordinary, being one of the unchanging facts of my own life, still I believe that, even as a child, in some way I always saw how little he belonged. His daily routine consisted of a singular path to and from the alehouse. He had his own table there and read or wrote for those who needed it enough to pay. It was well-known that, although he would initially insist upon a payment of cash, he could be persuaded to accept drink instead. If no one came with contracts or letters, then he would find a way to drink anyway. He was an educated man, a civilized man, who took no interest in educating or improving me. He avoided strangers and sweated like a horse, himself, at the sound of horse's hooves on the road. These were things I knew though I thought about them no more than another child might notice that his father's hair was red or that he sometimes shouted in his sleep. He was just my father and generally I saw very little of him until dusk when, his cup having been refilled many times, my mother would send me to lead him home. Holding my shoulder in a pretense of intimacy, but in fact, to hide his unsteady feet, I could feel the long yellow nails of his hand catch in the cloth of my shirt. Then he might tell me, in a voice he wrongfully believed to be quiet and private, that the king was mad.

His words carried into the open doorway of our home. "What does it matter?" my mother might or might not answer. "The sun rises, the sun sets."

"Stupid, stupid woman!" I can see my father throw his arm out in a wide arc. "His forest, his road, his fields. Right outside our door."

My mother continues her work. Her hand dips and rises. She is mending a shirt, she is ladling soup, she pulls on the rope to raise water from our well, she brushes my sister's hair into braids for bedtime. We left the women behind the day we fled into the forest and my father never seemed to care if we saw them again.

Eodmund, the trader, arriving home told my father he had met a party of King Halric's hunters who were coming to chase boar in the king's forest. We could already see their dust down the road, hear the hooves of their horses. My father's face shone with sweat. The horses were approaching fast, too fast to suggest that they were nearing the end of a long ride.

"Hunters?" my father said, his voice breaking under the double strain of panic and drink. "Hunters?" We fled immediately with only those provisions and possessions we carried every day, over the fence and into the double darkness of the night and the trees.

Of course he was followed. A child sees a fence as a challenge more than a discouragement and they had all been through this particular fence many times before. The man who owned the property had done everything he could to curtail this, had even called the police on two occasions. It was not that he disliked children, he told them, it was only that the boys upset the delicate ecological balance of the creek.

In the summer the creek evaporated entirely, exposing all manner of evidence to support his concern—pop cans, tennis balls, unmated socks, school papers carelessly or deliberately lost, and last year, a gruesome manifestation which turned out to be a headless doll.

But now the creek was filled with clean, new water and even the algae growth was confined to the very edges. Wystan slid down the creek bank on the seat of his pants, leaving a wide, flat, muddy slide behind him. He set the toad free and ran into the water, slipping once as the mud attached itself to his shoes. He was wet to the knees, and quite unpleasantly so, when he reached the other side, but he was too small, too awkward to keep his lead under ordinary circumstances. His only chance seemed to lie in a direct route. He could hear Jason shouting behind him. His pursuers had just made the fence.

Up the creek and slightly to the left, on the very edge of the cultivated lawn, was a tree Wystan had found about a year ago when he was chasing fireflies. This tree had an unusual trunk which curved about an open space like the letter C. A child, anyone not too big, could squeeze through the opening and be surrounded on three sides by living wood. Wystan had a faint hope that he was the only one who knew this tree. He thought it possible that no one else had ever ventured so far onto the property or gone so near the house. If he was wrong, he would be trapped inside.

The boys' voices behind him moved to his right. They were heading for the slender fallen trunk which bridged the creek. Wystan scrambled up the bank, his pant legs clinging wetly together, parting noisily with every step. He sprinted for the tree and curled his body into it. Then he tried to quiet his panicked breathing, which pounded in his ears like the tree's own heart.

There were paths into the forest, but none went very deep and my father ignored them. Soon the trees stood so close together we had to break their branches to move between them. My father led us, urging me often to follow more closely, apparently unaware that if I did this I would take many stinging branches in the face and arms. Still, my father's speed surprised me. We might have run for more than an hour before he was spent and collapsed against a rock, gasping in air. He did not try to speak until his breathing had become more even.

"What now?" he asked despairingly. "What now?"

"Will we go back?"

"No." He shook his head; the hair damp at his temples did not move. "We couldn't go back even if I could find the way. Which I couldn't."

"I could," I told him. "We left such a trail of broken branches I could easily follow it home."

His eyes rolled back like a horse's, startled. "A trail? There must be no trail!" He rose heavily to his feet, gestured with one skinny hand for me to take the lead. "No trail," he repeated and though I could feel his impatience with my slow progress, could feel it like a heat on my back, he said nothing more and took care in how he moved, stopping for several long minutes to untangle the material one of his sleeves had left on a branch. All his shirts were old and very soft.

Soon it was too dark to see at all and we were forced to stop. We slept together in a place our feet alone chose for us. My father wrapped his cloak around us both and took several long tugs on his flask without offering to share. I smelled his liquor and his sweat. I imagine I rested better than he did, though I awoke several times to strange noises. In addition to royal hunters, to royal beasts, and to ruthless outlaws, my mother had told me of the forests' unnatural occupants. In Brenleah, when someone died, the corpse was beheaded to prevent it rising and walking in the forest at night.

When dawn came I slipped out of my father's arms and followed the sounds of water to a pretty stream where I drank and washed. My father found me there. His eyes were red and caked; his hands shook in the cold water of the stream. He spoke and the suspicion in his words surprised me. "Don't sneak away from me like that," he ordered harshly. "Every minute, I want to know where you are."

Over the sounds of his own breath, now successfully muffled, of his own heart, which refused to slow, Wystan heard an unfamiliar voice—male and authoritative. "I suppose you boys know you're trespassing?" it asked.

Enrique answered. "Sorry, mister. We were just playing a game."

Jason—God, Jason was much closer than Wystan had imagined—affected a tone of innocence. "We didn't hurt the creek, sir," he said.

"I'm sure there's been no harm done," the strange voice conceded. "Still, you know you're not welcome here. If I mention this to my uncle, he'll have the police out again. But—if you go home now, I might forget to mention it."

The voices retreated. Wystan heard Enrique saying thank you; it sounded distant. Minutes passed. Wystan closed his eyes. He was as safe as a bird in his tree. He was as comfortable as a squirrel, except for his sopping footwear. He smelled tree all around him. It was a lovely smell. Wystan felt moved to say thank you, himself. He reached into his pocket for his boy scout knife. He had been a cub once for about thirty minutes when his parents had hoped it might ease the way to social acceptability. He opened the blade and carved a large and wonderful W into the inner bark of the tree.

He dropped the knife with a start. The strange voice he had heard in the distance was speaking to *him*. "You can come out now," it said, then its tone changed. "What the hell are you doing to the tree?"

Wystan did not answer. He leaned forward, hugging his wet knees. He became a small and pitiable ball of a boy. It was not a plea a child would have responded to, but an adult might. Unfortunately the face which had appeared in the opening of the trunk was not clearly identifiable as one or the other. Older than Wystan, certainly. Lots older. But not old enough to be a parent or a teacher. The face was not looking at Wystan, anyway. It was focused on Wystan's W, an undeniably clean, new wound in the side of the tree. Wystan looked at it, too. The tree was bleeding; he had not expected this. He felt horrible and slid his left foot forward, ever so slowly, until it covered the open blade of his knife.

"What does the W stand for?" the young man asked. His voice hovered somewhere between the friendly, "You can come out now," and the hostile, "What the hell are you doing. . . ?"

"Wystan," Wystan said.

"That your name?"

Wystan nodded. When the man looked away again, he slid his right foot forward to cover the knife handle, although the W was still there and no one was going to believe he'd done it barehanded. To Wystan the knife suggested premeditation. Or malice. He really hadn't meant to hurt the tree.

The man was expressing his opinion of Wystan's name by whistling quietly. He shook his head. "Bet you hate it."

This was patently obvious. Wystan did not respond.

"You could tell them to call you Stan. That wouldn't be so bad. I knew a couple Stans."

This was stupid. He could *tell* them to call him Rex. What difference would telling them make? "It's a poet's name," he offered.

"So is William Williams. That's no excuse." The

young man inserted a hand through the opening of the trunk. "I'm Carl," he said. Wystan shook Carl's hand; Carl withdrew it and his face disappeared. Wystan snatched up his knife, closing it and shoving it deep into his pocket. He wriggled his shoulders through the tree trunk, emerging on the grass at Carl's feet. Carl was lighting a cigarette. "Don't ever start smoking," Carl told him. "You already know that, right?"

Wystan nodded. Carl had a sharp nose, light brown hair, and gray eyes with enormous irises. He breathed out a stream of smoke, tapped on the cigarette with a fingernail. "You going to get home all right?" Carl asked.

Wystan shrugged.

"I could walk you."

"No. Thanks." Wystan began to move in the direction of the fallen trunk bridge. If he crossed the creek there, then cut over two neighboring lots he could emerge far down the bike path. He reached the top of the bank, then Carl called after him.

"Wystan? Stan?"

Wystan turned. "My uncle's in Europe," Carl said. "I'm watching the house for him. You can come back and play if you want to. Down at the creek or up here. It's okay."

"Okay," said Wystan.

"Don't carve up any more trees, though."

"Okay," said Wystan. He picked his way down the creek bank, leaving no tracks, making no noise. He was a white man, stolen by Indians from his natural parents, trained in Indian ways, accepted by the tribe like a brother, loved by the chief like a son. He was on his name-walk, the ordeal which would make him a warrior, which would determine the secret name his tribe would have for him. Wystan crossed the bridge from one world into another with great expertise.

My one wish was to go home. I wept whenever I thought of my mother and sister and I could have left my father at any time, but it would have been his death and I knew it. He had no idea what could be eaten safely and what would grow in the belly like a plague. He depended on me. I bound my knife to a branch and caught fish. I found nests with eggs in them. We talked about traps, but never had the food to spare for bait. My father grew skinnier; the meals clung to his beard but not to his body. He suffered from cramps in his stomach and legs. One by one he broke the yellow nails from his fingers, but his hands were no more useful without them. His flask was empty. He was morose.

"Happiness," he said, "comes from doing what you are suited to do. I knew this happiness once. Long ago. Long ago."

"Let's go back," I pleaded.

"Never."

We lived in a cave some bear had abandoned to the fleas. They were glad of our company. We chose it for its depth. It had inner chambers and went back farther than we dared explore. One chamber held a surprise, a faded painting on its flattest wall. We examined it by torchlight. It showed a great beast driven to its knees by a slender stake which pierced its back and protruded from its chest. A small man danced before it, his arms and legs sticklike, delicate, but triumphant. I could not identify the beast with any assurance, a bear, perhaps. A giant boar? I asked my father what he thought, but the subject held no interest for him. "We could retreat this far," he said. "If we needed to. We could put out the torches and still find our way out in the dark. And not be found, ourselves, unless the cave was searched thoroughly."

We went back to the cave's mouth and the fire I had started with my father's strike-a-light. Usually he put it out immediately when the cooking was done; he worried about the smoke. This night he was more relaxed. I had caught and cooked three fish. We sat and picked over the bones, watched the suggestive shapes of the flame shadows on the cave walls. I heated water in my father's flask, not too hot, and made a weak tea out of bitter nuts, leaves, and fish bones. My father was thoughtful. "I suppose this is what prison would be like," he suggested. "Without the fire and the opening, of course. Would you go mad in the dark without them, do you think? So mad that light and freedom couldn't heal you?"

"Is it prison you're afraid of?" I asked him. He seemed so relaxed I was willing to risk the question. I didn't expect an answer and I didn't get one. He didn't say another word.

We saw the sun directly only at noon. I'm not sure how many days passed. Not as many as I have made it sound, I suppose. A handful only. No seasons passed. The stars did not change their courses. My father began to teach me to read. I scratched the letters of my name in the dirt and he corrected them. "I once taught a king's son," he said suddenly. "I was once well paid for these instructions."

"Halric," I guessed. Our young king.

"No. Cynewulf. His eldest brother. I taught him his letters. I taught him history. I taught him statecraft. When he became king I advised him on everything." I waited. A question from me and the story would end. It might be ended in any case. But after a long silence my father went on. "Cynewulf was a good king. He brought peace after a century of hostilities. The countryside had been bled of money and men. I wrote the treaty, he signed it and sent Halric as a hostage to seal it."

"His brother?"

"Half brother. They'd never met. Different mothers. Oh, Halric's mother was completely mad. Heard angels and devils. Dangerous woman. Removing Halric from her influence was one of the advantages to the treaty. And you mustn't think he was ill-treated. He took his own servants, had his own rooms. In cruelty, I doubt it compared with what we now suffer." My father scratched his own name above mine. His hands shook whenever he required small, controlled movements of them. "Halric was six years old and seven people stood between him and throne. Who knew he would someday be king? An assassination, a hunting accident, the plague. Suddenly the boy has to be ransomed and brought back to rule. A boy who knows nothing of his own country, nothing of how to be king, and worse, has inherited his mother's weakness." My father dropped his stick, rubbed out our names with his boots. He fell on his knees and howled suddenly like an animal. It surprised and frightened me. "And all he wants is revenge. Revenge on those of us who brought this peace we still enjoy." He collapsed on his side, curling his legs to his chest, his mouth slack with soundless weeping. He lay and rocked in the dust and never made a sound.

Carl had a cold. Carl got lots of colds. He sat on the lawn chair in full sun, and his skin, Wystan thought, had taken on a chilly hue. He had heard Wystan down by the creek and invited him up to the grass. "I looked up your name," he said. "You know every name has its own story and its own meaning. The story is hard to find, but the meaning is usually pretty accessible. Yours is Celtic and old. It's the name of a weapon, a particular sort of battle axe." He blew his nose into a white Kleenex, dropped it with several others beside his chair. "I thought it might help. It's a warrior's name."

"What does Jason mean?"

"I can find out," said Carl, and the next day, same time, same place, he had. The lawn chair was in its reclining position; the tissues had been replaced by an untidy pile of library books. "Healer," Carl told him. "Jason means healer."

Wystan laughed an adult, ironic laugh.

"Not accurate?" said Carl. "Too bad. I was trying to find a picture of your axe, but the library here is pretty minimal." He pulled a large book onto his lap and opened it to the photographic plates. "Look here."

Wystan pulled his chair closer; Carl tilted the book in his direction. Various artifacts were shown, the fruits of a single grave. There was a Celtic penannular brooch, a cruciform brooch, a ring sword with a skeuomorphic ring, whatever that was, and an iron strike-a-light.

"You like this old stuff?" Wystan asked.

"I like stuff even older." Carl dumped the book from his lap and fished up another. "Look at this," he said. "This is a cave painting. Cro-Magnon."

This plate was colored. Wystan examined the picture as best he could; the way Carl was holding it, it was upside-down to him. He thought it a rather clumsy drawing and said so. "I could do that."

Carl laughed excitedly. "You did do it." He bent forward in Wystan's direction. Wystan drew back. "You did!" Carl's voice was insistent. "I'm thinking of that W you left inside the tree. Same impulse, or so I imagine. 'I was here,' in four quick strokes." He fell back again, tapping the plate with his index finger. "The need to change the world is so basic—to mark it, to direct it. Anthropologists say these kind of paintings may have covered the world once, everywhere humans lived. And we're still doing it. Like your W. This is the challenge the small human makes to the large world—I will change you to suit me."

Wystan's W had been intended as a W of celebration, a W offered in gratitude to the natural world, but he remembered the bleeding tree and realized this would be hard to argue. He looked from the picture to Carl's thin, sharp face. Carl's eyes were closed. The veins branched over the lids like rivers, like roads.

"What a glorious vision of the world it was," said Carl. "And it's all come true. Except for the beast inside us. We can't quite eradicate that one. When are we human? When we deal with other men, when are we dealing with humans?"

We did not hear them come. My father was bent at the stream, drinking water from the cup of his hand. The noon sun flashed off silver and he froze, water dripping from his fingers. His last thoughts were for me. "Run," he screamed. "Run!" and then he became a deer and his flank was opened by the blade of a ring sword. It dipped and rose. The man who wielded it had a torn sleeve pinned together with my mother's brooch. I saw it and knew there was nothing to go back for.

So I ran. I made the cave and forced myself deeper and deeper, lightless inside it. My feet and my fingers led me to the inner chamber we had chosen and I hid there and believed whole days were passing.

I heard them at the cave's entrance, faint voices whose words were indistinguishable. The voices continued awhile, never growing louder, never coming closer and then they were gone. I crouched and wept. Hours passed before I dared make my way out again; our fire was cold and the cave was empty. I heard birds and knew no humans were near. Still I went back to the inner chamber to hide awhile longer. This time I slept. I dreamt I saw the painting again, in full sunlight, in full detail. I took the charred end of a used torch—I was moved to add to the painting and I wrote the sign for my name under the drawing of the man. Then I erased it dreamstyle, by having not done it. I put the mark under the picture of the felled beast instead and I woke up.

In that moment, and never afterwards, I faced the death of my family. There are some now who say it was inhuman not to seek revenge. They miss the point. I had stopped being human. I had no fires; my father's strike-a-light and the flask for carrying water were gone. I became a beast and I gave myself over to the protection of my enemy the forest. I thought of nothing but survival.

And I survived. My hair and my nails grew and I ate my food raw and there was never enough of it. When I was finally taken from the forest it was by force. Three men surprised me by the same stream. One seized me and I opened the veins in his arms with my teeth, so the humans struck me and bound me and carried me out of the trees on their backs. They took me to an unknown village where they told the other humans fanciful stories about me, stories I only began to understand after much repetition had reminded me of the meanings of words. They said that I had been raised by wolves, that I was half-wolf myself and twice as mad. The more I fought to escape, the more I behaved exactly as they wished.

They took me from village to village, showing the humans how I would eat meat thrown to me raw, how I could snarl, how frightened I was of fire. Until finally we came to Brenleah where I discovered I had been wrong. My mother and sister still lived there and they set about the formidable task of retaming me.

* * *

Carl was leaving. The friendship he had offered Wystan, the haven he provided had lasted only a few weeks. Carl's uncle was returning ahead of schedule and Carl was being put into a hospital. Wystan thought Carl was crying, but Carl said it was just another cold. "I want to stay out," he said, "as long as I can, but everyone else is in agreement. Villanueva is too wild for me. I need an absolutely human environment." Carl's voice was strained and sarcastic. He stood with Wystan together at the tree. Carl lit a cigarette. "No point in my quitting," he said, waving the match to extinguish it. "No matter what they say." He coughed and covered his mouth. "Back up," he said to Wystan. "I don't want to cough on you. Don't come close at all."

"What's wrong with you?" Wystan asked. In another year he would have known better than to ask it, though he still would have wanted to know.

Carl tried to smile, more a baring of teeth than amusement. "I have the plague," he said. "I have a monkey disease." Smoke came from his mouth. "My uncle had a hell of a time finding a hospital that would take me." If the planners of Villanueva had known about Carl's condition they would not have wanted him in Villanueva. They would have been relieved to know he was going.

Wystan felt desperately sad. "Will you get well?" he asked.

Carl's eyes glassed over. "Sure," he said. "Sure I will." He averted his face. "You better go home now."

Wystan left him in the shadow of the tree, holding his small flame to his mouth. Wystan slid toward the creek, knelt by the water, and watched long-legged bugs skate across it. The algae was spreading. A late toad hopped by his hand.

The humans were taking Carl away from him. Wasn't that what Carl had said? Very well. He, Wystan, had had enough of humans. He was giving his notice. He was signing on with the toads. Wystan took three hops on his long back legs along the side of the creek. He heard the boys above him on the bike path and straightened up hastily. He looked for more tenable alternatives.

He would probably have to ask for swimming lessons again. He would have to spend the whole summer at the pool where the lifeguards were paid to protect him.

THE VIEW
FROM VENUS

A CASE STUDY:

Linda knows, of course, that the gorgeous male waiting for her, holding the elevator door open with his left hand, cannot be moving into apartment 201. This is not the way life works. There are many possible explanations for the boxes stacked around his feet—he may be helping a friend move in, his girlfriend, perhaps. Someone equally blond and statuesque who will be Linda's new next door neighbor and Gretchen will point out that she is a *sister*, after all, and force everyone to be nice to her. Their few male guests will feel sorry for her, oppressed as she is by all that beauty, and there will be endless discourse on the tragic life of Marilyn Monroe. . . .

The door slides shut. Linda reaches for the second floor button, but so does he, and they both withdraw their hands quickly before touching. He takes a slight step backward, communicating his willingness to let her punch in the destination. She does so; the outline of the button for the second floor shines slightly. It is just below eye level. She watches it closely so as not to look at him and she can feel him not looking at her. They share the embarrassment of closely confined strangers. The elevator does not move.

Linda is upset because she is nervous. This nervousness is in direct proportion to how attractive she finds him. She is very nervous. She tells herself sharply to stop being so juvenile.

He reaches past her and represses the button. "It's always like this," Linda tells him. "When you're in a hurry, take the stairs."

He turns slowly and looks at her. "I'm Dave Stone," he says. "Just moving in."

"Linda Connors. Apartment 203." So he *will* be living here. He and his girlfriend will move in together; they will both be neighbors, but she will still be a sister and no one will be allowed to rip off another woman's man.

The elevator groans and shudders. It begins to lift. "I'm transferring up from Santa Barbara," Dave says. "Have you ever been there? I know how this is going to sound, but you really do look familiar."

"Nope." The elevator jerks twice before stopping. Linda is expecting it and is braced against the side. Dave stumbles forward. "Maybe you've confused me with some movie star," Linda suggests. "A common mistake." She gives the door a slight push to open it. "My roommate Lauren says I have Jack Lemmon's chin," she adds and leaves him struggling to unload his boxes before the elevator closes up and moves on.

Inside the apartment Linda gets herself a glass of milk. Her mood now is good. She has stood next to a man, a strange man, and she has talked with him. She actually spoke first instead of merely answering his questions. And she tells herself, though it is hard to ever be sure of these things, that nothing about the conversation would have told him this was difficult for her.

The truth is that men frighten Linda. The more a particular man appeals to her, the more frightening he becomes. Linda knows almost nothing about men in spite of having had a father practically her whole life. She believes that men are fundamentally different from women, that they have mysterious needs and assess women according to bizarre standards on which she, herself, never measures very high. Some years back she read in "The Question Man," a daily column in the *San*

Francisco Chronicle, that men mentally undress women when they pass them on the street. Linda has never recovered from the shock of this.

One of Linda's roommates, a red-haired woman named Julie, is curled up on the couch with a book. It is a paperback entitled *The Arrangement*. Julie likes books with explicit sex. Julie already knows she is destined to be some married man's lover and has told Linda so. Linda reads Jane Austen. For fun.

"Have you seen what's moving in next door?" Julie asks.

"I met him. Big, blond. . . . His name is Dave."

"Chiseled features," says Julie. "That's what you call those. And he's not the only one. There's a little dark one, too, and a couple of brothers who haven't arrived yet."

Four of them. And four women inside Linda's own apartment. There seems to Linda to be a certain inescapable logic at work here. She pictures a quadruple wedding (where she is the only one technically entitled to wear white, but no one need know this) and then life in a cozy suburban quadru-plex. It is only with some effort that Linda remembers that Dave did not really seem to be her type, being unquestionably more attractive than she is. *Not my type* is the designation that Linda applies to men who pay no attention to her. It is an infinite set. Those few men who are Linda's type she invariably dislikes. She drinks her milk and makes the realistic decision to forget Dave forever. They'll always have their elevator ride. . . .

Welcome to Comparative Romance I. You have just experienced the Initial Encounter. The point of view is female; we shall be sticking to this perspective through most of this term. And we shall access only one mind at a time. This gives a more accurate sense of what it would be like to be an actual participant. It is not uncommon for those inexperienced in the process of absorption to have an uncomfortable reaction. Is anyone feeling at all queasy? Claustrophobic? No? Good.

Then let me make a few quick points about the

Encounter and we will return. You must remember, owing to the time required by Transmission and Processing, that these events are not current. We are involved here in an historical romance. The location is the city of Berkeley, before its secession. The year, according to local calculation, is 1969, a time thought by some to have been critical in the evolution of male/female relationships. Can anyone here provide a context?

Very good. In addition to the war, the assassinations, and the riots, we have a women's movement which is just becoming militant again. We have many women who are still a little uncomfortable about this. "I believe in equal rights for women, but I'm not a feminist," is the proper feminine dogma at this time. To call oneself a feminist is to admit to being ugly. Most women are reluctant to do this. Particularly on the West Coast.

Are there any questions? If not, let's locate ourselves and Linda at Encounter #2. Are we all ready? Well? I'm taking that as affirmative.

Linda meets Dave again the next morning on the stairs. He is returning from campus and invites her in for a cup of coffee in exchange for her advice in choosing classes. She is on her way to the library, but decides it would be more educational to see the inside of apartment 201. She has an anthropological curiosity about men living together. What do they eat? Who does the dishes? Who cleans the toilets? Her hands are cold so she sticks them into the opposite cuffs of her sweater sleeves as she follows Dave back up the stairs.

Her first impression is that the male sex is much neater than the sex to which she belongs herself. Everything has already been unpacked. There are pictures on the walls, tasteful pictures, a small print of Rembrandt's thoughtful knight, the gold in the helmet echoing the tones of the shag carpet, a bird's-eye view of the Crucifixion, a bus poster which reads "Why do you think they call it dope?" The dishes all match; the avocado formica has been sponged so recently it is still wet. Linda is so busy collecting data she forgets to tell Dave she doesn't really want coffee. He hands her a steaming cup and she notices wit... dismay that he has not even left her room to soften the taste with milk. She uses the cup to warm her hands, smells it tentatively. "Did you know," she asks him, "that in Sweden they have a variation on our bag ladies they call 'coffee bitches'? These are supposed to be women who've gone mad from drinking too much coffee. It gives you a whole new perspective on Mrs. Olsen, doesn't it?"

She hears a key turning in the door. "Kenneth," says Dave, and Kenneth joins them in the kitchen, his face a little flushed from the cold air, his eyes dark and intense. Kenneth gives Linda the impression of being somehow concentrated, as if too much energy had been packed into too small a package.

"This is Linda," Dave tells Kenneth.

"Hello, Linda," Kenneth says. He starts moving the clean dishes out of the drainer and into the shelves. "I love this place." He gestures expansively with a plastic tumbler. "We were right to come here. I told you so." He is sorting the silverware. "I've been over at Sproul, what—half an hour? And in that time I got hit with a frisbee, someone tried to sign me into the Sexual Freedom League, I listened to this whole debate on the merits of burning New York City to the ground, and a girl came up out of nowhere and kissed me. This is a *great place*."

"What was the pro side to burning New York?" asks Dave. "I've got relatives there."

"No more blackouts." Kenneth puts a coffee cup away, then takes it out again immediately. Linda sees her chance.

"Take mine," she urges. "I haven't touched it. Really." She gives Dave an apologetic smile. "Sorry. I meant to tell you before you poured. I hate coffee."

"It's okay," he says evenly. "I'll never ask you over for coffee again." He turns to Kenneth. "Tell Linda what happened last night."

"Oh God." Kenneth takes Linda's coffee cup and sips at it. He settles into the chair next to her, leaning back on two legs. Linda decides she is attracted to him as well. She looks away from him. "Last night," he begins, "this guy came to our door looking for a friend of his named Jim Harper. I said we were new to the building, but I didn't think there was a Jim Harper here."

"I don't know a Jim Harper," Linda says. "In fact, you're practically the only men. Except for . . ."

"So he says Jim might be living under an alias and have we seen any little brown guys around? I say, 'Is he a Negro?' and he says, 'No, he's just a little brown guy.'"

"So," Dave finishes, "Ken tells him we'll set out some snares tonight and let him know in the morning if we've caught anything. Who are the other men in building? Are they little and brown?"

"There's only one. Dudley Peterson. And no. He's middle-aged, middle-sized, medium coloring. We think he's a CIA agent because he's so cunningly nondescript and he won't tell us what he does."

"You could live your whole life in Santa Barbara without anyone coming to your door looking for small, brown men," Kenneth tells Linda. "I love this place."

Linda does not respond. She is thinking about Dudley. Last summer he'd gone to Hawaii for two weeks, on vacation, he said, but she wasn't born yesterday. She knows a Pacific Rim assignment when she sees one. He'd asked her to water his ferns. Apparently she'd been overzealous. She wouldn't have thought it possible to overwater a fern. There'd been bad feelings on his return. But while she had access to his apartment she'd found a shelf of pornographic books. Quite by accident. She'd brought them downstairs and shared them with her roommates. Really funny stuff—they'd taken turns reading it aloud. "He had the largest—hands Cybelle had ever seen." "'No,' she moaned. 'No.' Or was she saying 'More. More'?" "Her silken breasts swelled as he stroked them. She drew his head down until his mouth brushed the nipples."

It all reminded her of an article *The Chronicle* had once run in the women's section. An expert in female psychology (an obscure branch of the larger field) had argued that small-breasted women were using their bodies to repress and reject their femininity because they would rather be men. Under hypnosis, with the help of a trained professional, these women could come to accept themselves as women and their breasts would grow. This happy result had been documented in at least three cases.

What had struck Linda most about the article was its very accusing tone. Men liked women to have large breasts; it was highly suspect, if not downright bitchy, the way some women refused to provide them. Linda feels Kenneth looking at her. Mentally undressing her? Why, even as they speak, Dave and Kenneth are probably asking themselves why her breasts are so small. Because she is cold and nervous, Linda has been sitting with her arms crossed over her chest. Now she deliberately uncrosses them. "When do the rest of you arrive?" she asks distantly.

Dave looks himself over. "I'm all here," he says. "This is it."

"No. Your other roommates. The brothers."

There is a moment's silence while Dave and Kenneth drink their coffee. Then they both speak at once. "We couldn't afford the apartment just the two of us," Kenneth says while Dave is saying, "The Flying Zukini Brothers? You mean you haven't met them yet? You are in for a treat."

"They're here already," Kenneth adds. "God, are they here. They have presence, if you know what I mean. Even when they're not here, they're here."

"Go home while you can," advises Dave. "Go home to your small brown men." His eyes are just visible over the tilted rim of his coffee cup.

Footsteps stamp at the doorway. There is a sound of keys. "Too late," says Dave ominously as the door swings open. Two clean-cut men in T-shirts which show their muscled arms try to come through the door together. They catch, in a charmingly masculine fashion, at the shoulders. They are nice-looking, but somehow Linda knows that the quadruple wedding is off. No one would take the last name of Zukini anyway, not even if they hyphenated it.

"I got a car!" says the first of the brothers through the door. "I mean, I put the money down and it's sitting in the basement. I drove it home!" He accelerates into a discussion of RPMs, variations in mileage, painless monthly payments. Man talk. Linda is bored.

"Linda, this is Fred," says Dave. "The other one is Frank. You want to go see the car?"

"I got a class."

"Good thinking."

Linda shifts from one foot to the other, feeling awkward and grateful for Fred's noise which makes it less obvious. She wants to say something intelligent before she pushes her way through the clot of men blocking the doorway and the longer she puts it off the more awkward it becomes. She gives up on the intelligent part. "Thanks for the coffee," she says to Dave. She narrowly misses Fred's fist which has swung good-naturedly past her ear and settled on Kenneth's shoulder.

Kenneth covers the spot with his right hand. "Don't do that again, Fred," he says, his tone deceptively light. And then Linda is out in the hall and the door closes behind her.

We have reached the end of the second Encounter. Let's take a moment to reorient ourselves and then perhaps you have questions I can answer. Yes? You. In the back.

The Chronicle? No, I believe it is a *major* newspaper with some particularly well-known columnists. Did you have another question?

Well, yes. I know it wasn't painted by Rembrandt and you know it wasn't painted by Rembrandt and in fifty years everyone will know it wasn't painted by Rembrandt, but in 1969 it was a Rembrandt. There was another question, wasn't there? Yes. You. Speak loudly please.

Well, I'm not sure I want to answer this. We are experiencing these events as Linda does; to give you an objective assessment of Linda's physical appearance would taint this perspective.

Let's imagine a reality for a moment, an objective, factual *you*. How do others perceive this you? How do you perceive others' perceptions of this you? We are now at two removes from the objective reality; we have passed it through two distorting filters: others' perceptions of you and your perceptions of others, and yet, for the purposes of relationships this is absolutely the closest to reality anyone can come. So, this is where we will stay. Linda is small and thin; you experience this with Linda. She perceives of herself as ordinary so you will share this perception. But I will point out that, although Linda imagines her appearance to be a liability, still she dresses in ways that support it. She cultivates the invisibility she feels so hampered by.

The point you raise is an interesting one with its own peculiarly female aspects. The entire issue, women's perceptions of their own bodies, is strange and complex and one of you might consider it as a possible term paper topic. Let's collect a little more data and then discuss it further. We'll pick up the third Encounter a bit early to give you a chance to see the women together first. And let me just give you this bit of insight to ground your thinking on this subject. There are four women involved in this next Encounter, four relatively intelligent women, and yet all four share the same basic belief that anyone who looks at them closely will not love them. They feel that their energies in a relationship must go primarily to the task of preventing the male from ever seeing them clearly.

Are we ready? All right.

Dinner is over and the women of apartment 203 are still sitting around the table. They are holding a special financial meeting. Item one: Someone has made two toll calls to Redwood City and is refusing to acknowledge them. This is of interest only to Linda; the phone is in Linda's name. Item two: Was the Sara Lee cake which Julie consumed unassisted a cake bought with apartment funds or a personal cake?

Julie's position is completely untenable. She argues first that it was her own private cake and second that she most certainly did not eat it alone. It is the most flagrant case Linda can imagine of trying to have your cake and

eat it, too, and Linda says so. Julie is a closet eater and
has developed a number of techniques for consuming
more than anyone realizes. She will open the ice cream
container from the bottom and shovel away unnoticed
until someone else tries to serve themselves and the ice
cream collapses under their spoon.

Julie can seldom decide if she is dieting or not. This
ambivalence forces her to rely on an ancient method of
weight control. If, after polishing off a chocolate cake, it
turns out she is on a diet after all, she throws it up. Of
course this step, once taken, is irrevocable. Julie thinks
that she is fat although in the whole time Linda has
known her she never has been.

"Self-induced vomiting is hard on the stomach
lining," says Gretchen. Gretchen is as short as Linda,
but more muscular and athletic. She is a feminist and
says so. "This is what finally destroyed the Roman
culture."

"Lead in the pipes," contends Linda.

"What?"

"They used lead in their water pipes. Eventually
they all were brain-damaged."

"The process was accelerated by self-induced
vomiting."

Julie is not listening. She is holding her red hair in
her fingers, isolating single strands and splitting the
ends. Julie does this routinely although she spends extra
money on special shampoos for damaged hair. Gretchen
bites her fingernails. Lauren, who is black and so
beautiful that strange men approach her on the street
and say, "Hey, foxy lady" to her, pulls out her eyelashes
when she is nervous and has done such a thorough job
she now wears false eyelashes even to class. Linda bites
her lips. She was told once as a child that her eyes were
her best feature; she ceased to have any interest in the
rest of her face. And then later she read in Chekhov that
an unattractive woman is always being told she has
beautiful eyes or beautiful hair. Linda's most recent
compliment is that she has nice teeth. It is hard to get
excited about this.

Someone knocks on the door. The women's hands all drop to their laps. "Come in," says Lauren.

It is Dave. Linda's breath quickens slightly. He has brought a penciled sign which he claims to have found scotch-taped to the doorknob of 201. "Attention!" it says. "Emergency!!! Clothes drier in basement refusing to function. Suzette."

"What do you make of this?" Dave asks. He is wearing a dark blue T-shirt which reads "Kahoaluah Summer Camp—Turn your life around." It looks good on him.

"Suzette lives directly above us," Linda tells him. "Apartment 303. Just guessing, but I'd say she's got a load of wet laundry and she'd like you to fix the dryer. She's a foreign exchange student from France," she adds. "Which explains the exclamation marks."

Gretchen shakes her head, moves her dark and heavy bangs off her forehead with the back of one wrist. She has to shampoo daily and even so her hair is oily by evening. "It's because you're male, of course. She thinks mechanical abilities are linked to the Y chromosome."

"It's shaped like a little wrench," Julie points out.

"Or maybe she read your aura." Lauren's smile is particularly innocent. She examines her fingernails. "I wonder what color an electrician's aura would be?"

"Bright?" suggests Linda. Dave is looking at her. He is waiting for an explanation. "Suzette's a little strange," she tells him. "She communicates with Venusians. She writes herself notes from them; they guide her hand. It's called automatic writing. I think. And she reads the magnetic field around people's heads." Linda swallows uncomfortably. "She's very pretty."

"If you like pretty," says Gretchen. It is a test question.

Dave dodges it. "I don't know how to fix a dryer."

"I'll tell you what." Lauren folds her hands and smiles up at him. "You go up there and explain that in person. I imagine she'll forgive you. Apartment 303. Just above this one. You can't miss it."

Dave takes his note and edges back out the door. Linda feels her aura dimming around her ears.

"I bet they thought living in an apartment building with nothing but women in it would be outtasight," says Gretchen. Her tone suggests malicious satisfaction. "Serves them right if it's just one broken dryer after another."

"Is the dryer broken?" Julie asks. "I used it this afternoon, fading my jeans. It was working fine then." She looks at Lauren and they both start to laugh. "Poor, poor Dave. He'll never leave Suzette's apartment alive. He'll walk through that door and one thing will lead to another."

One thing is always leading to another in Julie's own romances. The phrase mystifies Linda who feels that, logically, a gaping chasm must separate polite "Hello, I got your note" sorts of conversation from passionate sex. "What does that mean, Julie?" she asks, perhaps more vehemently than she might have wished. " 'One thing leads to another.' That never, ever happens to me. Can you describe that?"

Julie looks embarrassed, but more on Linda's behalf than her own. "Oh, come on, Linda," she says. "*You know.*"

Linda turns to Lauren. "Tell me about the first time one thing led to another when you were out with Bill."

"Don't be a voyeur," says Lauren.

Julie laughs and Linda looks at her questioningly. "Sorry," she offers. "It just struck me as funny that you should be accused of voyeurism. You're the last of the prudes."

"How the hell can you tell?" Linda demands. "Have I passed up a number of opportunities to be licentious? Alert me when the next one comes along."

"She's not a prude," Gretchen objected. "Just naive. And very smart. It's an unexpected combination so nobody knows what to make of it. And, of course, men don't care about smart anyway."

Linda rises from the table with dignity. "I'm going to my room now," she says, "because my presence appears to be having such a dampening effect on your desire to discuss me." She starts down the hall and it occurs to her that the route is absolutely identical to the one between the kitchen and bedrooms in apartment 201. Or 303. She dredges up a parting shot. "There's no way I'm going to pay for two phone calls to Redwood City I didn't even make. I'll take out the phone first. Try me." She goes into her (and Gretchen's) bedroom and closes the door. She lies across the bed she has very sensibly decided never to make. It would just have to be done again tomorrow. Every tomorrow. The blankets form comfortable little hills and valleys beneath her. And above her? Directly over her head, one thing is leading to another. She tries to imagine it.

> Dave: I got your note. I came as soon as I could.
> Suzette: I've been waiting. (Their eyes lock.)
> Dave (gazing at her): I don't know how to fix a dryer, Suzette. I wish I could.
> Suzette: It doesn't matter. Nothing matters now that you're here.
> (Dave steps through the door. Suzette closes it slowly, sensuously behind him. She presses against it with her back. They are both breathing audibly.)
> Suzette: I was just about to slip into something more comfortable. (She removes her sweater.) Would you like to watch?
> Dave (grabbing her): Suzette!

(Her silken breasts begin to swell.) Linda makes them swell larger and larger until they pop like balloons. It is a fleeting satisfaction. She consigns the phrase "one thing leads to another" to the large set of things she doesn't understand and nobody is ever going to explain to her, a set which includes the mysterious ailment known as hemorrhoids.

Gretchen comes into the room, ostensibly to find her English Lit assignment, but the quarter has not even started yet, Linda is not fooled. Gretchen just wants to see if she is angry. "Julie made the calls," Gretchen says. "Of course."

"Has she admitted it?"

"Any moment now." Gretchen fusses with the things on her desk. "Hey, Linda?"

Linda rolls onto her side and looks at Gretchen.
"Yeah?"

"We all love you just the way you are."

"I know that," says Linda.

All right. That was Encounter #3. Let's take a
moment to stretch and shake off the effects of the
absorption. Or sit quietly. Return to yourselves. When
you feel ready, we'll discuss what we've just absorbed.

Yes? Is everyone back now? Good. Questions?

Very good. You are very quick; I wondered if anyone
would pick this up. We do have an agent on the scene,
although our control of her is limited to suggestion only.
The note, for example, was our idea, but the spelling was
all her own. We communicate with her in the manner
Linda described and we have identified ourselves as
Venusians, a wildly implausible cover which she
accepted without hesitation. We hope with her help to
have some input into the pacing of the romance. At
present it is not unusually slow, but cannot be said to be
developing quickly either. And we have so much ground
to cover this term.

I did say we'd come back to this topic and I take
your point. Lauren would be an interesting focus for us
later; certainly the additional variable of being black in a
predominantly white culture adds yet another complication to the issue of women and their bodies. The other
three women represent differentiated approaches to the
topic: Julie dislikes her body and abuses it; Gretchen
dislikes her body, but believes politically in the injustice
of current standards of physical beauty and is attempting
to substitute standards of health and strength instead;
Linda is interesting because, in fact, she likes her body
quite well, she just doesn't expect anyone else to. Linda
perceives her major shortcoming to be the size of her
breasts, although she is mystified as to the reasons men
desire more here. As long as Linda is our focus, we will
share this mystification. Later in the term, when we
switch to the male point of view, these things may
become clearer. Let me just emphasize that it is hard to

exaggerate the importance of these physical aspects, perceptions, and self-perceptions to the question of romance. Yes?

I must tell you that I find your remarks both alarming and repelling. It is one thing to agree, as we all must for the sake of the study, on the principle of physical relativity. We can accept that they find each other attractive even if we do not find them so. We can do our best to dispose of our own physical standards and prejudices in those areas where they seem likely to cloud the study. We can even remind ourselves that they might find us just as repellent as we find them. But it is quite another thing to speculate as you have just done on their physical intimacies with such a specificity of detail. You are in danger of losing your academic detachment and, frankly, I will not be able to allow your continued participation if I see any more evidence of such imaginative and sympathetic absorption. Is that clear?

Yes? No, this is a good question. Of course you have not heard of Redwood City. No one important has ever lived in Redwood City and no one important ever will. The mystery is not that anyone would deny having placed phone calls to such an area; the mystery is that anyone could find someone there to call in the first place.

We are going to skip the fourth and fifth Encounters. They are brief and concern themselves only with a discussion of possible professors and classes. You will remember them once absorbed. And I'm going to time our approach so that we pick up another critical memory of the period which has lapsed. Are you ready? Stay with me now.

The boys in apartment 201 had decided to give a party. Kenneth had come in the evening to extend his invitation. It was to be a small affair, limited to people who lived in the building and a few who could be persuaded to spend the night since the city of Berkeley was under curfew.

"We'll just sit out on the terrace and yell 'Fascist

pigs' at the passing police cars," Kenneth said. "It'll give
us a chance to meet our neighbors in a relaxed social
setting."

Two days later he invited the entire Cal ROTC on
an impulse. Linda hears him arguing with Dave about it
as she rises slowly toward the second floor in the sticky
elevator. "It's going to be fine, Dave," Kenneth is saying.
"You worry too much. Getting arrested for violating
curfew will radicalize them." Linda gets out of the
elevator and Kenneth catches the door with his hand,
batting it back so that he can get in. "Later," he says
cheerfully as the door closes, making him disappear from
the left to the right.

Dave looks at Linda sourly. "Did you hear?" he asks.
"Can you imagine what our apartment is going to look
like after a bunch of cadets have partied there? What if
they just don't go home? What if they pass out all over
the place? They're all going to be physical as hell." They
hear Kenneth's feet below them, pounding the sidewalk.
He has an 11:00 class. Linda can see, reading Dave's
watch sideways, that it is 11:02. Dave moves his arm
suddenly to brush his hair back with his hand. The watch
face flashes by Linda. She likes Dave's hands, which are
large and rather prominently veined. She tries to find
something not to like about Dave. "Come on in," Dave
offers. "I'll make you a cup of hot chocolate."

"I hate chocolate," says Linda.

"Of course you do. I knew that. Come in anyway.
I've got a problem and I'm surrounded by Zukinis. Did
Kenneth tell you that Frank registered Peace and
Freedom last Monday? Yesterday he switched to Repub-
lican. I don't even pretend to understand the intricate
workings of his mind."

Linda follows Dave into apartment 201. Her palms
are sticky with sweat, which strikes her as adolescent.
The whole world is wondering when she is going to grow
up and she is certainly no exception. Linda has hardly
seen Dave since the night he went up to Suzette's. She
wishes she could think of an artful way to find out how
that evening had ended. Or when it had ended.

Dave puts a yellow teapot on the stove. Not a stray dish, not a fork left out anywhere. The avocado formica gleams. Before Linda believed they were neat. Now she is beginning to feel there may be something unhealthy about it. The neatness seems excessive.

Fred Zukini is sitting at the kitchen table. The wastebasket is beside his chair; every few moments he crumples a piece of paper and drops it in. There is a stack of library books by his left elbow. His arm is bent to support his head. "Please don't make a lot of noise," he requests.

Dave lowers his voice. "You want to know his class load? This is the absolute truth. He's got music for teachers, math for teachers, and volleyball."

"Is he going to be a teacher?" Linda asks.

"God help us. We spent all yesterday listening to him learn to sing 'Twinkle, twinkle, little star' by numbers. I don't know if it was music or math. Today, at breakfast, he demonstrates the theory of the conservation of milk."

"The what?"

"How you can pour one large glass of milk into two small ones with no resulting loss in volume. Then he asks me to correct a paper he's working on. The assignment is for two pages; he's done ten. I can't say I was enthusiastic, but I wouldn't want it said that I discourage initiative. So I look at it. He's hovering by my elbow, all nervous because it's his first college paper and I'm a seasoned junior. Eight pages are a direct quote. One quote. Out of one book. I tell him, 'You can't do that,' but he says it's exactly what he wants to say."

"How are your own classes?" Linda asks. "Did you get into MacPherson's?"

"I did, but I had to lie about my major. And you didn't tell me he threw chalk."

"Only when he's provoked. It's no fun if you're not surprised. Did he throw it at you?"

"No, but I jumped about a foot out of my chair anyway." Dr. MacPherson teaches Economic History and is one of Linda's favorite professors. He can tell you about the Black Plague so that you feel you're actually there. If you are momentarily overcome, however, and he thinks your attention is wandering, he sends a piece of chalk singing past your ear.

The teapot whistles asthmatically. Dave gets out the instant coffee, makes himself a cup in a green enamel mug and puts the coffee jar away. They tiptoe past Fred, who groans for their benefit and crumples another piece of paper. They sit on the living room couch at a respectable distance apart. No one's leg touches anyone else's. "You said you had a problem," Linda hints. Please, please don't let it be Suzette.

"Yeah," says Dave. He blows on his steaming cup. "Yeah. I do. It's Mrs. Kirk up in the penthouse. She hates me. She started hating me Tuesday morning and she refuses to stop. It's because of the sign I had in our window. Maybe you saw it?" Linda shakes her head. "Well, I'd spent a bad night because a number of neighborhood cats were out looking for each other. And I made this small and tasteful sign for our window. It said, 'The only good cat is a dead cat.'" Dave blows on his coffee again and takes a quick sip. Linda remembers how silly she always thought it was, as a child, the habit grown-ups had of making drinks so hot they couldn't drink them and then having to wait until they cooled. Sometimes they waited too long and had to heat the drink all over again. A bad system.

"How can you drink that?" she asks. "Thirty seconds ago it was boiling."

"You blow right next to the side," Dave says, "and then you only drink the part you've blown on. I could teach you, but when would you use it? Tea? Do you drink tea?" Linda shakes her head. "No, you hate tea. Am I right?" Linda smiles and watches Dave blow and take another sip. It's a larger sip. She thinks he's showing off.

"It was a small and tasteful sign," Dave repeats. "A very restrained response considering the night I'd just been through. You probably heard them, too?" Linda shakes her head again. "Well, I can't explain that," Dave says. "You must be a very sound sleeper. So Mrs. Kirk thinks my sign was aimed at her particular cats who are, apparently, too well-bred to yowl all night. She's called the manager and she's threatening to call the SPCA. The manager asked me to go and smooth it over with her since she's an old and valued tenant in contrast to myself. And I did try. I'm not proud. She won't even open the door to me. She thinks I'm only pretending to be sorry in order to gain access to her apartment and bludgeon her cats. She told me she just wished we lived in England where they know how to deal with people like me, whatever the hell that means."

"So what do you want from me?"

Dave smiles ingenuously. "You're very popular, Linda. Did you know that? I can't find a single person who doesn't like you. I bet even Mrs. Kirk likes you. Couldn't you go up and tell her you and I were having this casual conversation about cats and I just happened to mention what models of catdom *her* cats are? Invite her to the party. Invite her cats."

Linda doesn't respond. She is too surprised by the assertion that she is popular. She is liked by other women; she always has been. In high school she had seen clearly that girls who were popular were almost always those not liked by other girls; this was, in fact, the most reliable indication of popularity, the dislike others of your own sex had for you. It was the price a woman paid for being beautiful and Linda knew of women who were not so beautiful, but insisted other women hated them in an attempt to fool men into thinking they were. Sometimes Linda had even seen this work. Surely being popular has nothing to do with Mrs. Kirk's opinion.

"Please," says Dave. "It's a small favor."

"No, it's not," Linda informs him. Mrs. Kirk is the ex-wife of a state senator. He has been married twice since, and although he is now free as a bird again, his interest in sending her alimony checks on schedule has dwindled. Six months ago, shortly after the dissolution of this last marriage, he was picked up for drunk driving. A small newspaper article reported the event. Page 29. Mrs. Kirk cut it out and posted it in the elevator in case anyone had missed it. She added her own caption. "Would you vote for this man?" But Mrs. Kirk is a bit of a

drinker herself. Any visit to the penthouse is an occasion
for Bloody Marys and long discussions on the inadvisibil-
ity of giving your heart and the best years of your life to
swine. It is not the conversation that Linda wishes to
avoid, however. She likes Mrs. Kirk. It is the drinks.
Linda can hardly face tomato juice alone; add liquor and
it becomes a nightmare. And there is no way to refuse a
drink from Mrs. Kirk. Linda looks at Dave's hands. "But
I'll do it anyway," she says.

Fred slams a book closed. "Could you be a little
quieter?" he calls from the kitchen. "I really have to
concentrate."

"Don't respond," Dave warns her. "Don't say anything. He's fishing for help. He's dying to tell you what
his assignment is." They sit quietly for a moment. The
sun has moved down the wall to Linda's face; on the
opposite wall the painted sun illuminates the knight's
helmet in the Rembrandt and never moves. Dave shifts
closer to Linda on the couch, but still does not touch her.
Linda focuses on the painting. She feels very warm, but
she tells herself it is the sun. "We'll make a deal," says
Dave. He has lowered his voice, but his tone is nothing
more than friendly. "You go talk to Mrs. Kirk for me
and I'll get Dudley Petersen's fingerprints for you at
the party. Then we'll be even. Are your roommates
coming?"

"Yes," says Linda. But she is lying. They have no
intention of attending and they all told her so last night.

She goes home and tries to persuade them again. "I
don't think I can lose fifteen pounds by Friday," says
Julie. "I can't have fun at a party if I'm fat."

"Sorry. Bill and I are going to a movie," says
Lauren. "If we can agree on something. *The Dutchman*
is on campus, but he wants to see the new Joey
Heatherton epic in the city."

"It's about Vietnam," says Julie. "Give the man a
break. I'm sure his interests are political."

"Listen to this," says Gretchen. She is holding *The
Chronicle*, folded open to the women's section, in two
white fists. The strain in her voice tells Linda she is
about to read from Count Marco's column.

"I don't want to hear it," says Linda. "Why read it?
Why torture yourself?"

There is no stopping Gretchen. "He's complaining
about the unattractiveness of women you see in hospital
emergency rooms," she says. "'Set aside a flattering
outfit, loose, no buttons, of course, and a pair of fetching
slippers. *Think ahead* a little.' He's concerned that in the
case of an emergency, we may become eyesores. God!
I'm going to write *The Chronicle* another letter."

"Any attention you pay a columnist, they consider
good attention. The more letters he provokes, the more
secure his job. He's ridiculous. Just don't read him."

"It's not trivial," says Gretchen. "You think it is, but
it's not. They pay this flaming misogynist to write
antifemale poison and then they put it in the women's
section. Can't they just move his column? Is it too much
to ask? Put it in the goddamn sports section." Her voice
has risen steadily in volume and in pitch until she hits its
limits.

Linda reaches out and brushes Gretchen's bangs
back with one hand. They won't stay; they fall back into
Gretchen's outraged eyes. "It's important," Gretchen
says.

"About this party . . ."

"I don't want to go." The newspaper crackles in
Gretchen's hands. "I told you that."

"Why not?"

"I just don't like them. They look like fraternity
escapees. Jock city. Fifties timewarp. Have you ever
tried to have a conversation with Frank Zukini? He
thinks Bernadette Devlin is a French saint. He told me
he saw the movie about her."

"Dave and Kenneth are nice."

"Shall I tell you about this party?" Gretchen asks.
She takes a deep breath; she is talking more slowly and
has regained control of her voice. "I know about this
party. We're talking party games. We're talking people
passing oranges around using only their chins and
everyone maneuvering to be the lucky guy who gets his
orange from the woman in the low-cut blouse with the
Mae West body. We're talking beer cans that people

have crushed with their hands, collecting like flies on the windowsills."

"They've ordered a keg," says Linda.

"Excuse the pun, but I rest my case."

Lauren is standing behind Linda. She clears her throat in a way that makes Linda turn to look at her. She is combing her hair higher and wider. "Julie says you've got a thing for Dave. But Gretchen says you don't." Her voice is quiet. "Who's right?"

Linda tries to think what answer she wants to give. She takes too long.

"If we thought you liked him we would never have sent him up to Suzette's. You've got to know that," Lauren says.

"Even if he is all wrong for you," adds Gretchen.

"It's all right," Linda tells them. "He was going to meet Suzette sooner or later." But come to the party with me. You're supposed to be my friends. She doesn't say it out loud so nobody does it.

Are we all back? Does anyone have any questions or comments to make?

Actually the curfew was more of an annoyance factor. If you could demonstrate persuasively to the police that your reasons for being out were nonpolitical then you were likely to get off with a warning and the instruction to go right home. Later the National Guard brought tanks into Berkeley and stationed them at critical intersections, but even this was primarily for show. Though you must remember that there was real fighting and some serious injury.

Well, cats are one of those topics on which you find only partisans. You love cats or you hate cats; no one is indifferent. I can't explain this. Perhaps these questions are taking us a little far afield. The course is Romance. The point of view is female. Does anyone have a question that is a little more penetrating?

No, no, we will be looking at the romances of older (and younger) women later. Mrs. Kirk will not be a focus, although we will be meeting her. Her partiality for alcohol would make her a difficult subject. Absorption is tricky enough without the added complication of chemical abuse. Let me tell you though, that on the two occasions when Mrs. Kirk's husband has remarried, his wives have both been thirty-three years of age. He, himself, was fifty-two and then fifty-eight. Mrs. Kirk herself is now fifty-eight and in 1969 if she had become enamored of a man of thirty-three, even in Berkeley, this would have been considered humorous or pathetic. Yet, Mrs. Kirk at fifty-eight, judging by appearance alone, has aged less than Mr. Kirk at fifty-eight. There may be variables in this situation, the significance of which we have not yet grasped. Keep the issue in mind, though for the purpose of our current case study all the participants are contemporaries. In the back there?

He was not really a Count. Yes?

Those changes are sexual. The course is Romance. We will not be discussing them this term, although you will find them even more pronounced when the subjects are younger and male.

I must mention to you the possibility of sensory overload at this next Encounter. We are going with Linda to the party. The room is smoky and hot; the music is loud and primitive. This will be an exercise in academic detachment. Ready? We're going now.

Gretchen had offered Linda grass before she left, but Linda had refused. She wanted to keep her wits about her, but now, standing in the open doorway to 201, she realizes suddenly that in couple of hours she will be surrounded by drunken strangers. And she will still be sober. There is nothing to drink but beer and she finds the taste of beer extremely vile.

The Doors are on the record player; "Twentieth Century Fox." Linda is glad Gretchen is not there. Just yesterday Gretchen had called Leopold's to ask them to remove records with sexist lyrics from the bins. She had a list of the most outrageous offenders.

"Sure," the salesman on the phone had said. "Anything for you chicks. Why don't you come down and we'll talk about it. Are you a fox?"

"No, I'm a dog," said Gretchen, slamming down the phone and repeating the conversation to Linda. "Male chauvinist pig!"

Linda passes Dave on her way in. He is in the kitchen washing some glasses. Suzette is with him, perched on the countertop. She has dressed for the evening as Nancy Sinatra, short skirt, white boots, mane of sensuous hair. She is leaning into Dave's face, saying something in a low, intimate whisper. Linda can not hear what she says, doesn't even want to know. Anything Suzette says is rendered interesting and charming by that damned accent she has. Linda doesn't say hello to either of them.

She finds Kenneth and he hands her a beer, which she accepts tactfully. "I was just thinking of you," Kenneth says. "I'm glad you're here. I've got someone I think you'll like." He uses his elbows to force a path through the ROTC, Linda has to follow very closely; it closes up behind them like water. At the end of the path is the living room couch. On the couch is a thin, pale woman with eyeliner all around her eyes. She's done her lashes like Twiggy, tops and bottoms. No lipstick, but she's wearing a skirt and nylons. This surprises Linda, who glances around quickly and sees that a lot of people in the room have legs. She is wearing jeans, herself, not Levis, since Levis doesn't make jeans small enough to fit her, not even boys' jeans, which are too large at the waist and too small through the hips, but as close to Levis as she is capable of coming. They should have been appropriate for any occasion, but Gretchen was right. Linda finds herself in the fifties, where it is still possible to underdress. Where did Kenneth find these people?

Next to the woman on the couch is a man and this is who Kenneth introduces her to. "Ben Bryant," he says. "A writer. Ben, this is Linda Connors." He looks pleased. "A reader," he adds. "She reads everything. She reads nonfiction." He starts to introduce the woman, his hand is opened in her direction, but he never finishes. "And this is—" he says. "Margaret! You made it! Far out!" and he is gone, a little heat remaining where he had been standing. Linda moves into it.

A man behind her is talking above the music in a loud voice. "But *Sergeant Pepper* is the best album ever made. The Beatles have ennobled rock and roll."

Another man, higher voice, responds. "Ennobled? They've sanitized it. It used to be black! It used to be dangerous!"

Linda smiles at Ben even though she is nervous and he is wearing a thin sweater vest with leather buttons, which she doesn't think looks promising. "I don't really read that much," she says. "Kenneth is easily impressed."

"Melanie and I," says Ben, "were just discussing the difference between male and female writers. I was comparing Jane Austen to Joseph Conrad."

"I like Austen," says Linda warningly.

"So do I. What she does, she does well. But you must admit the scope of her work is rather limited."

"Must I?" Linda's uncomfortableness is disappearing.

"The difference between the two, as I was just telling Melanie, is the difference between insight and gossip."

Linda looks at Melanie. Her face is impassive. "I'm not so sure a clear distinction can be made between the two. Who knows more about people than the gossip?"

"You're playing devil's advocate," says Ben comfortably.

"I'm expressing my true opinion."

Ben settles back in the couch, crossing his arms. "I don't want you to think that *I* think the differences are biologically determined. No. This is a sociological limitation. Women's writing is restricted because women's lives have been restricted. They're still capable of writing well-crafted little books."

Linda opens her mouth and Gretchen's voice comes out. "You've lived a pretty full life?" she asks.

"I've traveled. Extensively."

"So have I. I was in Indonesia when Sukarno fell. Grown men circumcised themselves in the hopes of passing as Moslems." Linda sees Ben shift slightly in his seat. "Circumcised *themselves*. Someday I may want to write about the things I've seen." She has won the argument, but she has cheated to do it. Linda has never even been to Santa Barbara. Dr. MacPherson was in Indonesia when Sukarno fell and has described it so vividly Linda knows she can carry it off if she is challenged. She isn't. Ben is looking at his lap. Linda's mood is black. Dave and Suzette are still in the kitchen. She has been at the party maybe fifteen minutes and already she has betrayed her sex. Worse, she has betrayed Jane Austen. She isn't fit to live. Linda punishes herself by taking a large sip of beer. And another. She holds her breath and swallows and decides she has paid enough. She abandons her glass by the couch and pointedly directs her words to Melanie. "Excuse me," she says. "There's someone I have to talk to."

Linda shoves her way over to the record player and Kenneth. "Don't introduce me to any more writers," she says.

"Didn't you like Ben?" Kenneth asks. "Fred, let Linda pick out a record." Fred Zukini is just about to put The Association on. It is a lucky thing Linda came along. She asks for *Big Pink*. She wants to hear "The Weight."

Kenneth turns the music up. He has one arm draped around Margaret; he kisses her on the neck. He smiles at Linda, but it is definitely a get-lost kind of smile. Linda responds, spotting an empty chair in a corner and retreating to it.

She sees Dave again, sitting under the Rembrandt, talking with Dudley Petersen. She cannot quite hear their words, though the young man with the high voice who disliked the Beatles so is still clearly audible. "No, no, no," he is saying. "We're talking about the complete failure of the dialectic."

Suzette has found Dave again, too, and in the sudden silence between "Tears of Rage" and "To Kingdom Come" Linda hears Suzette ask Dave if she can sit on his lap. Well! Linda can't help feeling this is somehow lacking in subtlety. Her father told her, advice she has never needed, not once, that boys do not like to be chased and he was a boy himself and should know, but there Suzette is, settling herself in, laughing like Simone Signoret, and this appears to be just one more area in which Linda has been sadly misled. The situation is hopeless. Linda looks at her shoes and wonders how early she can go home. In fact, Linda likes Suzette for being so brazenly weird. Gretchen likes her, Julie likes her, Lauren likes her—add them together and it should have been enough to prevent such popularity.

Linda leans back and closes her eyes, listening to the conversations close to her. To her right, two women are laughing. "So he doesn't have a condom," one says. "'I figured you'd be on the pill' he tells me and I say 'Listen, buster, we have a saying among my people—the person who plans the party should bring the beer.' 'Your people?' he asks and I say, 'Yeah, my people. You know. Women.'" The second woman's voice is soft and throaty. "Probably just never heard women called people before," she offers.

Farther from her she hears someone suggesting a party game. Everyone is to lie down with their heads on someone else's stomach and then all laugh simultaneously. Score another one for Gretchen.

She hears Frank Zukini asking some woman what her major is. Penetrating question, Linda thinks. "Drama," the woman answers. "I'm a thespian." There is a long pause and Frank's voice when he responds betrays shock. "Whatever's right," he says, at last.

And then Suzette's voice, close to Linda's ear, indicates that Dave's lap is unoccupied again. "I have a message for you," Suzette tells her.

Linda sits up and opens her eyes. "For me?"

"Yes. From the Venusians. They're very interested in you, Linda. They ask about you a lot."

"How flattering," says Linda. "Extraterrestrial attention. What's the message?"

Suzette's hair is the color of the knight's helmet and surrounds her face like an aura. "They said not to do anything they wouldn't do."

"Suzette," says Linda, smiling at her. "Tell them to relax. I never do *anything*."

Dudley Petersen passes. Linda knows he sees her

but he goes in another direction. Still brooding about his
ferns. But Mrs. Kirk joins her, carrying her beer in a
pewter mug with a hinged lid and a glass bottom.
"Marvelous party," says Mrs. Kirk. "No hippies. Just a
lot of nice young people enjoying themselves."

"I'm not enjoying myself," Linda tells her. "I'm
having a terrible time."

"It's because you're not drinking. Kenny! Kenny!"
Mrs. Kirk waves a plump hand and her bracelets ring out
commandingly. "Linda needs a beer!"

Kenneth supplies one, giving her an empty glass
wrapped in a paper towel at the same time. "The glass is
a gift from Dave," he informs her. "And Dave says not to
handle it too much. Would you like to tell me what the
hell is going on?"

Linda takes the glass and her spirits lift ridiculously.
But briefly. "It's evidence," she says. She watches
Kenneth weave his way back to Dave. Kenneth wants to
invite the police department, any off-duty officers and
anyone they are willing to let out of jail. He argues with
Dave about it; Dave is holding the phone clamped
tightly together and refusing to release it.

"Hey, Linda." It's Fred Zukini. "You still haven't
seen my car. You want to? I got a tape deck, now, and I
put a lock on the gas cap and I put sheepskin on the
seats."

Linda takes a long drink of her beer and then sets it
and the empty glass back under the seat where they'll be
safe until she can retrieve them. She follows Fred to the
elevator, passing through a nasty, acrid smell by the
couch where Ben Bryant is smoking a pipe. With tobacco
in it.

Fred doesn't seem the sort to seduce her in the
basement. Too much risk to the car, for one thing, and
Linda doesn't like him so she is relaxed and calm,
picking her way through the couples who have left the
party and opted for romantic subterranean lighting.
Fred stops at a polished red VW bug and runs his hand
over the curves of the trunk. "I got extra locks on the
doors, too," he says. "Because of the tape deck. I'm
going to get leather for the steering wheel."

Linda leans over, peering into the car's interior. Above the soft and snowy sheepskin, next to the steering column, a set of keys dangles. "You've left your keys in it," Linda tells Fred. "Anyone could take it."

Fred pushes her roughly aside, pressing his forehead against the window. "It's locked." His voice breaks. "It's all locked up. The keys are locked inside."

"Oh," says Linda. She thinks for a moment. "Maybe you could get in with a coat hanger. I've seen that done."

"Linda, the windows are closed. And it's got *special* locks."

"Oh." Linda thinks again. "I guess you'll have to break a window."

Fred runs a hand through his hair, but it is too short to be disarranged. His face is anguished. "Could you let me think this through?" he requests. "God, Linda, could you be quiet and leave me alone for a bit?"

Linda makes her way back to the elevator, the heels of her shoes snapping on the cement floor. A white-faced cadet stumbles across her path. He moans once, a pathetic, suffocated sound. "Oh, no," he says. He falls against the first of the washing machines, claws it open and throws up into it. He looks at Linda and throws up again.

There is a message here, Linda decides. A message from the Venusians. The message is to go home. Go home to her roommates who were so right when she was so wrong and Linda feels that all she will ever ask for the whole rest of her life is not to forget and wash her clothes in the first machine or to spend another second with anyone named Fred or Frank or Kenneth or . . .

The elevator opens slowly, suspensefully, and Dave is inside. "I thought you might need rescuing," he says. "Mrs. Kirk gave me the keys to the penthouse. She says you can see all of San Francisco from there. Want to come?"

"Why not?" Linda answers coldly. "As long as I'm in the elevator anyway." She joins him. They face front. No one's shoulder touches anyone else's. The elevator does not move. Linda jabs the topmost button. And again. The elevator gives a startled lurch upward. About the third floor Linda asks where Suzette is. Maximum aplomb. A casual, uninterested question. She is merely making conversation.

"Sitting on Frank's lap. Apparently he's a very old soul. A teacher. A guru, would you believe it? He has a yellow aura. Suzette just about died when she saw it."

"Too bad for you," says Linda. The elevator has stopped, but its door is sticking. Linda has to wedge her foot in to force it open.

"I'm not interested in Suzette." Dave sounds surprised. "Linda, the woman communicates with Venusians." He fits Mrs. Kirk's key into the lock. "You seem angry," he says. "You're not drunk, are you? I mean, not even a little. You hate beer?"

"Yes."

"Just a lucky guess."

"But I'm working on it," Linda tells him. "I'm growing. I'm changing."

"Oh no. Don't do that," says Dave. They enter the penthouse and are attacked by a mob of affectionate cats, escaping to the terrace with their lives and a quantity of cat hair. The evening couldn't be more beautiful, absolutely clear, and the lights on the hills extend all the way to the water, where Linda can actually see the small shapes of the waves, forming and repeating themselves endlessly over the bay. The air is cold and somewhere below she hears the sound of breaking glass.

"Did that come from the basement?" Linda asks with some interest.

Dave shakes his head tiredly. "The apartment. That's what I get for leaving Kenneth in charge." He moves closer to Linda, putting his hands around her shoulders, making her shake. She can't think clearly and she can't hold still. The entire attention of her body is focused suddenly on those places where his hands are touching her. "My apartment is full of drunks and it's after curfew," Dave says. "I'm going to kiss you now unless you stop me."

And what Linda feels is just a little like fear, but no, not like that at all, only it is so intense that she is not quite able to participate in the first kiss. She does better on the second and by the third Dave has moved from her mouth to her neck and is telling her that he fell in love with her the first time he saw her, that first day in the elevator, when he saw that she had Jack Lemmon's chin.

Well. There we are. This seems to me to be a natural breakpoint, and although I can't deny that we could learn a great deal more by going on here and, time permitting, we may return and do this later in the term, for now I want to bring this experience to some kind of close. The course is, after all, Romance and the focus is courtship, not mating, and, let me add that the process of absorption is rather, well, untested in situations involving actual chemical changes in the subject's physical system. We don't really want to find ourselves as subjects in someone else's test, now do we? Of course we don't. Let's let the lab work this out first.

We did go far enough with Linda to make some final observations concerning women and the physical aspects of romance. These are the sort of concerns which will continue to occupy our attention, as we determine whether or not they are universal, specifically female or merely manifestations of a particular personality type.

I'm speaking, most specifically, of the body/mind split which occurred at the moment Dave touched her. I thought it was very pronounced. Did anyone *not* feel this? Yes, very pronounced. Linda's body began to take on, in her own mind, in her own perceptions, a sort of otherness. Partly this was inherent in her conscious decision to feel whatever her body was feeling. A decision to be physically swept away is a contradiction in terms even when carried out successfully and I feel Linda was relatively successful. But this is only the most straightforward, simplest aspect of the split.

Linda's arousal was dependent upon Dave's. Not upon Dave himself. Upon Dave's arousal. Did you notice? In the earlier encounters we didn't find this. Linda responded to his hands, to his face, to his voice, to various secondary-male characteristics. She found him attractive. Mentally and physically. But toward the end she was much more aroused by the fact that he found her attractive. I don't want to get into a discussion of evolution or of psychology. I merely point this out; I ask you to consider the implications. We have a sort of loop between the male and the female and the conduit is the female's body. It has been said, and we will be trying to determine as we move on to other subjects, different ages, different locations whether it has been oversaid, that any romantic entanglement between a male and a female is, in fact, a triangle and the third party is the female's body. It is the hostage between them, the bridge or the barrier. At least in this case. Let's be cautious here. At least for Linda. I'm ready for questions.

I would imagine that being told you had a nice chin was about as exciting as being told you had nice teeth. But this is just a guess. Linda was hardly listening at this point.

They went to *The Dutchman*, a movie in which a white female seduces and destroys a black male. It made for an uncomfortable evening. Yes?

Well, the Joey Heatherton choice would have been problematical, too. No, I understand your interest. We'll look at Lauren more later. I promise.

Nobody has a clue as to what the lyrics to "The Weight" mean. I doubt that the man who wrote it could answer this question. He was probably just making it rhyme.

Are there any more questions?

Anything at all?

Then I'm ready to dismiss you. Be thinking about what you've absorbed. Next time we'll begin to look for common themes and for differences. It should be very interesting. The course is Comparative Romance. The point of view is female. We'll start next time with questions. When you've thought about it some more I'm sure you'll have questions.

PRAXIS

The price of a single ticket to the suicides would probably have funded my work for a month or more, but I do not let myself think about this. After all, I didn't pay for the ticket. Tonight I am the guest of the Baron Claude Himmlich and determined to enjoy myself.

I saw *Romeo and Juliet* five years ago, but only for one evening in the middle of the run. It wasn't much. Juliet had a cold and went to bed early. Her nurse kept wrapping her in hot rags and muttering under her breath. Romeo and Benvolio got drunk and made up several limericks. I thought some of them were quite good, but I'd been drinking a little myself.

Technically it was impressive. The responses of the simulants were wonderfully lifelike and the amphitheater had just been remodeled to allow the audience to walk among the sets, viewing the action from any angle. But the story itself was hardly dramatic. It wouldn't be, of course, in the middle of the run.

Tonight is different. Tonight is the final night. The audience glitters in jewels, colorful capes, extravagant hairstyles. Only the wealthy are here tonight, the wealthy and their guests. There are four in our own theater party: our host, the Baron; his beautiful daughter, Svanneshal; a wonderfully eccentric old woman dressed all in white who calls herself the Grand Duchess de Vie; and me. I work at the university in records and I tutor Svanneshal Himmlich in history.

The Grand Duchess stands beside me now as we

207

watch Juliet carried into the tombs. "Isn't she lovely?" the Duchess says. "And very sweet, I hear. Garriss wrote her program. He's a friend of the Baron's."

"An absolute genius." The Baron leans toward us, speaking softly. There is an iciness to Juliet, a sheen her false death has cast over her. She is like something carved from marble. Yet even from here I can see the slightest rise and fall of her breasts. How could anyone believe she is really dead? But Romeo will. He always does.

It will be a long time before Romeo arrives and the Baron suggests we walk over to the Capulets' to watch Juliet's nurse weeping and carrying on. He offers his arm to the Duchess though I can see his security cyber dislikes this.

It is one of the Baron's own models, identical in principle to the simulants on stage—human body, software brain. Before the Baron's work the cybers were slow to respond and notoriously easy to outwit. The Baron made his fortune streamlining the communications linkup and introducing an element of deliberate irrationality into the program. There are those who argue this was an ill-considered, even dangerous addition. But the Baron has never lacked for customers. People would rather take a chance on a cyber than on a human, and the less we need to depend on the poor, the safer we become.

The Duchess is looking at the cyber's uniform, the sober blues of the House of Himmlich. "Watch this," she says to me, smiling. She reaches into her bodice. I can see how the cyber is alert to the movement, how it relaxes when her hand reappears with a handkerchief. She reverses the action; we watch the cyber tense again, relaxing when the hand reemerges.

The Baron shakes his head, but his eyes are amused. "Darling," he says, "you must not play with it."

"Then I shall walk with Hannah instead." The Duchess slips her hand around my arm. Her right hand is bare and feels warm pressed into my side. Her left hand is covered by a long white glove; its silky fingers rest lightly on the outside of my arm.

The Baron precedes us, walking with Svanneshal, the cyber close behind them. The Duchess leans against me and takes such small steps we cannot keep up. She looks at the Baron's back. "You've heard him called a 'self-made man'?" she asks me. "Did it ever occur to you that people might mean it literally?"

She startles me. My eyes go at once to the Baron, recognizing suddenly his undeniable perfection—his dark, smooth skin, his even teeth, the soft timbre of his voice. But the Duchess is teasing me. I see this when I look back at her.

"I like him very much," I answer. "I imagine him to be exactly like the ancient aristocracy at their best—educated, generous, courteous. . . ."

"I wouldn't know about that. I have never studied history; I have only lived it. How old would you guess I am?"

It is a question I hate. One never knows what the most polite answer would be. The Duchess' hair, twisted about her head and held into place with ivory combs, is as black as Svanneshal's, but this can be achieved with dyes. Her face, while not entirely smooth, is not overly wrinkled. Again I suspect cosmetic enhancements. Her steps are undeniably feeble. "You look quite young," I say. "I couldn't guess."

"Then look at this." The Duchess stops walking and removes the glove from her left hand. She holds her palm flat before me so that I see the series of ciphers burnt into her skin. IPS3552. It is the brand of a labor duplicate. I look up at her face in astonishment and this amuses her. "You've never seen anything like that before, have you, historian? But you've heard perhaps how, in the last revolution, some of the aristocracy branded themselves and hid in the factories? *That's* how old I am."

In fact, I have heard the story, a two-hundred-year-old story, but the version I know ends without survivors. Most of those who tried to pass were detected immediately, a human cannot affect the dead stare of the duplicates for very long. Those few who went into the factories gave themselves up eventually, preferring, after all, to face the mob rather than endure the filth, the monotony, and the endless labor. "I would be most interested in interviewing you," I say. "Your adventures should be part of the record." *If true*, but of course that is something I do not say.

"Yes." The Duchess preens herself, readjusting an ivory comb, replacing her glove. We notice the Baron, still some distance away, returning to us. He is alone and I imagine he has left the cyber with Svanneshal. The Duchess sweeps her bare hand in the direction of his hurrying figure. "I am a true member of the aristocracy," she tells me. "Perhaps the only surviving member. I am not just some wealthy man who chooses to call himself *Baron*."

This I discredit immediately as vanity. Revolution after revolution—no one can verify a blood claim. Nor can I see why anyone would want to. I am amazed at the willingness of people to make targets of themselves as if every time were the last time and now the poor are permanently contained.

"I must apologize." The Baron arrives, breathless. "I had no idea you had fallen so far behind."

"Why should you apologize," the Duchess chides him, "if your guest is too old for such entertainments and too proud to use a chair as she should?" She shifts herself from my arm to his. "Verona is so lovely," she says. "Isn't it?"

We proceed slowly down the street. I am still thinking of the Duchess's hand. When we rejoin Svanneshal it is as though I have come out of a trance. She is so beautiful tonight I would rather not be near her. The closer I stand, the less I can look. Her eyes are very large inside the dark hood of her gown, which covers her hair and shoulders in a fine net of tiny jewels. In the darkened amphitheater the audience shines like a sky full of stars, but Svanneshal is an entire constellation— Svanneshal, the Swan's throat, and next to her, her father, the Dragon. I look around the amphitheater. Everyone is beautiful tonight.

Juliet's nurse is seated in a chair, rocking slowly back

and forth in her agony. She is identical to the nurse I saw
before and I tell the Baron so.

"Oh, I'm sure she *is* the one you saw before. I saw
her once as Amanda in *The Glass Menagerie*. You didn't
imagine they started from scratch every time, did you?
My dear Hannah, anyone who can be recycled after the
run certainly will be. The simulations are expensive
enough as it is." The Baron smiles at me, the smile of the
older, the wiser, to the young and naive. "What's
amazing is the variation you get each time, even with
identical parts. Of course, that's where the drama comes
in."

Before, when I saw *Romeo and Juliet*, Friar Law-
rence was killed on the second night, falling down a
flight of stairs. That's mainly why I went. I was excited by
the possibilities opened by the absence of the Friar. Yet
the plot was surprisingly unchanged.

It makes me think of Hwang-li and I say to the
Baron, "Did you know it was a historian who created the
simulations?"

"I don't have your knowledge of history," he answers. "Svanneshal tells me you are quite gifted. And
you have a speciality . . . forgive me. I know Svanneshal has told me."

"Mass movements. They don't lend themselves to
simulation." The Duchess has not heard of Hwang-li
either, but then only a historian would have. It was so
many revolutions ago. I could argue that the historians
are the true revolutionary heroes, retaining these
threads of our past, bringing them through the upheaval.
Many historians have died to protect the record. And
their names are lost to us forever. I am glad for a chance
to talk about Hwang-li.

"Hwang-li was not thinking of entertainment, of
course. He was pondering the inevitability of history. Is
the course of history directed by personalities or by
circumstances?" I ask the Baron. "What do you think?"

The Baron regards me politely. "In the real world,"
he says, "personalities and circumstances are insepa-
rable. The one creates the other and vice versa. Only in
simulation can they be disjoined."

"It follows then," I tell him, "that if you could intervene to change one, you would simultaneously change both and, therefore, the course of history. Could you make a meaningful change? How much can depend upon a single individual taking a single action at a single moment? Or not taking it?"

"Depending on the individual, the action, and the moment," the Duchess says firmly, "everything could change."

I nod to her. "That is what Hwang-li believed. He wished to test it by choosing an isolated case, a critical moment in which a series of seeming accidents resulted in a devastating war. He selected the Mancini murder, which was manageable and well-documented. There were seven personality profiles done on Philip Mancini at the time and Hwang-li had them all."

The Baron has forgotten Juliet's nurse entirely and turned to me with gratifying attention. "But this is fascinating," he says. "Svanneshal, you must hear this." Svanneshal moves in closer to him; the cyber seems relieved to have both standing together.

"Go on," says the Baron.

"I was telling your father about Hwang-li."

"Oh, I know this story already." Svanneshal smiles at the Baron coquettishly. "It's the murder that interests him," she says to me. "Aberrant personalities are sort of a hobby of his."

The Baron tells me what he already knows of the murder, that Frank Mancini was killed by his brother Philip.

"Yes, that's right," I say encouragingly. This information survives in a saying we have—enmity is sometimes described as "the love of the Mancinis."

It is the Duchess who remembers the saying. But beyond that she says she knows nothing of the case. I direct my statements to her. "Frank Mancini was a security guard, back in the days when humans functioned in that capacity. He was responsible for security in the Irish sector. He had just learned of the terrorist plot against Pope Peter. The Pope was scheduled to speak in an open courtyard at noon; he was to be shot from the window of a nearby library. Frank was literally reaching for the phone at the moment Philip Mancini burst into his study and shot him four times for personal reasons."

Svanneshal is bored with the discussion. Although she is extremely intelligent, it is not yet something she values. But she will. I look at her with the sudden realization that it is the only bit of inherited wealth she can be certain of holding on to. She is playing with her father's hair, but he catches her hand. "Go on," he says to me.

"Philip had always hated his brother. The murder was finally triggered by a letter Philip received from their mother—a letter we know he wrongly interpreted. What if he had read the letter more carefully? What if it had arrived ten minutes later? Hwang-li planned to replay the scene, running it through a number of such minute variations. Of course he had no simulants, nor did he need them. It was all to be done by computer."

"The whole project seems to me to raise more questions than it answers." Svanneshal is frowning. "What if the Pope had survived? How do you assess the impact of that? You cannot say there would have been no revolution. The Pope's death was a catalyst, but not a cause."

I am pleased to see that she not only knows the outline of the incident, but has obviously been giving it some thought. I begin to gesture emphatically with my hands as though we were in class, but I force myself to stop. This is after all a social occasion. "So, war is not averted, but merely delayed?" I ask her. "Another variation. Who would have gained from such a delay? What else might have been different if the same war was fought at a later time? Naturally nothing can be proved absolutely—that is the nature of the field. But it is suggestive. When we can answer these questions we will be that much closer to the day when we direct history along the course we choose."

"We already do that," the Duchess informs me quietly. "We do that every day of our lives." Her right hand smoothes the glove over her left hand. She interlaces the fingers of the two.

"What happened in the experiment?" the Baron asks.

"Hwang-li never finished it. He spent his life perfecting the Mancini programs and died in a fire before he had finished. Another accident. Then there were the university purges. There's never been that kind of money for history again." I look into Svanneshal's eyes, deep within her hood. "It's too bad, because I've an experiment of my own I've wanted to do. I wanted to simulate Antony and Cleopatra, but make her nose an inch longer."

This is an old joke, but they do not respond to it. The Baron says politely that it would provide an interesting twist the next time *Antony and Cleopatra* is done. He'll bring it up with the Arts Committee.

Svanneshal says, "You see, Daddy, you owe Hwang-li everything. He did the first work in synthetic personalities."

It occurs to me that the Baron may think Svanneshal and I are trying to persuade him to fund me and I am embarrassed. I search for something to say to correct this impression, but we are interrupted by a commotion onstage.

Lady Capulet has torn her dress at the collar, her hair is wild and uncombed. Under her tears, her face is ancient like a tragic mask. She screams at her husband that it is his fault their baby is dead. If he hadn't been so cold, so unyielding . . .

He stands before her, stooped and silent. When at last she collapses, he holds her, stroking the hair into place about her sobbing face. There is soft applause for this gentleness. It was unexpected.

"Isn't it wonderful?" Svanneshal's face glows with appreciation. "Garriss again," she informs me although I know Garriss did the programming for the entire Capulet family. It is customary to have one writer for each family so that the similarities in the programming can mirror the similarities of real families created by genetics and upbringing.

The simulants are oblivious to this approval. Jacques tells us, every time, that the world is a stage, but here the stage is a world, complete in itself, with history and family, even the random stagehands, death and disease. This is what the simulants live. If they were told that Juliet is no one's daughter, that everything they think and say is software, could they believe it? Would it be any less tragic?

Next to me I hear the beginning of a scream. It is choked off as suddenly as it started. Turning, I see the white figure of the Duchess slumping to the ground, a red stain spreading over her bodice. The gloved hand is pressed against her breast; red touches her fingers and moves down her arm. Her open eyes see nothing. Beside her, the cyber is returning a bloody blade to the case on its belt.

It was all so fast. "It killed her," I say, barely able to comprehend the words. "She's dead!" I kneel next to the Duchess, not merely out of compassion, but because my legs have given way. I look up at the Baron, expecting to see my own horror reflected in his face, but it is not.

He is calmly quiet. "She came at me," he says. "She moved against me. She meant to kill me."

"No!" I am astounded. Nothing is making sense to me. "Why would she do that?"

He reaches down and strips the wet glove from the warm hand. There is her lifeline—IPS3552. "Look at this," he says, to me, to the small group of theatergoers who have gathered around us. "She was not even human."

I look to Svanneshal for help. "You knew her. She was no cyber. There is another explanation for the brand. She told me . . ." I do not finish my sentence, suddenly aware of the implausibility of the Duchess's story. But what other explanation is there? Svanneshal will not meet my eyes. I find something else to say. "Anyway, the cybers have never been a threat to us. They are not programmed for assassination." It is another thought I do not finish, my eyes distracted by the uniform of the House of Himmlich. I get to my feet slowly, keeping my hands always visible and every move I make is watched by the Baron's irrational cyber. "The autopsy will confirm she is human," I say finally. "Was human."

Svanneshal reaches for my arm below the shoulder, just where the Duchess held me. She speaks into my ear, so low that I am the only one who hears her. Her tone is ice. "The cybers are all that stand between us and the mob. You remember that!"

Unless I act quickly, there will be no autopsy. Already maintenance duplicates are scooping up the body in the manner reserved for the disposal of cybers. Three of them are pulling the combs from her hair, the jewels from her ears and neck and depositing them in small, plastic bags. The Baron is regarding me, one hand wiping his upper lip. Sweat? No, the Baron feels nothing, shows no sign of unease.

Svanneshal speaks to me again. This time her voice is clearly audible. "It tried to kill my father," she says. "You weren't watching. I was."

It would be simpler to believe her. I try. I imagine that the whole time we were talking about the Mancinis, the Duchess was planning to murder her host. For political reasons? For personal reasons? I remember the conversation, trying to refocus my attention to her, looking for the significant gesture, the words which, listened to later, will mean so much more. But, no. If she had wanted to kill the Baron, surely she would have done it earlier, when the Baron returned to us without his cyber.

I return Svanneshal's gaze. "Did anyone else see that?" I ask, raising my voice. I look from person to person. "Did anyone see anything?"

No one responds. Everyone is waiting to see what I will do. I am acutely conscious of the many different actions I can take; they radiate out from me as if I stood at the center of a star, different paths, all ultimately uncontrollable. Along one path I have publicly accused the Baron of murder through misjudgment. His programs are opened for examination; his cybers are recalled. He is ruined. And, since he has produced the bulk of the city's security units, Svanneshal is quite right.

We are left unprotected before the mob. Could I cause that?

I imagine another, more likely path. I am pitted alone against the money and power of the Himmlich's. In this vision the Baron has become a warlord with a large and loyal army. He is untouchable. Wherever I try to go, his cybers are hunting me.

The body has been removed, a large, awkward bundle in the arms of the maintenance duplicates. The blood is lifting from the tile, like a tape played backward, like a thing which never happened. The paths radiating out from me begin to dim and disappear. The moment is past. I can do nothing now.

In the silence that has fallen around us, we suddenly hear that Romeo is coming. Too early, too early. What will it mean? The knot of spectators around us melts away; everyone is hurrying to the tombs. Svanneshal takes my arm and I allow myself to be pulled along. Her color is high and excited, perhaps from exertion, perhaps in anticipation of death. When we reach the tombs, we press in amongst the rest.

On one side of me, Svanneshal continues to grip my arm. On the other is a magnificent woman imposingly tall, dressed in Grecian white. Around her bare arm is a coiled snake, fashioned of gold, its scales in the many muted colors gold can wear. A fold of her dress falls for a moment on my own leg, white, like the gown of the Grand Duchess de Vie and I find myself crying. "Don't do it," I call to Romeo. "It's a trick! It's a trap. For God's sake, look at her." The words come without volition, part of me standing aside, marveling, pointing out that I must be mad. He can't hear me. He is incapable of hearing me. Only the audience turns to look, then turns away politely, hushed to hear Romeo's weeping. He is so young, his heart and hands so strong, and he says his lines as though he believed them, as though he made them up.

The Baron leans into Svanneshal. "Your friend has been very upset by the incidents of the evening." His voice is kind. "As have we all. And she is cold. Give her my cape."

I am not cold, though I realize with surprise that I am shaking. Svanneshal wraps the red cape about me. "You must come home with us tonight," she says. "You need company and care." She puts an arm about me and whispers, "Don't let it upset you so. The simulants don't feel anything."

Then her breath catches in her throat. Romeo is drinking his poison. I won't watch the rest. I turn my head aside and in the blurred lens of my tears one image wavers, then comes clear. It is the snake's face, quite close to my own, complacency in its heavy-lidded eyes. "Don't look at me like that," I say to a species which vanished centuries ago. "Who are you to laugh?"

I think that I will never know the truth. The Duchess might have been playing with the cyber again. Her death might have been a miscalculation. Or the Baron might have planned it, have arranged the whole evening around it. I would like to know. I think of something Hwang-li is supposed to have said. "Never confuse the record with the truth. It will always last longer." I am ashamed that I did nothing for the Duchess, accuse myself of cowardice, tears dropping from my cheeks onto the smooth flesh of my palms. In the historical record, I tell myself, I will list her death as a political assassination. And it will be remembered that way.

Next to me Svanneshal stiffens and I know Juliet has lifted the knife. This is truly the end for her; the stab wounds will prevent her reuse and her voice is painfully sweet, like a song.

One moment of hesitation, but that moment is itself a complete world. It lives onstage with the simulants, it lives with the mob in their brief and bitter lives, it lives where the wealthy drape themselves in jewels. If I wished to find any of them, I could look in that moment. "But how," I ask the snake, "would I know which was which?"